THE SECRET KEEPER

THE SECRET KEEPER

THE WITCH OF FROGNOT COUNTY™
BOOK ONE

MARTHA CARR
MICHAEL ANDERLE

DISRUPTIVE IMAGINATION®

Copyright © 2024 LMBPN Publishing
Cover by Fantasy Book Design
Cover copyright © LMBPN Publishing
A Michael Anderle Production

LMBPN Publishing
2375 E. Tropicana Avenue, Suite 8-305
Las Vegas, Nevada 89119 USA

Version 1.00, December 2024
ebook ISBN:979-8-89354-320-9
Print ISBN: 979-8-89354-407-7

THE SECRET KEEPER TEAM

Thanks to our JIT Readers:

Christopher Gilliard
Dave Hicks
Jackey Hankard-Brodie
Jan Hunnicutt

CHAPTER ONE

During the summer in Frognot County, afternoon thunderstorms rolled off the San Juan mountains with factory precision, giving the small town an unearned sense of importance. But the locals knew better—storms here were just a reminder that nature had its own agenda, especially when it came to the Santa Sangre River. Cursed, or so they said, though no one would admit it out loud.

Carrie Moonshadow stood on the balcony of her Victorian home, watching the storm clouds gather. Her house sat precariously on the river's edge, defying both nature and town gossip with each new flood. She knew what they whispered about her, that she was as cursed as the river, her house spared from the floods only by some strange magic. But she never let it bother her. Not anymore. Carrie had bigger things to worry about, like the rotting balcony joist she was trying to fix with a spell.

Carrie sighed as she examined the rotting joist. This would take more than a quick fix. But magic always had a price, and the energy had to come from somewhere—

whether it was drawn from the earth, the moon, or from her own life force. Too much magic, and the debt to nature would come due in unexpected ways. She had learned that lesson the hard way, and now she was more careful.

As she began to trace runes along the wood, she felt the familiar tingle of power sparking through her fingertips. It was always a delicate balance, using just enough to get the job done but not so much that it would cost her more later.

She glanced at the river below, swollen and muddy from the week of rain, and raised her hand in a half-salute to the raft of tourists from Dallas that Jack Landry was guiding through the rapids. He ignored her, which was fine by her. The less attention, the better. Carrie did not mind being left alone—unless the town made it impossible.

She had just started muttering the incantation under her breath, fingernails scraping at the wet wood, when she heard the familiar rumble of Alethea Monroe's Jeep pulling into her driveway. Frognot's only hydrologist always showed up after a storm, as if she expected to find Carrie's house washed away at last. No luck today, Alethea.

The afternoon thunderstorms were erupting with their usual timeliness. Heavy clouds from the high wild peaks were dropping their moisture off in the middle of town before making a beeline to the border with New Mexico. When it rained like this in Seattle, people zipped up their raincoats and powered through, but in Frognot an afternoon thunderstorm was a big wet pause button. At Marigold's bookstore, antsy tourists dripped on the hardwood floors as they perused field guides to Colorado wildflowers. Blacktree Perk coffee shop did brisk business on lattes and muffins, and tourists got wet dashing from shop to shop looking for umbrellas that they would not need in an hour.

Carrie glanced at the raft fighting the rising water, the passengers bobbing along as Jack shouted orders. The Santa Sangre river was popular among whitewater rafters and kayakers in spite of—or possibly because of—the rumored curse. It had rained hard every day this week, and the river was flowing high enough that the whitewater rafting company had made the Texans sign an extra waiver. Landry was a hard-bodied old-timer. Heavy rains were not enough to slow down business.

She gently shook her head. She knew he was already planning which of his customers he would dump off the raft at which rapids. The twenty-something in the cowboy hat might enjoy a swim through the Washing Machine, which was plenty bouncy at these flow levels. People who fell out of their rafts tipped more, he would brag to any locals that would listen. He had actually tracked it on a spreadsheet one summer—and who was he to deny them their thrills?

"Best be careful," muttered Carrie. "People struck by lightning on a whitewater rafting trip don't tend to tip at all."

The Santa Sangre River divided the town of Frognot into two neat halves, both of which had strong opinions about the other. According to the pamphlets printed by the Frognot tourism bureau, the fifteen-thousand-person town had sprung up during the gold rush of the late 1800s. Martha Sage, who ran Frognot's three-room Ute Indian Cultural Center, was irked by the suggestion that the town had appeared spontaneously, as if the buildings had pushed up through the soil along the river one day, like cattails. Martha frequently handed out her own hand-annotated versions of the official tourism pamphlets. In truth, the town had been imposed on the valley in an orderly Victorian grid, by a railway company looking to build a depot that would service the Frognot mining district.

Men had come to dig gold out of the mountains, and shrewd shovel salesmen had come to dig gold out of the miners' pockets. The luckiest left rich; the unluckiest never left at all. There were plenty of secrets buried in the boarded-up mineshafts dotting the surrounding mountains.

A hundred miles upstream from Frognot, the headwaters of the Santa Sangre poured straight out of a stony gash in the side of Blacktree Peak. Near the river's source, the iron-rich water ran blood red. Mary Cardoso, who at one hundred and two years old was the oldest resident of Frognot, adamantly told anyone who would listen that the river water was cursed. She attributed her long life to drinking only bottled mineral water imported from the Swiss Alps. This was ridiculous, of course. A spring in Switzerland could be cursed as easily as a river in Colorado, and it was harder to untangle yourself from magic that had originated so far away. Swiss covens were probably really well organized, too.

Carrie Moonshadow hadn't decided if she believed the river was cursed. If it was, the curse didn't have anything to do with her. Or maybe she was cursed as badly as the river, and so they got along. Carrie lived right on the banks of the Santa Sangre, but the spring floods always spared her. The denizens of Frognot whispered about it to one another, when sheds and decks were flushed away from houses just up- or downstream.

It was true that Carrie lived on a lucky piece of land. Well, more than lucky, in fact. Her old Victorian home was located smack dab in the middle of an oxbow in the river, on the Northern edge of town where the river slowed and meandered through flat green pastures. The house was an eclectic gingerbread confection of dormer windows, Greek pediments and Queen Anne shingles topped by a soaring circular tower with a peaked roof and a distant view of the barren summit of Blacktree Peak.

Every sane flood insurance underwriter had assured Carrie that her home would be washed away by the next light drizzle. It had managed to stay standing for a hundred years before she arrived, but somehow, the town still blamed her for her good fortune, trading cruel whispers every time she emerged unscathed from a flood or a forest fire. It was as if, by not sharing in their pain, she had taken something from them.

At the moment, the swollen river was the color of hot chocolate, lapping right against the bars of the wrought iron fence that surrounded her property. Carrie watched as an inflatable blue raft bobbed downstream over the waves. Jack Landry glanced at her window as he shouted a command to his eager crew, who dipped their paddles in the water with something significantly short of military precision. When she raised a hand in a wry salute, he frowned and looked away.

By now, the rain was down to a bare sprinkle, and Carrie went out onto her balcony to huff the smell of fresh-washed mountains and scrutinize a rotting joist. The joist's condition had been worsened by the week of heavy rains, but Carrie was loath to replace it. Modern lumber couldn't compete with the Victorians' sturdy hardwood. Plus, she rebelled at the thought of bringing noisy contractors and prying workmen into her home.

She was going to try and fix it herself, and hope her luck held. She thought she'd be able to manage the repair by tweaking a spell for encouraging tree growth and was eyeballing how many angelica stems she would need to give the incantation power. As she prodded the wet wood with an acid green fingernail, a truck rumbled off the road onto her gravel driveway.

Alethea Monroe drove her big Jeep up to the oxbow after every big rain, ostensibly to check on Carrie's well-being. "You're crazy to live there," she told Carrie whenever they ran into one another. These occasions usually involved Alethea blocking an exit.

Leaning over the balcony railing, Carrie waved at Alethea's truck. When she straightened back up, her hand caught a splinter on the railing, and a droplet of ruby-red blood welled up from her skin. She would have to get back to the spell after Althea left. Wincing, she plastered on a smile. She would have to pick a few angelica stems for herself.

Carrie knew the townspeople found her uncanny, some more than others. Alethea, she suspected, was disappointed to find Carrie high and dry. If Carrie's house had disappeared, Carrie might have gone with it.

Carrie, to her knowledge, had never done anything to deserve this grudge. She and Alethea had first crossed paths in the gardening section of the hardware store, where they'd both reached for the last bag of fertilizer. Carrie had let Alethea have it, but the token generosity hadn't softened the old woman up.

Maybe she should make one more friendly overture. The jeep was still idling just outside Carrie's iron gate, and on a whim, she grabbed a large bucket and went out the back door, making her way to an orange barrel of fresh, dry compost. She shoveled in about a foot of rich soil and headed for the Jeep. Her sudden approach startled Alethea, whose hand hovered on the gear shift. It was too late, though—Carrie had already waved her down.

"Quite a storm, huh?" Carrie said cheerfully.

Alethea's lips pursed as she glanced disapprovingly at Carrie's still-standing house.

"The river's running high," Alethea said.

Carrie held up her peace offering. "I have a gift for you."

Alethea sniffed the bucket warily. "Oh?"

"Some of my compost. Fresh out of the barrel. It'll do wonders for your roses."

Everyone in town knew that Alethea grew prizewinning roses. Even Carrie knew it, and she tried to actively avoid Frognot gossip. Alethea told everyone who would listen about her upcoming competitions, and whenever she won a blue ribbon, she wore it around town for a full week. Carrie often ran into Alethea at the garden center, where the older woman frequently roped green-vested employees into lengthy debates on the merits of various irrigation systems. Their mutual love of gardening should have made them friendly, but Alethea still acted like she was eager to put some of her outstanding blooms on Carrie's grave.

It was time to let bygones be bygones, dammit.

Carrie smiled cheerfully at an earthworm poking its head out of the compost. Alethea should have been grateful at this bounty, but instead, she looked afraid. "You're trying to poison my roses, aren't you!" she barked.

Carrie took an instinctive step back. Her foot slipped on the gravel and the bucket flew out of her hand as she tried to right herself.

"Why would I want to poison your roses?" she asked, genuinely mystified. Her tastes ran to wildflowers, but she had nothing against the more formal blooms.

"There's something wrong with this place," Alethea said. "There's something wrong with you. The Santa Sangre should have reclaimed that land years ago."

"And yet, it hasn't."

"By all rights, you ought to have drowned in the river." Alethea was babbling now.

"I'm sorry to disappoint you." Carrie's eyes blazed. She was tempted to do something outlandish like cackle, or wave a broom around, or steal a small terrier from a girl with pigtails. But she didn't want to give Alethea the satisfaction.

"Keep your poison," Alethea said, punching a button to roll up her window. She threw the car in reverse and backed up rapidly, hitting the overturned bucket of compost. The orange plastic cracked beneath the Jeep's wheels, and Alethea's tires left a track in the rich, dark compost. Carrie hoped the earthworms had avoided the worst of it.

"Stay away from my house!" Carrie shouted after the retreating Jeep. She doubted Alethea heard her. When the hum of the Jeep's engine disappeared into the distance, Carrie collected the broken fragments of the plastic bucket and hurled them into her trash bin. Then, she carefully scooped up the loose compost with a trowel and carried it into her garden to put it to good use.

Flowers, trees, and medicinal plants flourished on every square inch of the property. Carrie's gardens were startlingly large. Larger, in fact, than the dimensions of the property should have strictly allowed. But under Carrie's watch, there was somehow always room for another row of agrimony or columbine, or another trellis for sweet peas. Her upstairs and downstairs porches were packed from end-to-end with potted greenery, and against the southern wall she had built a small glass greenhouse.

As Carrie circled the house, she paused at the leaded glass door, fingers brushing the thick chain and padlock that held it shut. The metal was embossed with intricate interlocking runes. The work was as beautiful as it was powerful. Vines crawled up the sides of the door in orderly twists, with flax string tied to the stems at regular intervals. Carrie tapped the glass and turned back to the open gardens for now. The situation with the joist was not quite dire enough to require opening up the greenhouse.

The vines of a trellis brushed against Carrie's skin, the still-wet leaves moistening her dark hair as she walked down to her herb garden. She had been meaning to cut back her overgrown fleawort patch for several days and was glad to have a use for the culled plants. Dropping to her knees, she thinned the fuzzy stalks by hand, depositing her harvest in a hand-woven basket she'd gotten from the annual Frognot craft fair last Christmas.

As she collected plants, a strange protrusion rose up from under one of the paving stones that wound down the garden towards the ten-foot circular meditative labyrinth located at the high point of the property. The paving stone shivered several times, dislodging the dirt surrounding it, then fell flat. Carrie locked eyes with a small ceramic garden gnome guarding the path. The lawn ornament had a conical red hat and a mischievous expression. As Carrie watched, the gnome shivered, and then leapt an inch in the air. She blinked as the ground below the path roiled, throwing off the smell of wet soil and raining errant earthworms onto the paving stones. With a sodden grunt, a figure emerged from the churned-up soil below the ceramic garden gnome. The statue tumbled from the figure's head onto a paving-stone and cracked in two. Carrie took a step back as the soil-encrusted figure shook itself off like a dog. Finally, two wide, gray eyes opened under the crust of dirt.

Standing barefoot—and he was always barefoot when he ventured underground—Finn was just under five feet tall. When he went out into town, he wore heeled cowboy boots. He insisted this was a style preference, but Carrie thought he liked the boost. His hair and beard weren't visible under the muck, but they were snowy white. Before he went earth-diving, he braided both hair and beard into tight, sturdy braids. Which meant that out and about, he tended to look like his hair had been through a crimper. Carrie considered it a nostalgic nineties throwback.

"You owe me a gnome," Carrie said peevishly.

"That's not a gnome. It's an atrocity," Finn grumbled. His voice was always gravelly. When he was annoyed, it rumbled like an earthquake. He poked at the halves of the lawn ornament with one foot.

"Jealous?" Carrie asked. "Afraid there's only room for one garden gnome in this town?"

"I'm not a garden gnome," Finn growled. "I'm a gnome in a garden."

Carrie's eyes sparkled. "My apologies." Finn was the only gnome Carrie knew, and accordingly much more of an expert.

Carrie cheerfully collected the ceramic gnome shards under her arm and deposited them in her basket.

"Hose me down?" Finn asked.

Shaking loose dirt off herself, Carrie walked with Finn back up to the house. He waited patiently on the brick patio as she screwed the high-pressure sprayer nozzle onto the hose.

"You buy these things just to grind my gears," Finn said, holding up the two halves of the gnome. "They're a terrible representation of my people."

"You're right." She grinned as the layers of grime sloughed off onto the bricks. Muddy runnels of water ran off into the garden. If they weren't sucked up by the plants, they would soon join the Santa Sangre as it flowed into the San Juan and made its way towards Mexico. Muddy water filled the halves of the gnome. "It doesn't look at all like you. Your hat is much uglier."

Finn was now dripping wet but largely clean. He was wearing a tight-fitting silver bodysuit. He insisted that the suit's construction was a gnome secret, but he'd hinted that it was woven from some kind of metallic thread. The texture reminded Carrie of steel wool. Even if humans could make it, she doubted it would be appearing on Paris runways anytime soon.

"I have fantastic taste in hats," Finn growled. He dropped the pieces of the ceramic gnome, made a rude gesture, and stomped away towards his rooms at the back of the house. Carrie sighed and went to inspect the hole where he'd emerged from her garden. Admittedly, the ability to move through solid earth was quite useful. She suspected that he was able to do it by way of small skin vibrations, possibly with the help of the fine, wiry hairs that covered his body. He looked like an unusually hairy human, but sometimes people stared.

Finn refused to answer her questions on a wide range of topics: gnome magic, gnome culture, gnome anatomy, and most especially his own biography. Although she watched, and learned, and made hypotheses, he remained largely an enigma. For all she knew, there were a hundred more gnomes living in the soil right below her feet, and Finn was the black sheep of the family gone to seek his fortune above ground.

Carrie had met Finn in an abandoned mineshaft the year she'd moved to Frognot. Although "met" was incomplete. It was more accurate to say that she'd stumbled over his half-dead body. She was in the mineshaft chasing rumors that a cursed jackalope had built a warren underground in the area. Her mission had been totally harebrained—even if she'd been powerful enough to trap an ensorcelled beast, she could have easily died in a cave-in. Instead, she'd tripped over Finn, slamming into a rotting support and nearly bringing the roof down on both of them. But she'd gotten Finn out, and after realizing he wasn't human, taken him home to nurse him back to health. He'd lived there ever since and made himself indispensable in the process.

Carrie returned to the garden and replaced the flagstone Finn had dislodged. She patted the earth back down around it and made sure all the upturned earthworms found nice loamy patches of soil to dig into. Then, she went back to picking fleawort.

A few minutes later, Finn emerged from the house.

"Where's your hat?" Carrie asked. Recently, he'd taken to wearing a wide-brimmed green straw hat tied with a crocheted blue ribbon. It was truly an assault on the senses.

Finn glared at her from below exuberantly bushy white eyebrows. "Sun's down. Don't need a hat," he said, twirling a tube of superglue between his fingers. She smiled, and he went to find the pieces of the ceramic gnome he'd broken. By the time she had finished clearing the fleawort bed, the gnome was fixed and back in its spot on the freshly turned soil of the garden path.

Carrie wondered if all gnomes could pass so easily as humans, or if Finn was unique. Sure, Finn's silvery manbun drew odd looks when he went into town. Additionally, Finn's stony eyes were wider set than most people's, and Carrie was pretty sure he had an extra transparent eyelid that protected his eyes when he was burrowing through the soil. Other than his height, the main thing that set him apart from other people was his appalling fashion sense. At the moment, he wore leggings printed with smiling yellow suns, his platform flip-flops dangling off the edge of a hammock that was strung between her house and the squat mountain alder that shaded her back patio.

"Have you got time to help me with a spell? I'm going to try something new with that rotting joist on the balcony."

"This is what happens when you build with wood," Finn said, shaking his head disapprovingly. "Show me an underground granite vault with rot problems."

Carrie rolled her eyes. "If you'd like to buy me an underground granite vault I'd be happy to relocate."

Finn scratched his beard. "Count me in. What time?"

"As soon as the moon rises," Carrie said. Finn grunted in agreement and closed his eyes. By the time Carrie made it up the porch steps, he was snoring again.

The gnome wasn't much of a conversationalist, but Carrie knew she could count on him. The moon was waning, so it would be nice to have a little extra oomph behind her spell. Finn might mock the human propensity for building with wood, but at the end of the day, he needed a roof over his head as much as she did.

Carrie ground down the fleawort with a pestle. She scraped most of it into a bowl to save it for later, then added aloe and marigold. She spread the fragrant herbaceous paste onto the cut on her hand, then sat down to read for an hour with a library copy of Jules Verne's *Journey to the Center of the Earth*. She read a lot of classic science fiction, and as she thumbed through the pages, she wondered how far Finn could tunnel underground before he got into trouble. Surely he wasn't backstroking through lava pools? At least, she didn't think so. It was one more mystery to ponder.

When the twilight had faded from gray to navy, Carrie

collected her fleawort paste from the kitchen and headed up to the balcony. Finn joined her a minute later, keeping his distance from the railing. He wasn't a fan of heights, which made sense for someone from a ground-dwelling species.

As Carrie sat down beside the rotting joist, Finn tossed her a small black marble. Carrie admired the smooth onyx.

"Polished it up myself," he said. "Will it work?"

"It'll work just fine," Carrie said, carefully unrolling a leather carrier across the planks. About the size of a yoga mat, the leather was laden with pockets and tool loops, each carefully embroidered with intricate symbols. Carrie unhooked a leather loop to retrieve a long silver scoop—about the size of a Slurpee straw—and carefully assessed her options. After a moment, she selected a pouch marked with the rune for strength, and added some of the powder inside to the fleawort paste. Carefully resealing the pouch, she tapped the silver scoop against the boards.

"What do you think? Longevity? Or abundance?"

"You don't need abundant joists," Finn grumbled. "Just one good one."

"Longevity it is," Carrie said, flicking open the clasp. The paste inside was a ruddy mess—Carrie had purchased it from a trapper over in Silverton and hadn't dared to ask about its origins. By itself, the reddish longevity paste was rank, but the herbs in the stone bowl brought out different notes, and the whole thing smelled vegetal and alive. Carrie took a deep breath. It was like she was smelling an entire forest. Not just the living trees and animals, but soil, rotting vegetation, crumbling bones and decomposition. An ecosystem in a bowl.

Finn had already chalked a signaling circle onto the balcony platform. Carrie looked over his marks.

"You're becoming quite the witch," she said. Finn ignored the comment, but when she handed him a protective amulet, he slung it swiftly around his neck. She did the same, and then dolloped fleawort paste into the center of the chalk circle. When she was done, she placed the black marble gently inside.

Taking the chalk from Finn, Carrie drew three runes on the rotting joist. One for growth. It was wood, after all. One for youth, and one for protection against disease. When she was satisfied with her work, she traced the chalk lines over with the fleawort paste. Energy crackled under her fingers as she worked, tiny pinpricks that jolted across her skin as the energy for the spell flowed out of the marble and into the runes. The sensation wasn't painful, but it wasn't pleasant, either, and she winced as she finished the lines. When she was done, she scooted back, letting as much moonlight as possible fall across the circle. Under the watery silver glow, threads of power flowed out of the onyx marble and into the runes on the joist, an opalescent milky way of promised magic. The runes on the joist grew brighter and brighter, and there was a creak of wood, almost sub-audible, as the rot began to heal itself.

The mystery never failed to awe her. Visible only under moonlight, the magic was mesmerizing. That could be dangerous. If you used too much power, you could rack up a bill you couldn't pay. Carrie pulled a delicate three-minute hourglass from her leather kit and upturned it. There was nothing particularly magical about it—the timer on her cell phone would work just as well—but she liked collecting antique hourglasses. This one was a Victorian egg timer she had found at an antique store in the middle of Kansas, and she'd bought it for herself as a reward for completing a particularly difficult piece of work.

As the last grains of sand flowed through the neck, Carrie retrieved a set of long silver tongs from her kit.

"Have you got the jar?" she asked Finn.

He made an affirming noise and placed a small metal cup on the balcony beside her. Working carefully, Carrie grasped the marble with the tongs and pulled.

The marble didn't move. Cursing, she tightened her grip on the silver and pulled. A threatening hiss echoed through the air, and then the marble came loose. It was incredibly heavy and very unstable, oozing with errant loops of magic now that it was unbound from its circle. She had to grab the silver tongs with both hands to lift it into the iron cup. When it clinked into the bottom, Finn slammed an iron lid on top, screwing it on tight.

Carrie sighed in relief as the twinkle of magic faded from the air. This was the most dangerous part of any spell. She took a few minutes to collect herself, then grabbed the iron jar and scrambled to her feet.

"You could leave it until the morning," Finn said. "You know my jars are good for it."

"They're the best. But I don't like to wait," Carrie said, fingers pressed into the grooves around the lid.

All magic had a price. The energy to heal a wound or dowse for water or strengthen your own muscles had to come from somewhere. Even a witch couldn't escape the second law of thermodynamics. A good witch could, however, hide from it for a few days. That was the essence of magic. The black marble was now a cosmic IOU. The jar would prevent the universe from collecting its due, but not forever. Carrie, who understood the cost of an overdue cosmic bill all too well, liked to pay her debts as quickly as possible.

"You're probably right. Remember the last time you tried to delay a debt like this?" Finn asked, his tone light but his eyes sharp.

Carrie looked away, memories rushing back. "I remember."

Finn chuckled darkly. "That storm didn't just wash away half your garden. It took a whole week of crops with it. Nature doesn't forget when you steal from it."

Carrie rubbed the back of her neck, feeling the phantom ache of that past mistake. She had tried to avoid payment for a water spell, but when the rains came, they had come with a vengeance. Floods that had torn through her carefully planted beds, leaving destruction in their wake. She had been lucky not to lose the house.

As they stepped outside, the smell of burning leaves hit her. A rose bush withered at the edge of her garden, one of the sacrifices she'd been planning to make. The moment her foot touched the ground it shed an arc of loose magic. The bush shriveled, its deep red petals turning to ash in an instant. The marble pulsed again, lighter now, its demand partially satisfied. But the air still buzzed with static. It wasn't over yet.

"Let's get this over with," she said. "I'll buy you a slice of pie afterwards."

Carrie's blue truck was fifteen years old, and it would last another fifteen if she had anything to say about it.

Admittedly, Finn's uncanny ability to duplicate just about any metal object she gave him made it significantly easier to get parts.

"Where are you thinking? Somewhere up on the peak?" Finn asked.

Carrie grinned. "I had a more...urban destination in mind," she said.

"You have a soft spot for trouble," Finn grumbled.

Carrie didn't argue with him. Instead, she grabbed her cloak and checked the time on her phone. Magic had a way of twisting reality, and it was well past midnight now. Most of the houses on the hillsides were dark. She slowed the truck as she reached the north side of town, which had once been an entirely different city from Frognot, before the railroad had sucked up the whole valley. Parking the truck at the end of a quiet cul-de-sac, she scrambled out.

"Stay here," Carrie instructed. Finn shrugged and leaned his seat back, closing his eyes.

Frognot was located at an altitude of about 7,000 feet, and even in the summer it was cold at night. Even colder after the recent rains. Carrie's hooded velvet cloak was an affectation, but it was warm and comfortable, and it added to her mystique. She had dyed the velvet herself, using midnight blue pigments from plants in the garden. It was the color of a starless sky, and in the dark, it made her almost invisible. She clutched the cloak's worn blue edges close to her chest as she strode silently among the neighborhood's old Victorian homes.

Carrie stared down the block of houses, trying to remember the house number. Just as she was about to risk looking at her phone, she spotted Alethea Murrow's cherry red Jeep behind a tall iron gate. Bingo.

Carrie hurried up the driveway, grateful that the iron gate was unlocked. She was awfully tired from climbing fences. The gate squeaked as it opened, and Carrie had to duck behind the Jeep as a light flicked on in the house. Breathing hard, Carrie imagined Alethea staring out the window with her beady, busybody eyes. The hair stood up on the back of her neck. When the light turned off, Carrie continued around the side of the house.

Where Carrie's garden was a riot of haphazard herb beds, Alethea's was scrupulously orderly. Military, even. A smooth concrete path ran straight down the center of the lawn towards a small marble fountain surrounded by rose trellises.

Carrie moved silently to the nearest trellis. In the low light, the white wood looked like peeling skin. The roses, outlined against the dark concrete, filled the night air with a heady, romantic fragrance. They smelled so lovely that Carrie almost felt guilty as she retrieved a trowel from her pocket and dug a six-inch hole in the soil below the trellis, slicing through thread-like roots. A thorn snagged her, leaving a long red scratch along her wrist. Fair play to the rose. When she was done, she unscrewed the lid from Finn's sturdy iron jar and tipped the black marble into the hole, covering it quickly with moist soil.

Magic always extracted a price. Today, it would extract that price from Alethea Murrow's award-winning roses. She stood back, and a beam of moonlight fell on the nearest flower. The petals were bloody red for a moment, and then began to fade. Leaves rustled faintly as the color drained out of the roses, turning the petals a gummy flesh color before they cracked into dead rot. The thorny green stems lost color and withered, the points of the thorns crumbling away. A circle of grass surrounding the hole where Carrie had deposited the marble died off as she watched, leaving patchy earth behind. Alethea could flush that soil and fertilize it with fresh-fallen manure, but nothing would grow there for years. The spirit realm was collecting its debt with interest. Within a few minutes, the pace of the decay slowed, and then stopped entirely. The black marble had sucked up the life it was owed. On a whim, Carrie speared her trowel back into the dirt. After inspecting the black marble for any errant traces of magic, she slipped it into her pocket. A memento, for the next time her refusal to drown disappointed Alethea Murrow. *Congratulations on your latest prize. You've got the deadest roses in Frognot.*

A light turned on at the back of the house, and a cat in the distance yowled. Carrie melted back into the shadows and left quickly. As she walked back to the truck, a faint note of guilt twanged. But they were just roses, and Alethea had plenty more.

She wasn't normally so petty. Usually, after she finished a spell, she took the debt-stone out to the middle of the forest, to a tree riddled with mountain pine beetles or half-dead from invasive dwarf mistletoe. There were more direct ways of transferring power, of course. Those ways were bloodier than using debt-stones, although less dangerous to the witch. But Carrie didn't need to have some local farmer up in her business about why she needed so many goats all the time. A rose bush, she thought, was a reasonable price to pay.

Not just any rose bush. An award-winning rosebush. She allowed herself a wicked smile as she climbed back into her blue truck.

"Ready for pie?" she asked Finn.

"Always," he said.

Carrie would have gone hungry without the Wildcat Diner. Unlike everything else in Frognot, the tiny vintage burger joint was open all night, except on Christmas and Valentine's Day. It was busier than usual at the moment, rowdy with a long table of Texan tourists who had clearly just left the bar down the block. Their server was the diner's owner, Binita, a wizened scrap of a woman who was either an ancient forty or a cherubic sixty. Binita glared at Carrie and Finn, standing well back from the table as she took their order of pies and coffees.

"Who put mine tailings in her coffee?" Carrie muttered to Finn as the server cast a long, suspicious look over her shoulder on her way to the glass dessert case up front.

"She can probably sense you're a floricidal maniac," Finn said.

"Hey!" Carrie narrowed her eyes. "How do you know that?"

"We didn't risk sneaking around suburbia so that you could kill some random tree," Finn said. "Besides. The roots talk to me." He waggled his bushy white eyebrows, pulling his purple knit beanie down over his head.

"Is that a joke?" Carrie asked.

He shrugged mysteriously, and before Carrie could question him about it further, Binita returned with two slices of warm strawberry rhubarb pie and two cups of coffee, one black and one with cream. The diner's owner might not like Carrie, but she remembered how she took her coffee, which counted for something.

"Thanks, Binita," Carrie said. The woman made a small sign against evil and skittered away. Carrie sighed. "I may not have the warm regard of my community, but at least I have hot pie." Binita always heated the pie up in a toaster oven rather than a microwave, a detail Carrie appreciated.

When the bell on the door rang, she was too engrossed in the excellent strawberry rhubarb pie to look up. A moment later, however, quick footsteps approached the booth. Carrie looked up in surprise to see a thin young woman with mousy strawberry blonde hair looking down at her. Her arm shook as she raised one hand and pressed it into the dark tattoo on the back of Carrie's right hand.

"It's not polite to poke strangers," Carrie said, drawing her hand back.

The young woman ignored her. "You're the witch," the young woman said. By the way her words mushed into one another, Carrie thought that she was a little drunk. Overhearing her, one of the Texan tourists looked their way and chuckled. Something about Carrie's expression, however, made him look away.

"I'm Carrie. It's nice to meet you." Her words came out ironically sharp.

"I– I need your help. I'm sick," the young woman stammered.

There was a thin film of sweat on the woman's upper lip, and her hair lay lifelessly against her head. Carrie thought that the young woman was pretty—or at least, she had been. Was she on drugs? "It's late. You should sit down and get something to eat. I can order you something before we go–"

Nodding to Finn, she slid halfway out of the booth. But the young woman grabbed her arm with a surprisingly strong grip. She traced the outlines of Carrie's tattoos with a yellowed fingernail. "I don't need food. I need help," she said insistently.

"Well, I can't help you right now," Carrie barked. She regretted speaking so sharply, but it was true. The icy languor that came over her after she worked magic was surging up inside her. The price, perhaps, of her stunt with the rose bush.

"Your hand is freezing," the young woman said, fingers digging into Carrie's bones.

Carrie rubbed her eyes and reassessed the young woman. She looked more distraught than dangerous, wearing a dingy white fleece jacket over a long denim dress.

"What's your name?" Carrie asked.

"Emily. I saw your truck out front. That's why I came in."

Binita approached now with a sour look on her face. "If you're going to cause trouble, you can cause it somewhere else," she said, looking straight at Carrie as she spoke.

Carrie put her hand on top of the young woman's. It was warm in comparison with her own, but very frail, the bones sharp under stretched skin. "Will you sit down?" Carrie asked.

Emily tugged her hand away, eyes darting to Binita for

an instant before drifting back to her own worn leather boots.

"I'm sorry. This was a mistake. I shouldn't have come." She turned to go, but Carrie reached out and caught at her sleeve. It was damp with sweat.

"Wait," Carrie said. After all, she had to make a living somehow. "You know where I live? Out on the oxbow?"

Damp strings of hair obscured Emily's face, but she nodded.

"Come by tomorrow," Carrie said, then added "Not too early."

The bell over the door clanged away; the frightened young woman was already halfway across the parking lot.

"Think she'll come?" Finn asked.

Carrie shrugged. "Or she'll sober up and realize she needs a different kind of help."

"Think she can pay?"

"Everyone can pay. One way or another." Carrie shivered. The cup of coffee between her hands was already cold. She put a few bills and a generous tip on the table. "Can you drive? I'm about to faceplant into my pie crumbs."

CHAPTER TWO

I f someone had asked Sheriff Caleb Thorne about what made him good at his job, he'd have said patience. Heaps and heaps of patience. A full mountain range of patience, soaring and majestic. Of course, no one ever did ask the sheriff about his job. They were too busy lodging wild complaints. Just this morning, Jed Menkin, who was the younger and significantly more troubled of the two Menkin boys, had dropped by the station to report that a bat-winged monster was draining the local cattle of their blood. Jed hadn't actually seen the monster, of course, but he had inferred its shape from the puncture wounds in a steer's neck and a tuft of black hair that had been left nearby in a patch of sagebrush.

Thorne often daydreamed about moving far away from Frognot. He could get a job somewhere like south central LA, where there would be a lot of nice simple murders and very little bovine vampirism.

"-are you even listening to me?" Alethea Murrow's voice cracked his reverie wide open.

"I'm listening, Ms. Murrow. Someone took a weed whacker to your rose bush?"

"It's *Doctor* Murrow. And you're not listening *at all.* Good luck getting my vote in the next election, mister. You know I have a lot of pull with the local landscaping community."

"I'm sorry."

"I don't want an apology. I want you to *listen.*"

"I'm listening, I'm listening." Thorne gulped down his coffee. Although truthfully, there was not enough coffee in the world for this.

"That *witch* killed my prize Polyantha roses with black magic."

Thorne's heart sank at the word *witch.* He hoped with some futility that she might be talking about a particularly unpleasant member of Frognot's cutthroat rose gardening community.

"When you say *witch−*"

Alethea leaned over his desk, flooding the space with a very pleasant faint floral odor. He wondered if it was a perfume, or if she simply rubbed herself with homegrown rose petals every morning. The vivid image disturbed him. "Carrie Moonshadow," Alethea whispered, so loudly that Theo, his administrative assistant, looked curiously through his open door.

"You saw Carrie Moonshadow trespassing in your garden?" Now there was a woman who would look good rolling around in a pile of rose petals. Thorne pushed this image away before his cheeks could turn red.

"I didn't have to *see* her. The evidence is as plain as a

bear in the road!" She shoved her phone under his nose. He glanced at the desiccated rose bush in the photo.

"Maybe you're overwatering them...?" he said, taking a little mean pleasure at her face's immediate transformation into a good imitation of a ripe summer tomato.

"I defended a dissertation in hydrology before you were born, young man. I assure you my roses are perfectly irrigated." She underscored this point by poking him in the chest.

"Ow," he said, as Alethea scrolled through a series of identical photos of dead roses.

"Roses don't just die overnight," she said.

Thorne sighed. "You're a scientist," he said, appealing to her better nature. "Do you really believe in witches?"

At this, Alethea looked slightly embarrassed. He hoped this might be enough to get her to drop her complaint, but after a moment, she shook her head.

"You're right. I'm a scientist," she said. "If it was a fungus, the other roses would have been affected. Same with the irrigation system. If it was a bad strain, I would have seen problems before now. A healthy trellis doesn't simply die overnight of natural causes. And that's not all. Have you seen Carrie Moonshadow's house? Right in the floodplain. It simply shouldn't exist. It defies everything I know about hydrology. Which, as I've stated—"

"Is quite a lot. I know," Thorne said, trying to think of a way to divert the conversation. "How about poison?" he asked brightly. He regretted it the moment he said it. He was trying to get Alethea to leave, not to escalate her claim.

"I thought of that. The second I saw my poor rotting trellis I sent a soil sample to a friend who works in the chemistry lab over at Fort Clark. I haven't gotten the results back yet."

Thorne sighed. The problem was, he believed her. If Alethea Murrow had been crazy, he could have dealt with it. But she wasn't crazy. Irritating, maybe, but she was a respected researcher whose work on water conservation had saved one of his favorite local fishing streams from being turned into an ugly reservoir. And there was something uncanny about the Moonshadow woman. Her green eyes drew you in and fixed you in place like a butterfly under glass. She was beautiful, yes. But there was more to it than that, a fundamental otherness that kept her apart from the rest of the town. He could easily believe her house was held up by magic.

"I can't arrest someone for witchcraft," he blurted, frustration building.

To his great surprise, this seemed to mollify Alethea. "Have you checked?" the old woman asked after a moment. "Maybe there's a crazy old law on the books from back in the 1800s."

"Even if there is, dragging it out of some dusty law register isn't going to do any lasting good. I'm not turning Frognot into a laughingstock with some kind of harebrained Crucible re-enactment."

"Well then, what am I supposed to do?" Alethea demanded. At this point she seemed to be asking the universe as much as him.

"If you really believe that Carrie Moonshadow is a witch," he said in a low voice, "then maybe you should stop pissing her off." Alethea turned red again and was about to open her mouth for another run of complaints, when he held out a pacifying hand. "I'll go talk to her. Okay?"

Alethea sniffed. "You tell her to stay away from me. And my roses."

"I will." Sheriff Thorne put on his best, most patient smile. "Help yourself to a muffin on the way out. Orange-cranberry. Theo made them."

Narrowing her eyes, Alethea nodded sharply and turned to go, crossing paths with Theo, who was on his way into Thorne's office.

Theo was the department's newest administrative assistant. Thorne had hired him straight out of college. The young man had earned his place in the office with his steady competence but had really won Thorne over with his baking. As he came in, he placed a muffin on Thorne's desk. Thorne sensed it was an emotional bribe.

"Problems?" Thorne asked.

Theo frowned. "I think I used too much ginger. Chelsea says she likes the bite, but I think it overshadows the cranberry. I'm taking an informal poll."

Thorne smiled patiently. "The muffins are terrific. That's why I've already had three, which is the only reason I'm resisting eating this one immediately. But that's not what I meant."

"Oh. Uh, sure. We got a call while you were in with Dr. Murrow. Some hikers spotted a fire out at the old Becker-meir cabin. The fire department sent a helicopter to check it out. They think the afternoon rain will take care of it. But the fire chief's sending a few guys on foot to finish the job. Just thought you should know."

"I should, thanks." Thorne frowned, and after a long

moment, picked up the muffin and bit through the chewy golden top. Summer wildfires were normal—increasingly normal, unfortunately—but the incidents this summer weren't. It was possible someone had tried sheltering in the cabin—or that teens dicking around had started a fire for kicks—but it was still weird. Two weeks ago, a single massive ponderosa pine on Blackthorn Ridge had sponta-neously ignited and burned to fine ash. The fire chief said it had to have been a lightning strike, only there had been no lightning in the area for at least a week. At the very least, it was weird. And while Thorne was unwilling to embrace the existence of cow vampires, the Menkins had lost an unusual number of cattle this year. Even if Carrie Moonshadow was a witch, he couldn't lay *all* of that at her feet. She was strange, sure, but not malicious. Maybe she would have some insight about what was going on in town.

CHAPTER THREE

C arrie greeted the next day with a pile of crispy bacon, which she cooked up on her ancient cast iron skillet and took into the garden. *A witch and her spells need fuel,* as her mother used to say. She had made it onto her feet just before noon and passed a pleasant hour breakfasting and assessing the state of her fleawort beds. She'd gone through almost all her plantings this summer and was down to a measly patch at the edge of the row. If there was a big rush on healing spells in the near future, she'd be out of luck. Carrie carefully collected some seeds and got them started in a big terra-cotta pot she could move to her kitchen if the weather got cold early.

When that was done, she slung a canvas bag over her shoulder, dropping in a few novels to return to the library. The ground was wet, and she considered driving into town, but the weather would be stunning for another few hours, and it was only a mile's walk. She laced on her hiking boots over her sweatpants and set out along the shoulder of the road.

A cool breeze livened her senses, and she listened for birds. A red-tailed hawk circled lazily overhead. The spring wildflowers had faded to profuse green. Halfway to the library, she made a detour up the hill to a patch of wild sage. After checking around for cars, she collected several of the stems, placing them gently in a cloth bag. She could grow sage in her garden, she supposed, but it was basically a weed in this part of the world, and growing it would be a waste of effort.

Carrie took a moment to admire the view from the hillside. A few fluffy swirls of clouds decorated the brilliant blue sky on the horizon, but otherwise everything was drenched in pale yellow light. The sediment-rich water of the Santa Sangre lapped at its banks as it wound through the green valley below the piney hills.

The only thing out of place was a column of smoke rising up from behind the hills to the west. Something about the smudge of darkness made her uneasy, but she shrugged. The nearly perpetual fire ban of recent years had been partially lifted, courtesy of the heavy rains. Maybe someone was taking advantage of the window to roast s'mores. The smoke marched higher in the sky, and the breeze turned cold, turning her sweat clammy. On instinct, she picked an extra handful of sage. Already feeling productive, she clambered down the hillside and walked the rest of the way to the library with a spring in her step.

The Frognot Library was the oldest building in the county, originally put up by the railway as its headquarters in the late 1800s. Made of solid red brick, it had survived the various fires that had swept through the frontier town. It was also Carrie's favorite place in town, although not because of its historic significance. Whenever she walked through the glass doors, she had the feeling that she might get lost, that the library could swallow her up. It was a rambling place, overflowing with books, the stacks pruned occasionally by the enthusiastic town librarian, Maggie Lane.

Carrie headed straight to the circulation desk, where Maggie was checking out a stack of books almost as tall as the scrawny girl who had selected them. Carrie stood back a little bit. Today, Maggie was wearing a flowery minidress straight out of the seventies. Maggie had a nose for vintage clothing, which, unlike Carrie, she preferred for aesthetic reasons. A cheerful plastic clip shaped like a daisy secured her auburn curls.

"Are you on your bike, Kaylee? Are you sure you can carry all of these? They'll be awfully heavy," Maggie dubiously compared the height of the books relative to the height of the girl.

Kaylee nodded. "I've got a basket with a top that zips up. And I've got my backpack." She held out a spacious black nylon backpack.

Maggie pushed an auburn curl behind her ear, never one to discourage a young reader. Kaylee put her hands on her hips. "I wouldn't have so many, only the librarian who was here last week wouldn't let me check out the Edith Whartons I wanted. He said I should try *Diary of a Wimpy Kid.*" She snorted contemptuously, and Carrie had to put her hand on her mouth to stop herself from laughing. "Those are kids' books. And anyway, I've read them."

Maggie didn't find this as funny as Carrie. Instead, she looked troubled, tapping the protective plastic on *House of*

Mirth with one finger. "Well, I won't keep you away from Edith. And I'll talk to Archie about our circulation policies. Come on, I'll help you carry these out to your bike."

She spotted Carrie, and a warm smile spread across her face. "Carrie, will you hold down the fort while I'm outside?"

"Hey, Mags. Hello, Kaylee. I'm on it." Carrie put a protective hand on the circulation desk.

The girl's eyes widened when she saw Carrie, but she held her ground, which made her braver than most Frognot adults. When she nodded a wary greeting, her pigtails bobbed.

"How do you do, Miss Moonshadow?" she asked formally.

"I'm great. Enjoy your Wharton," Carrie said lightly, as Maggie and the girl labored away under their stacks of books.

Maggie swept back into the library a minute later to take possession of Carrie's library books. In addition to *Journey to the Center of the Earth,* she had a few old Agatha Christie mysteries she'd consumed without understanding a single thing about how any of the crimes were committed.

"How were they?" Maggie asked.

"Oh, you know, buttoned-up British people hemming and hawing over gruesome murders, and they all gather in a big room at the end for Poirot to explain things."

"That about sums up Agatha Christie."

Carrie leaned over the table to see what Maggie was reading. Her friend was always in the middle of a book, and often had good contemporary fiction recommendations. Today, however, she was being squirrely, blocking Carrie's view with her hand.

"What are you reading? Ooh! Is it something scandalous?" Carrie asked.

Maggie's cheeks reddened slightly, and she let Carrie push her hand away. The cover of the book showed a shirtless kilted Scotsman grasping a buxom redhead in well-muscled arms. The title was *The Hills of Loch Lomond.*

"Scotland's got a lot of ample hills, and this guy really seems to be enjoying them," Carrie teased.

"The *most* scandalous thing about this book is its butchering of the English language," she said primly, then coughed. "But yes, there's a lot of sex in it. Don't tell the other librarians you caught me reading this, I have a reputation to uphold. I would have put it in a different cover, but the plastic's stuck on."

"Not up to Wharton's standards?" Carrie asked.

"Barely up to Wharton's horniest chambermaid's standards."

They flung a few more barbs back and forth. Maggie endured her teasing with a good-natured grin. She was lighter on her feet than usual today, skipping from task to task with bouncing cheer. Maggie liked the Romantics, but she was not, personally, a romantic. Being a single mother in a small town had eroded her capacity for extravagant hope.

"What's going on? There's something different about you," Carrie said.

Maggie looked around to guarantee they were alone, then leaned forward. "I'm seeing someone," she said.

Carrie smiled. Maggie deserved a break. And Carrie

approved of any man who could drive her friend into the library's swooning section.

"You seem really happy," Carrie said.

Maggie smiled brightly, then stifled her expression, then smiled again. "I have a good feeling about this guy, Carrie."

"Tell me all the juicy details! Well, maybe not *all*. But I could probably handle a few medium-temperature details."

"I don't want to jinx it!" Maggie said, and then promptly continued talking, words flowing out in a hushed but enthusiastic clip. "His name is Marcus. He's a land surveyor."

"He has the technical background to appreciate ample hills."

Maggie slapped her with the paperback, then blushed. "Yes," she said. "Yes, he does."

"I'm happy for you."

Maggie surveyed Carrie's pale face and stained sweatpants. "How are you?" she asked. She was polite enough not to add the obvious, which was that Carrie looked terrible.

Carrie looked around to make sure no one was listening. "I've been working a lot lately. It's draining," she said in a low voice. Maggie was one of the only people in town who understood the extent of Carrie's powers. She also knew the price Carrie paid.

"You have to pace yourself. Are you eating enough? I'm due for my break. Want to go for a coffee? On me," Maggie offered. When confronted with friends in trouble, Maggie's default was mothering.

Carrie was sad to decline. "I ought to get back to the

house. I'm expecting company. Well, not company. A new client, I think." She quickly sketched out last night's encounter at the diner with the troubled young woman.

"Can you help her?" Maggie asked.

"I don't know. If she's ill or on drugs, I might not be the right person *to* help her."

"Hmm, I won't keep you then. But you owe me a visit! Reg misses you. He's going to visit his dad soon. You should come over before he leaves."

Reg was Maggie's ten-year-old son. The two of them had a little house up on the ridge, and Maggie was always trying to rope Carrie into family dinners. Reg's father, Orin, had skipped town when he was three months old, and Maggie had struggled in the wake of the breakup. Orin had shown up five years later asking to see his son, probably in an attempt to convince a new girlfriend he was marriage material. Allowing Reggie to build a relationship with his dad had nearly killed her, but Maggie always put her son first. Still, her eyes roiled with a mix of anger and sadness any time she talked about her ex. This was going to be Reg's first long trip visiting his dad. Maggie was worried but trying not to let it show.

Carrie sometimes wondered if their friendship was a drag on Maggie's life. The town kept her at arm's length, and she didn't want the hushed whispers and dark gossip rubbing off on Maggie. Carrie made a non-specific promise to set up a dinner.

"At least let me send you away with a book. More Christie?" Grinning, Maggie adjusted the daisy clip in her hair. "Or something else? I don't think Kaylee cleaned out *all* my Wharton."

"That might be a little advanced for me," Carrie sighed. "But I hear great things about *Diary of a Wimpy Kid.*"

To Maggie's great distress, Carrie left empty-handed. The walk, while pleasant, hadn't replenished her energy, and she didn't feel like shouldering more weight. She promised to correct the slight soon, however, and headed out.

CHAPTER FOUR

When Carrie got back to the house, Finn confirmed that Emily hadn't stopped by. She considered taking a nap, but decided against it, and went out to the balcony instead to see how her spellwork was holding up.

The rotten joist looked brand-new. A little too new, perhaps—a small twig had pushed its way out of the wood, unfurling paper-thin leaves into a nearby patch of sunlight. Carrie debated sawing it off but decided to leave it. It looked pretty at the corner of the house, if a little uncanny.

By the time she had finished a tuna salad sandwich, she had convinced herself that Emily wasn't coming. But in the middle of the afternoon, as she finished weeding the back garden and picked tomatoes for dinner, an engine rumbled in the distance. Carrie rinsed her hands off under the hose and was out front in time to open the gate for a beat-up red sedan puttering down the gravel driveway.

Emily was wearing massive black sunglasses that dwarfed her small frame. She declined to take them off inside Carrie's house, which was cool and shadowy behind its wooden blinds. She accepted an offer of herbal tea, however, and drank it without reservation, which wasn't always true of the Frognot denizens who came knocking on her door for help.

"My sister said you were a witch," Emily said, settling into Carrie's overstuffed blue sofa. A lot of people expected Carrie's home to be full of Victorian antiques—spooky hand-carved masks and bird skeletons and delicate glass bottles with dubious contents. True, she had some magical bric-a-brac up in her tower, including a basketball-sized jade orb she'd barely gotten up the stairs. But most of her furniture was from either Trixie's Treasures, the thrift store by Albertson's where Carrie also bought all of her clothes, or the IKEA in Denver, to which she made a biannual pilgrimage. Magic paid the bills, but no one was leaving investment banking for it.

Emily pointed at the coffee table. "I have the same table," she said, and went back to sipping her tea. She looked uneasy. Carrie didn't think Emily was afraid that she was going to do some kind of deviant black magic. No, she suspected the young woman was afraid that she wouldn't be able to do anything at all.

"What brought you to *me*, specifically? Have you been to a doctor?" Carrie asked, leaning forward and making her tone as warm as possible.

With shaking fingers, Emily reached up and removed her sunglasses. As she folded them carefully onto her lap, Carrie sucked in her breath. The young woman looked awful. Her eyes were red-rimmed, and her skin was yellow where it wasn't bruised. Carrie had never seen anything like it. Emily hadn't looked this bad last night, and Carrie felt a surge of regret that she'd sent the young woman away.

"Did someone hit you?" she asked, her voice deteriorating into a growl. Her fingers clenched onto the sofa in anger.

Emily shook her head. "No. I know it looks like it. I swear I'm not doing the thing where I say I ran into a door. I was by myself in my sister's house all night, and when I woke up I looked like this. It's—"

"What?" Carrie asked.

"It's happened before a few times. I've been sick for a while now, but the bruises. This is the third time. And it's getting worse."

"Have you been to see a doctor? Maybe it's a clotting disorder. Or you're sleepwalking."

"Dr. Redkar down at the clinic ran tests, but she says nothing's wrong. She told me to eat more spinach and try meditation."

Carrie's anger sparked at this almost as much as it had at Emily's bruises. Deep distress was too often pinned as the cause rather than the result of women's illnesses. She was used to being a last-ditch solution when doctors failed. Unfortunately, that often meant that she couldn't help either—or at least, that she couldn't afford to use the amount of power it would take to fix the problem. But something about the spark of hope in Emily's eyes tugged at her.

"I don't work for free," she said gently.

Emily swallowed and nodded uneasily. "I can sell my car if I have to."

Carrie took a deep breath. If she could produce a cure,

a car would be a reasonable trade. Good health was a bargain at any price. "I can't make any promises. But let me figure out if I can actually help before you go selling off your beanie baby collection."

Carrie rolled up the sleeves of her threadbare denim shirt, exposing a set of intricate tattoos on her tan skin. Intricate interlocking geometric designs circled both her forearms, extending down onto the backs of her wrists and crawling up her left pointer finger. Her throat caught briefly, and she had to blink very rapidly to stop her eyes from watering. These tattoos were visible symbols of her power, and it pained her so much to look at them that she was tempted to scream at Emily to leave, and to crawl back under her linen sheets. She had paid an incredibly high price for these tattoos—one she would take back in a heartbeat if she could. But that wasn't possible, and it would be worse not to use them, like hunting a deer and leaving its body to rot in the forest.

After collecting a few small bottles from an ornate apothecary cabinet on the kitchen counter, Carrie directed Emily to the dining room table and sat down across from her. "Put your hands on the table."

Emily's pale fingers quivered slightly as she rested them on the blonde wood. "Is this going to hurt?"

"No. I'm just going to try and figure out what's going on. Okay?"

Emily nodded meekly.

Repairing the house had drained Carrie's reserves. *If you find something terrible, don't go swooping in to fix it. Gather information first.* Carrie opened two small cobalt glass bottles. The first contained a fragrant herbal oil, which she rubbed into a symbol on her left arm that represented understanding. The second bottle smelled earthy and mineral, and she used it to trace a series of triangles on her right wrist.

"Palms up," Carrie instructed, and placed her olive-brown hands over Emily's palms, which were red and raw with worry.

Emily breathed in, feeling the same gentle tingle as Carrie. "Your hands are warmer today."

Carrie nodded, but didn't respond. She focused on her breathing, matching it to Emily's. She was attempting an empathic connection—basically, she was going to feel what Emily felt. Emily's inner life, combined with Carrie's understanding of magic, might alert her to the source of the problem.

The second she made the connection, fear rose in her throat. Emily was very afraid, and so Carrie was too. It was an exhausting, persistent sensation that flowed through Emily's body as surely as her blood, so familiar that she might not even realize she was living with it. The fear exerted a gravitational pull on the rest of Emily's emotions, tugging her life force down into a lower register, weighing down her joy and creativity. Emily was exhausting herself resisting the gravitational pull of it.

Carrie pushed deeper, spreading her awareness through Emily's body, starting with her fingers and toes, and working her way to the core. Emily's chest tightened with anxiety, and suddenly, Carrie's attention sparked to a unique sensation. There was a patch of darkness on Emily's breastbone, just above her heart. The flesh there was cold, and the rot in the marrow was more than just physical. A crab-like knot of dark energy had accumulated in the tissues, corroding Emily's spirit. As Carrie focused on the area, her fear flared, and every hair on her body stood straight up. She and Emily both breathed hard, and terror threatened to overcome her.

Carrie drew her hands away, and Emily gasped.

"What was that?" Emily asked. The ebbing of the doubled consciousness had hollowed her out.

"I was feeling what you feel," Carrie said.

Emily wrapped her arms around her chest. "You could have just asked me. I'm not trying to hide anything."

"I know. I'm not accusing you of anything. People don't always know what they're feeling. And they can know without understanding. But, you're right. I could have told you what I was doing."

"Did you fix what's wrong with me?"

"No. This was more like a diagnostic exam." Carrie tapped her fingernails on the table, and a flake of green paint chipped away. "Have you purchased any new jewelry? A necklace, specifically?"

There was a long pause, and Carrie knew her arrow had hit the target. But Emily said, "no, nothing," and stuffed her hands in her lap.

The small bones in Carrie's wrists and fingers ached with the effort of using magic two days in a row, and she flexed them. Pain and fatigue had eaten up her reserves of patience. "I'm trying to help you," she said. It came out almost as a yell.

Emily shoved her chair away from the table. Hands fluttering, she retreated to the front door. "I'm sorry. I shouldn't have come."

Carrie followed her, wondering why the comment about the jewelry had frightened her so much. Emily picked up her pace as she left, half-jogging down the driveway.

Dammit. Carrie forced her aching bones into a run. Emily recoiled when Carrie grabbed her arm, but Carrie held her in place. "Don't go. I think you've been cursed," she said.

This declaration was meant to scare Emily into submission. Instead, the young woman looked relieved. "Really?" she asked.

"Really," Carrie said. She raised one hand and lightly touched the spot on the younger woman's breastbone. The skin there was cold, and a foreboding tingle pricked at Carrie's fingers.

"I, uh, no. It's not possible. She wouldn't do this. I know she wouldn't," Emily said. The young woman looked like she wanted to sprint away from whatever she was about to tell Carrie.

"Who would do this?" Carrie tried to sound gentle, but she was so, so tired.

A rumble in the distance announced the arrival of another afternoon storm. Emily pulled her thin fleece jacket tighter at the moist breeze rolling off the hillside. "My sister. She bought me a bracelet, with a bunch of pretty silver charms. She said it would protect me. She's into this sort of thing." She waved her arm in Carrie's general direction, a sweep that encompassed her and her house.

"Do you have the bracelet with you?" Carrie asked. Emily shook her head. "What does it look like?"

"Like your tattoos," Emily said.

Carrie had many tattoos, all with different meanings. None of them, however, were curses.

"Would your sister have any reason to curse you?" Carrie asked.

Emily got very quiet. "I know she'd like the place to herself again. For me to go back to work."

Carrie nodded. If you wanted your sister back at work, poisoning her with a curse wasn't the way to do it. But then again, a lot of people were stupid and evil. Carrie knew all too well how twisted family dynamics could get. It was worth checking out.

"I'm coming with you back to your apartment. I want to look at this bracelet."

Based on the location of the rotten energy in Emily's chest, Carrie had suspected a cursed necklace. But the bracelet was worth checking out. And if it really was cursed, she didn't want Emily throwing it in the trash and passing the danger along to some unsuspecting garbageman.

"Now?"

"Yes, now! Unless you have a hot date," Carrie said. Emily, cowed, waved Carrie to her car. The second they were inside the red sedan, Carrie put her seat back and closed her eyes. If the bracelet was seriously bad news, she would need every last micron of energy. When they were halfway up Florida Road—which everyone in Frognot annoyingly pronounced Flo-ree-da—Emily ignored Carrie's clear fuck-off vibes and tapped her arm.

"How did you learn all of this?" she asked.

"You mean my superior napping skills?" Carrie grumbled. She tried to push the seat even further back, but it was blocked by a duffel bag in the back seat.

"I mean the magic. What you did back at the house? The tattoos and curses."

Emily had uncapped the well, and now a rush of dark feelings rose up unbidden, swirling through Carrie's guts. "I don't curse people. I only curse *at* people. And only when they ask me too many questions."

This was pointed enough to stick, and Emily turned on the radio. They listened to the back end of a National Native News broadcast as they finished the drive. According to the report, a forest fire around the Becker-meir cabin had spread to about twenty acres. That was probably the source of the smoke Carrie had seen earlier. She felt uneasy again but pushed it out of her mind. She had bigger things to worry about.

Emily lived with her sister in cheap apartments that mostly served agriculture students from Fort Clark. A makeshift fire pit had been thrown up at the far end of the parking lot, and several young people were tending a small campfire and drinking bottled beer. A young woman with dark hair raised a hand to wave to Emily, but stopped when she saw Carrie behind her, crossing herself instead. It was enough to make a girl want to learn a few curses. And not the four-letter kind.

Emily lived in a two-bedroom unit on the second floor of the building. "Dani's car isn't in the lot. If she comes home, though, don't say anything about the bracelet. Not until we know for sure." Her eyes were wide and fearful. Carrie stared at her until she unlocked the door.

The place was cheaply furnished, with windows that

faced a neighboring apartment complex and let in very little sunlight. Carrie's eyes narrowed immediately at the sight of several bright, brand-new looking tarot decks on the IKEA coffee table—as Emily had said, it was a twin to her own. A low wooden shelf behind the sofa supported a kaleidoscopic mass of crystals. The selection was random and unfocused—Carrie doubted the sister was getting much benefit from them. And the selection of books on witchcraft was preposterous. Volumes with pink and purple covers and titles like, *A Buffy Fan's Guide to Spellcraft.* Usually those books were harmless, full of poorly constructed spells whose only impact would be to waste the caster's time. Once in a while, however, a cheap grimoire would contain information that was downright dangerous.

"Does Dani use those books?" she asked, pointing to the shelf.

The spellbooks embarrassed Emily, who shrugged. "She looks through them, but she doesn't, like, do spells. Sometimes we read each other's tarot."

Carrie nodded. Most people were too lazy to make serious attempts at spellwork. *Maybe they're not lazy. Maybe they're smarter than you.* She made a show of looking over the tarot decks, which had all been designed and printed within the last four years. "Where's the bracelet?" she finally asked.

Emily led her down a carpeted hallway into a small bedroom, bare of the magical ephemera packing the living room. The blue Persian rug at the foot of the bed was spotless, and two large philodendrons flourished in the window. It was cooler in here, too, with less harsh sunlight streaming through the windows. A massive plush panda on the floral duvet gazed blankly out at the room.

The bracelet was in a lidded ceramic jar on the pine dresser. Emily removed the lid and offered it up without touching it. Before Carrie took the jar, she rubbed a small amount of salve onto the two intricate tattoos of stylized eyes on the soft undersides of her wrists. The eyes were ancient wards against evil, and the salve would reinforce them. The tattoos wouldn't protect her against everything, of course. They were like a sturdy raincoat, great in a thunderstorm but useless against a tidal wave. Carrie would have detected the presence of a powerful black magician in town, so whatever Dani had drummed up was unlikely to knock her socks off. The protective tattoos vibrated faintly, and her hands warmed.

Carrie plucked the bracelet from its container, arranging it so that she could see the charms, which were small silver discs, each a little smaller than a penny. The first one she looked at, etched with four interlocking triangles, was meaningless, the symbolic equivalent of gibberish. Carrie went down the chain, inspecting the charms one by one. The next three were like the first, with pretty but powerless designs. The last charm, near the clasp, was different. Carrie's focus sharpened at the spiral-in-a-square rune.

"Is it really cursed?" Emily twisted the drawstrings of her jackets in a nervous hand, hopeful that this had all been a terrible mistake.

"Yes." Carrie scratched her neck in confusion as she checked over the rest of the bracelet.

"Dani wanted to make me sick," Emily whispered.

The door creaked, and a hand slapped against the wood. Carrie and Emily spun.

"What are you talking about, Em?" the woman asked. This must be Dani. There was a clear resemblance between the women, who both had strawberry blonde hair and pale gray eyes. But Dani, who was in her late twenties, had a vitality that her younger sister lacked. Her face was fuller, her hair was shinier, and she marched immediately to take a stand between Carrie and her sister.

"You gave your sister a cursed bracelet," Carrie said, holding up the silver chain. It caught the light, the charms clinking softly.

Dani, face reddening, snatched the bracelet out of Carrie's hand, the friction from the chain leaving a red line on her palm. "You don't know what you're talking about."

"Actually, I know exactly what I'm talking about. It's how I make my living. Do you see the spiral near the clasp? That's an energy funnel. It's been siphoning off your sister's life force."

Emily had gone so pale that the blue veins in her eyelids were clearly visible below the skin. "Why? What's the point of draining my energy?"

"You'll have to ask your sister. The power's not even going anywhere. The way the bracelet is set up it's just flowing down a hole to nowhere."

Dani stormed closer. "You're lying. She's lying to you, Emily. I got you that bracelet to protect you."

Carrie caught Dani's arm. Drawing on the last of her energy reserves to fuel an empathic connection, she slapped her forearm against Dani's skin, shoving her awareness into the woman's body. Dani yelped in surprise, but Carrie held on tight, concentrating hard on the other woman's emotions. Dani was upset, and scared. Both of which might be true if she had tried to hurt her sister. But there was also an undeniable well of loving concern for Emily.

Carrie let go and sank into a crouch. Her teeth chattered as the spell subsided. She was in deep trouble now.

"If you didn't want me living here, you could have asked me to leave!" Emily said.

Dani was too shocked by the sudden intrusion into her feelings to respond.

"There's been a mistake," Carrie groaned. The sisters looked down. "I was wrong. Help me into the living room." She needed a blanket, stat.

"Are you okay?" Emily asked as they guided her down the hall.

"I used my own life energy to power the spell I just did," Carrie said.

"What spell?"

"She invaded me. She tried to read my mind," Dani accused.

"I did the same spell we did earlier. I wanted to know what she was feeling," Carrie said.

"What was she feeling?" The question was desperate, and Carrie didn't answer.

"I need sugar. Tea with honey. Or a Coke," Carrie said when they settled her on the sofa in the living room.

Emily offered to make cocoa. Dani offered to open a bottle of wine. Tempting, but it would only make her sick. Carrie said yes to the cocoa.

A few minutes later, Emily pressed a hand-thrown

ceramic mug painted with wild columbines into her hand. The sugar and fat restored a little of the energy she'd lost overextending herself. Dani settled herself on a chair, and Emily sat cross-legged on the floor.

"Where did you get that bracelet?" Carrie asked. The jangling silver strand was still in its ceramic container, sitting on the IKEA coffee table.

"I bought it from a store in Denver."

"A jewelry store?"

"No. A store that sells crystals and candles. Where they do fortune-telling in the back. I asked if they had anything for protection, and the woman working the desk gave me this. Sometimes I can tell when an object is–different."

Carrie raised an eyebrow. Dani really was a witch. Not a powerful one, maybe. Not with her current training. But she could pick up on magical currents, which was how all witches started. "You could tell that the bracelet was different?"

"Yes. I thought it was a protective spell. Like the woman said."

A little knowledge could be a dangerous thing. "It's not a protective spell. It's cursed. It's been draining Emily's energy. I'll dispose of the bracelet. You should start to feel better, soon." She tried to sound confident, but doubts still nagged at her mind, worsening when the sisters exchanged a look. She turned to Dani. "You bought that bracelet for protection. Why?"

After a moment of hesitation, Dani grabbed a leather-bound journal from behind her crystals. From between the pages, she retrieved a Polaroid. It showed a beaming Emily standing on a high mountain trail in front of a field of wildflowers. There was a sandy-haired man standing beside her, a possessive arm clutching her to him. His face had been scratched out with a safety pin. Emily looked happy in the photo, and much healthier. It made her deterioration since then seem even starker.

"She had this boyfriend, James." Dani said. "He was a real piece of work. Constantly running around with other women."

Emily hung her head.

"I told her to break up with him." Dani was irritated, even now. This had clearly been a longstanding argument between the sisters.

"Well, I did. And look what happened," Emily snapped back.

"He didn't take it well?" Carrie asked.

Emily looked guilty. "When I told him to move out, he apologized. He said we could work on our relationship. Things between us got better."

"And then they got worse again. I finally convinced her to leave him," Dani said.

"When I moved in with Dani, things got really bad," Emily said.

Dani was furious now. "James started dating the woman across the hallway so that he had an excuse to come around all the time. I told her about his cheating, and when she kicked him to the curb, I thought it was finally over. But he got a job with the maintenance department at the complex here. The kind of job where he had keys to our door. I put a deadbolt in for when we were home, but I can't be home all the time. A few weeks after he started working here, things in the apartment began moving around. And then he put a dead raccoon in Emily's bed. His boss told us that James was a 'nice guy' and hinted that Emily had put the raccoon in the bed herself, to try and 'ruin James's reputation.'" Dani snorted.

"He made me feel crazy, but I'm not crazy," Emily insisted.

"You have crazy taste in men," Dani shot back.

"I already feel terrible. Why are you still sniping at me?"

"Because none of this would have happened if you'd listened to me in the first place!" Dani turned to Carrie. "James and I went to school together. He was always bad news, and I told Em that when he first started sniffing around her."

"He was nice! If I dumped every guy you hate, I'd be alone forever," Emily said.

"Yeah, and you'd be better off!"

Their voices buzzed in Carrie's ears, and lightning-bolt-shaped dark spots flashed in the corners of her vision. In half an hour, she'd be flattened with a migraine. She had to make progress before then.

"Stop it!"

There was a moment of blessed silence. Carrie caught her breath, then said, "There's not a witch in the world who can change the past. Not you. Not me. Not anyone. If you want to fight over old terrain, do it when I leave."

Dani sighed, and Emily curled up on her corner of the sofa, wrapping her arms around her knees. Emily approached and put a hand on her sister's back. "I bought that bracelet to protect you. I swear."

When Emily met her sister's eyes, her face softened. She brushed a piece of hair out of her face. "It's okay. I know you did. You let me move in here, too." She looked up at Carrie. "I had a job, before. Working out at the Menkin ranch."

"Really?" Carrie couldn't picture Emily doing physical labor. Certainly not in her current state.

"I was good at it, too," Emily protested. "It was only part-time. But it was gonna help me with school."

"She was good at it," Dani added, shooting down Carrie's skepticism.

"I don't need your help," Emily grumbled.

"You clearly do," Dani shot back.

"I'll destroy the amulet, and you should start to feel better," Carrie said.

"Thank you. Truly," Emily said.

Carrie rubbed her temples, thinking about the copay on her migraine medication. You couldn't do magic to fix a problem caused by using too much magic. "In lieu of thanks, I accept cash," she said, staring down the sisters. Emily looked hopefully up at her big sister.

"For fuck's sake," Dani said, and reached for her wallet.

CHAPTER FIVE

Carrie counted the bills from Dani, then tucked them in her bedroom safe. If they lived frugally, the money would keep her household running for at least another month. Sometimes she dreamed about finding buried treasure out in the garden. That was a fantasy, though. Finn would have found it by now.

Picking up the ceramic box containing the silver bracelet, she contemplated her options. Finn kept a crucible in his small basement workshop. If she asked him to, he would happily melt the bracelet down. Wave a little sage over the whole thing and the curse would dissolve. She could even sell the silver for scrap.

Instead, Carrie tucked the ceramic box in the back of the safe, behind the sad wad of cash. Her finger brushed a bloodstained, heavily embroidered gray velvet pouch, and she pulled her hand away instinctively as a deep chill shot up her arm. *You really ought to buy a second safe.* Carrie grabbed a pointed black mule from under her bed and pushed the offending gray pouch safely back into the corner. Then, with a sigh, she removed the little ceramic box and put it back in her pocket.

Carrie collected dangerous magical objects like crows collected trinkets. It was a bad habit, and it was going to come back and haunt her one day. There was no reason she had to add the bracelet to the cursed horde. No, she wouldn't keep this one. She would be good and give it to Finn to destroy.

"Finn!" she cried. She hadn't seen the gnome since breakfast. She would make herself some willow bark tea, and then she would ask him to fire up his crucible.

Carrie closed the safe and activated the electronic lock, then stared reluctantly at the magical wards etched into the steel door. If she refreshed them tonight, the ache in her head would degenerate into a sleep-denying, jackhammering agony. She was dreading going to bed as it was. *Tea first.*

She sat at the table rubbing her temples, and when a pounding noise penetrated her awareness, she thought at first that it was her headache. After a moment, however, she realized there was someone at the door. She was so tired; she hadn't heard a car pull up.

Carrie peered out the peephole and opened the door.

Standing on the porch was Sheriff Caleb Thorne. His uniform was pleasingly tight on his well-muscled frame, but she was too tired for serious ogling. Plus, his uneasy posture and drawn face suggested he wasn't here for a social visit.

"Sheriff Thorne." Carrie stayed studiously neutral. He glanced inside the living room, eager to be invited inside. She let him stew in silence instead.

He cleared his throat. "Please, call me Caleb," he said, gazing at the waterfall of board-straight chocolate brown hair falling over her shoulder.

"Whatever you say, Caleb," she said.

Her sarcasm caught him off guard. "I'm, uh– I'm afraid I'm here on business," he said.

Carrie swung the door open and retreated into her kitchen. Falling over on her feet wasn't going to help her.

"Do you want some willow bark tea?" She gestured to the stove, where mushy bark was steeping in a pot.

Thorne grinned. "You know you can just take aspirin. It's the same active ingredient. Tastes better, too."

Carrie blinked in surprise. The sheriff was right. Willow bark tea contained the same compounds as aspirin. How did he know? "Be careful, saying things like that. People will think you're a witch."

He squirmed under her imperious gaze. Carrie admired the way it made his uniform tighten on his broad shoulders.

"I, um, need to ask you where you were last night," Thorne said. He looked embarrassed.

Had something happened to the sisters since she'd left? Carrie hoped not. "Is Emily okay?" she asked with genuine concern.

"Emily? Emily who?" Thorne's eyebrows went up, and she cursed her big mouth.

"Nothing. Just a little freelancing I'm doing."

"Does it have anything to do with Alethea Murrow's prizewinning rose bushes?"

Carrie froze for a fraction of a second, which she hoped Sheriff Thorne didn't notice. She had been told by multiple people—including several ex-boyfriends—that she was very hard to read. She mostly found this annoying, but once in a while, it was a boon. "Why do you ask?" She kept her voice careful.

"Alethea has it in her head that you killed one of her rose bushes."

"Why would I want to do that?"

He shrugged, clearly as unhappy with these questions as Carrie was. "I don't know."

"I've never done anything to Alethea Murrow. I don't know why she has a grudge against me." The first sentence was a lie, but the second one was true. Murrow had taken against Carrie years ago, well before Carrie had finally snapped and destroyed those perfect, blood-red blooms.

"Really?" Thorne asked. "No reason at all for any late-night deflowering?"

Carrie choked on her willow tea, and Thorne turned bright red. "I wouldn't deflower Alethea Murrow with a ten-foot pole," Carrie said icily.

It took a heroic effort, but he kept a straight face. When he spoke again, he was studiously casual. "You said you're a freelancer? What line of work are you in?"

"Do you work for the county or the IRS?"

Her sharp tone upset him. "I was curious, that's all."

"Like I said, I'm a freelancer."

"What kind of freelancer?"

"Odd jobs?"

"Like a task rabbit?"

Now there was an idea. Magical services, ordered up on an app. "Sure. Like a task rabbit," she said. Why not? It made as much sense as any other fabrication.

"People talk about you, you know," he said.

"I do hear the occasional whisper behind my back," she answered flatly. What did he want? Was he trying to get a rise out of her? Worse, was he trying to *flirt*? Was interrogating her in connection with floricide his version of pulling her ponytails on the playground?

He cleared his throat. "Frognot can't be a great place to freelance. What with the small population."

"That's my business. Literally."

"I just mean, I wonder if you'd find more community somewhere else. A larger city. People in small towns can be judgmental."

"So I've learned." Her face reddened as she spoke. The worst thing was, he thought he was being nice. Of course, people whispered about her. A few of them, like Alethea Murrow, did more than that. But she'd built a life here, and his casual suggestion that she leave town prodded at old wounds. "If you're here to run me out of town on a rail, sheriff, you'd better get it over with. Or are you going to come back later, with torches? There's a lot of agriculture in the Santa Sangre valley, I'm sure someone can drum up a pitchfork."

He winced, embarrassment clawing over his face. "I'm sorry. I didn't mean that. No one wants to run you out of town."

"We both know that's not true." Carrie glared. She was breathing hard now, a rush of adrenaline pushing back her exhaustion on all fronts. "Alethea Murrow takes my refusal to drown as a personal insult. I haven't done anything else to anger her." This conversation was quickly washing away any guilt she felt about the old crone's stupid flowers.

Thorne was clambering to his feet, clutching his hat in a sweating hand.

"Look, try to stay out of each other's way," he said.

"Tell her to stop nosing around my property every time it rains."

"I'll do that. In the meantime, if you need anything, here's my card." He placed it formally on her kitchen table.

Carrie still felt angry. Her heart rate was up, and a crimson haze clung to the edges of her vision, which only happened when she was really angry. The tiny ceramic box jostled in her pocket, and Carrie grinned. "You know, Sheriff, maybe there's something you can help me with."

"Of course," he said, straightening.

It would serve him right, coming to her house and trying to drive her out of town. She retrieved the ceramic box and shoved it across the table at him. Frowning, he opened the lid. When his calloused fingers touched the silver, he shuddered slightly.

"I found this on the road while I was walking," Carrie lied. "Maybe you can find its owner. You should check those charms, too, I think they might be gang signs."

"Really? Why?"

"They look suspicious," Carrie said.

Thorne was dubious about the extent of gang activity in the Santa Sangre Valley, but he tucked the bracelet in the front pocket of his shirt. Carrie smiled triumphantly. He wasn't going to sleep well tonight, not with that bracelet on him. It would serve him right. "I have a headache, and I think you'd better go." Her green eyes flayed him mercilessly as she herded him to the door.

Back in the kitchen, Thorne's business card stared at

her accusingly. "What do you want?" she muttered. She picked it up and headed for the trash, but some instinct made her transfer the number to the phone before she tossed it. She wasn't sure why. She was definitely never going to call that jerk.

CHAPTER SIX

As the door to Carrie Moonshadow's house slammed, Caleb Thorne wondered how he'd made such a mess of things. Carrie looked rather splendid when she was angry, like a beautiful mythological demon. The kind who lured unwary men onto sharp rocks. Because he enjoyed having all his limbs attached to his body, he would never tell her that. Why had he told her to leave town? She hadn't hurt anyone. He still had his suspicions about the roses, but even if she was responsible, it would hardly merit an arrest. There was no way Alethea Murrow was blameless in their conflict. The ridiculous woman cared about her roses more than most people cared about their dogs.

The meeting had been oddly tiring. His chest felt cold as he turned the heat up in his cruiser, his mouth opening in a wide yawn.

When he asked if Carrie had ever thought about moving, he hadn't meant it as a threat. It was more like asking a bright high school student if they were thinking of going to college out of state. Sometimes a place had nothing else to offer you, and you had to move on. Frognot hadn't been particularly kind to Carrie Moonshadow. She was an unusual person who deserved better.

He remembered the advice he'd given Alethea. *If she really is a witch, maybe you shouldn't piss her off.* He gave the crumbling Victorian house a final look as he pulled back onto the road. The sunset had turned the second-story windows into blazing orange eyes that watched him drive away.

Back on the highway, Thorne got a call about a cow blocking traffic on the highway near the Menkin ranch. Sighing, he pulled a U-turn and went to check it out. Maybe a vampire had let the cows out.

It was an easy drive. The Menkin ranch occupied four hundred acres of lush grassland east of the highway on the road up to Copperton. Along the edges of the property, trees interrupted the plains, and the land rose upwards into rolling hills.

Thorne heard the troublemaking cow before he saw it —or rather, he heard cars honking at it. Traffic was stopped in both directions, and Thorne turned on his flashing lights as he sidled along the shoulder. In the middle of the chaos, a massive black heifer loomed over the double orange lines. Paul Menkin, the ranch's semi-retired patriarch, was ten feet away, standing behind his truck. As Thorne got out of his car, the cow huffed and stomped a hoof at him. Jed might be off his rocker with his talk about vampires, but as Thorne got closer, he could see the source of the young man's unease. The cow's eyes were blood red where they should have been white, and milky liquid dripped out of the tear ducts. At the sound of Thorne's approaching car, the animal stumbled forwards, swaying unsteadily. Thorne considered taking a little detour to his gun rack, but ultimately decided against it. Menkin looked concerned, but not overly afraid.

"Hullo, Sheriff," Menkin said. The old rancher had been a big man when Thorne first met him, a football player gone doughy in middle age. About a decade ago, however, he had taken up the Atkins diet, cutting out everything but meat and salads—easy, Thorne supposed, when high-quality beef grew in your backyard. Now in his early seventies, he was as thin as the blades of grass his cattle munched on. Today, he looked frail, his belt tightened to its last notch and still hanging loose. Thorne didn't like the old rancher's odds against a two-ton beef animal, particularly not a sick one.

Menkin was chatting quietly with a sturdy, hard-faced woman. Sheila Kelley was a large animal vet who served both Frognot and Cypress, the next town over. She was dressed almost identically to Menkin, in jeans and a denim shirt, and there was a black medical bag beside her on the ground.

Sheriff Thorne greeted them both, although he kept an eye on the black Angus in his peripheral vision. "You're killing me, Paul. You've got to maintain your fences, or someone's gonna turn Bessie and themselves into hamburger taking a blind corner too hard," Thorne said. This was the third time this summer cattle had wandered off the ranch. The Menkin boys didn't have their father's work ethic, and often let maintenance work slide.

"I don't know how she got out. Doc Kelley and I walked

the whole paddock perimeter this morning. I swear on my mother's grave, Caleb."

"He's right. There's not a wire out of place," the vet said.

Just up the road, the breeze blew against a gate, jangling the metal chain. "You think one of the boys did it? Maybe Luke came in late and left it open?" He put extra emphasis on the word *late*. Luke and his friends often closed down McKellen's Pub. Marriage and kids had thinned Luke's crew of bar buddies, much to Luke's dismay. Instead of settling down, Luke had responded by partying even harder. After two DUIs for his trouble, he'd wised up and was now on a first-name basis with both of the town's Uber drivers. But it wasn't hard to believe he'd left the gate open in a drunken stupor.

But Paul shook his head. "The boys have their troubles, but this wasn't on them. I got a camera looking at the fence now. Takes a little video whenever someone drives up the road, motion sensor and everything. We live in a future my granddad coulda never imagined. Luke was home plenty late, but he left the gate latched. If you've got to write someone up, I guess the buck stops with me."

A car newly arrived to the traffic jam laid on its horn. Thorne winced, and when the noise died down, his left ear was humming. He shivered under his coat.

"You okay, Sheriff? You look a little peaky. Need Doc to take a look at you?"

The vet gave Menkin a disapproving look. But Menkin was right.

"I'm a little dizzy. Might be coming down with something." He rubbed his chest, and the silver bracelet in his breast pocket jangled, strangely cold through the fabric of his shirt.

"Wanna go up to the house?" Paul asked. "Get some coffee? Maybe a nice filet mignon?"

Thorne shook his head. "What would help is you getting your cow out of the damn road."

Paul nodded grimly, surveying the heifer. After an uneasy moment, he said, "The car horns should've scared her."

Another horn beeped, but the cow didn't respond. "What's the story with her eyes?" He looked at Doc Kelley, who stuck her hands in her jeans and eyed the heifer.

"That's a question I would dearly love the answer to," she said. She and Menkin exchanged a look that Thorne struggled to decipher.

"Is this about the, well, unusual wildlife situation Jed's been talking about?"

Menkin sighed. "You mean the man-sized vampire bat? Jed's been talking people's ears off with that ridiculousness."

Doc Kelley shook her head. "It's not that ridiculous."

This caught Thorne's attention. "Oh yeah? Has your practice been inundated by requests to neuter vampiric bat monsters?"

Before the vet could respond, Menkin butted in. "There's no goddamn vampire terrorizing the cattle, bat or otherwise. But the animals are sick, and it's not normal." He gave Doc Kelley another pointed look.

"You can't go around accusing people, Paul," the vet said. He'd caught them in the middle of a disagreement, and Menkin was itching to talk about it.

"Look Sheriff, what I'm about to say could be a coincidence."

Doc Kelley frowned at him. "Oh no you don't, Paul. You're leveling a serious accusation."

"Please. What are you two talking about?" Thorne asked.

"It's about one of my ranch hands. Well, former ranch hands. Young kid named Emily Leary."

Doc Kelley interrupted him, nostrils flaring. "She was volunteering with me earlier this summer. Thinking about going to veterinary school. Wanted to get a feel for large animal care."

"Doc brought her along to help vaccinate the cattle. She was so good at the work that I offered her a part-time job as a ranch hand. To help out with the things the boys can't keep up with."

"He poached my best volunteer." Doc Kelley's smile faltered, as she mulled the wisdom of adding relevant details.

"What is it? Something happened?" Thorne asked.

Before she could answer, the cow in the road panted and bellowed, hooves clacking on the asphalt.

Menkin shook his head. "The cattle got sick right after she started. As soon as things got really bad, she quit."

"And the cattle got better?"

Menkin's face screamed *no.* "They stopped gettin' worse. After she left," he admitted.

"And you think she tampered with them somehow?" Thorne asked.

Doc Kelley cut in. "We still don't know why they're sick. Even if a kid like Emily went crazy and wanted to take out a herd of cattle, she'd be hard-pressed to do it. We're not talking about some Russian arms dealer here. Some twenty-year-old kid from the wrong side of the tracks is not out here deploying novel bioweapons."

"Bioweapons?" Thorne's voice came out in a creak. His exhaustion vanished briefly, replaced by heart-pounding dread. "You think this was bioterrorism?"

"Whoa, cool your heels, Sheriff. Don't go calling Homeland Security just 'cause Doc made a bad joke," Menkin said.

Doc nodded. "Yeah. What's happening is weird, but not that weird. Not yet. We might be looking at some kind of new disease."

"Okay. What does that mean?"

"It means Paul'd have to cull the herd," she said grimly.

Thorne whistled. That would be a massive financial loss for the rancher. Maybe he had insurance, but still.

"What else?" Thorne asked.

"There's always a chance of a disease jumping species."

"Like swine flu? You think we could be dealing with, what? Cow flu?"

Paul was unhappy about this conversational turn. "Doc has a big imagination. The cows have been sick for a while, and me and the boys are doing fine. We're the ones who spend the most time out there, so we'd be first in line."

"What about Jed babbling about vampires?"

"Yeah, well, that isn't exactly a new development. And no one else in the valley is having problems. I called around and asked."

Thorne sighed. This wasn't how he'd imagined his day

going. Caleb Thorne, Cow Detective. "Could they have been poisoned?" he asked.

"I'm gonna do some bloodwork. Try and find out," Kelley said.

Sick cattle was one thing. Agricultural sabotage was another. Thorne added a visit to the ranch hand to his mental list. Had he heard her name before? "I'll check in with this woman. See if she can tell me anything."

"I can't stop you, but you're barking up the wrong tree. She's a good kid, I swear," Doc Kelley said. Menkin didn't contradict her, but Thorne could tell that he thought a visit to the Leary girl was a good idea.

The cow turned in their direction, its watering red eyes boring into Thorne. This animal was never going to make it to anyone's dinner table. "Want me to get my rifle?" Thorne asked reluctantly. He wasn't thrilled about the thought.

"No, no. You ever try to move a dead cow? Better to get her off the road. Luke's saddling up, should be trottin' out in a jiff."

Caleb nodded, and walked down the line of cars, letting people know what was going on. By the time he had put up a few cones, Luke Menkin was riding towards them on an elderly roan mare. Luke was in his early thirties, but his lifestyle made him look older. He had perennial stubble, and his face was covered with unnatural sweat. Thorne might have thought it was cow flu, only he knew the signs of a hangover all too well. He saw the same look on many a face leaving the Frognot jail.

Luke's eyes were bloodshot, and he rubbed the bridge of his nose between his fingers. The roan skittered when someone at the other end of the line blared their horn, but after a moment Luke circled around and got the cow moving back towards the ranch. By the time the hoofbeats had disappeared into the distance, Thorne was too tired to write Menkin a ticket.

"I'll let it slide this time."

"Thanks, Thorne. You know I appreciate it. How about you come up to the house and I send you home with some bone broth as a thank you. Best stuff in the world for what ails you."

In Thorne's opinion, the best cure in the world for what ailed you was a full course of modern antibiotics. But he didn't say that to Menkin. "Thanks, Paul, but I can't have people going around thinking they can get out of tickets by bribing me with bone broth."

Paul scoffed. "Believe me, Sheriff, if I wanted to bribe you, I'd do way better than soup. You want the best steak you've ever put in your mouth, you know where to find me. Change your life."

Sheriff Thorne tipped his hat. The thought of charred meat twisted his stomach, shooting acid into his throat. He still wasn't feeling great. He rubbed his chest again, coughing. "Nice to see you, Doc. If you learn anything about the disease, call me. I don't want to be playing catch-up on a national emergency."

"Will do, Sheriff. And, ah, when you talk to Emily, if you learn anything, and I'm not saying you will, I'd appreciate you returning the favor." The vet looked troubled. The sheriff promised he'd call her if he learned anything medically relevant.

As he pulled back onto the highway, his phone rang.

The voice on the other end chirped insistently. "Hello, sir!" his new deputy said. Her name was Dahlia Macintosh, and if she kept working as hard as she had during her first two weeks, she was going to steal his job out from under him before the snow melted next spring.

"Hey, Mac. I thought you were on the night shift tonight." He yawned, glad that his days working nights were over. *Don't kid yourself. Now that you're in charge, you're on call twenty-four-seven.*

"Yes, sir, Sheriff Thorne, but I started a bit early so I could talk to the fire chief. If you're worried about the overtime, I don't have to record those hours."

"You have to record all your hours. I'll figure out the overtime."

"…am I in trouble, sir?"

Thorne sighed. His new deputy had been the most qualified applicant by a mile, with top scores from the Dillon Mountain College's peace officer program. She was also painfully eager for his approval. When she'd started, he thought she might have a crush on him. That would have worried him less. She was a reasonable person, and crushes faded. But no, Mac was happily engaged to an equally earnest and hardworking dentist with the Indian Health Service. Her interest in Thorne was fatiguingly professional.

"You're not in trouble, Mac. But you will be if you burn out in a month." He tried to say this gently, but he could tell it stung.

"Yes, sir. But I think you're going to want to see what the fire chief sent over."

Fifteen minutes later, Mac met him in the small parking

lot at the side of the sheriff's office. She presented him triumphantly with a large blue cooler, which he eyed skeptically.

"I guess this isn't a cooler of beer that Fernandez sent over as a token of thanks?"

"No, sir. He said not to open it indoors."

Thorne cracked open the cooler, a decision he regretted deeply when he smelled the contents. If someone had used roadkill juice to put out a tire fire, well, he would have preferred smelling that to the odor in the box. The chill in his chest crawled down his spine, and Thorne yawned.

"Are you alright, sir? You look pale," Mac said.

"You can smell this, right?" he asked. The young woman was still smiling amid the stench—maybe he was having a stroke. But Mac nodded briskly.

"Yes, sir. Terrible, sir. Worse than the anatomy lab at school." He was relieved to see her smile crack a little.

"What *is* this?" he asked, yawning again. The smell seemed to be working its way up his nose and into his brain, and pain pulsed suddenly in his temples.

"The chief found it in the middle of the old Beckermeir cabin."

"Where the forest fire started?"

"Yeah. The guys he sent dug this out of the ashes. Stuck it in a haz bag and stuffed it in one of their coolers to bring it down the mountain."

He risked opening the insulated lid a little wider. When sunlight hit the contents, the smell seemed to fade slightly. He still couldn't make sense of the dark, palm-sized object inside.

It was a doll. Well, sort of. What kid would enjoy

playing with such a monstrosity? Maybe the little girl from *The Exorcist.* It looked a little like a corn husk doll, but made of choked hanks of black hair, formed into shape with greasy thread. Where was that smell coming from? When he looked at it, an ache in his chest pulsed more strongly.

"The chief thinks that someone burned down the cabin, and then left this inside?"

Mac shifted uneasily. "Well, that's the logical way of looking at it, sir."

"I didn't ask about logic, I asked what the chief thought."

She froze. "I know it's going to sound crazy, but I swear this is what he said. You can call him up and ask."

"I trust you, Mac," Thorne sighed.

"He thinks this thing survived the fire. That it was in the cabin while it was burning."

Thorne looked again, dubious. A fire could melt metal. It could certainly destroy a creepy hairball doll. A faint gray haze crept in at the edges of his vision, but before Thorne could blink to clear it, the thing in the cooler twisted. Thorne recoiled.

"What is it?" Mac asked.

He looked again, and the object was still. Damn doll. Thorne slammed the cooler lid down. "Nothing. Did Fernandez say what he wants me to do with it?"

"All he said was take a look."

Thorne cursed inwardly. The fire chief was probably pawning the thing off on him. Better it stay in the sheriff's offices than stink up the firehouse. Thorne couldn't blame him. He didn't want this thing hanging around, either.

Maybe he should order Mac to go drop it down the nearest abandoned mineshaft. But he couldn't order his employees to tamper with evidence.

"Thanks, Mac. I'll take this from here. Go get some food before your shift."

"Yes, sir."

Mentioning food sent a sudden wave of nausea through his body. Thorne grimaced. Maybe if he sat down for a few minutes, he would feel better. He waved Mac away and trudged into the office.

CHAPTER SEVEN

F inn crossed his arms, scrutinizing Carrie with a disapproving frown.

"You said this curse made the lass very sick," he said.

"I mean, she wasn't *dying* or anything. Not yet," Carrie said.

"You sound disappointed. Do you want this sheriff fellow to die?"

"What? Of course not!"

"But you want him to get very sick."

"No! I want him to regret trying to drive me out of town."

"He tried to drive you out of town?" Finn asked, spooning chicken soup into his mouth. The edges of his white moustache glistened.

"Not exactly. But he implied I should leave! And he accused me of destroying Alethea Murrow's rose bush."

"You're angry because Caleb Thorne accused you of something you did?"

"I wouldn't put it like that," Carrie spat.

"How would you put it?"

"In a different way," Carrie said. *One that doesn't make me sound like an evil witch.* "Emily had that bracelet for *months,*" she insisted. "It'll go into the evidence locker in a few days. Where it will probably be safer than it would be here." She drew herself up to her full height, plastering her most innocent expression on her face. The farce wasn't fooling Finn.

"I thought they auctioned off lost items. After a certain number of days."

She froze. "What?"

"They sell them to the highest bidder and keep the money. So that bracelet might not curse the sheriff at all. It might curse whoever buys it. Someone looking for a present for their little girl."

Carrie hadn't thought of that. She ate her soup grudgingly, marinating in this new information.

"He called me a witch." Was that true? *No, you called him a witch.*

"You are a witch," Finn said.

Carrie threw her soup spoon at him. He caught it nimbly, licked the chicken broth off it, and placed it carefully on the table. "You're impossible," she said, and pushed away from the table.

That night, sleep refused to come anywhere near her. Carrie twisted her sweaty wildflower-printed cotton sheets, imagining Sheriff Thorne sick in bed, a black spidery bruise spreading through his chest. He was shirtless in this nightmare, a detail she didn't care to interrogate.

Throwing off her sheets, she looked blearily over at the

glowing green numbers on her bedside clock. It was three in the morning. Before she could think about it clearly, guilt had tugged her out of bed. Carrie sighed, pulled on black drawstring pants and a t-shirt advertising a punk show in the basement of McKellen's, which was Frognot's Irish pub and the closest thing the town had to a goth club.

Light filtered out from beneath the door down to the basement, and on a whim, Carrie went to find Finn in his workshop.

The basement was another aspect of her house that was, by all accounts, physically impossible. This close to the river, it should have been underwater. But it wasn't— the plaster walls were dry and clean. Finn had built this place for himself shortly after moving in. Carrie couldn't detect any witch magic down here, but he must have done something to shore it up. *I should have invited Alethea for tea down here. She would have gone apoplectic, and I wouldn't have had to bother with her rose bushes.*

"You should be asleep," Finn said.

Carrie agreed entirely. "I need a cracksman."

"Adding breaking and entering to your criminal record alongside botanical sabotage?" His right eyebrow waggled with amusement. A single long white hair stuck out of it, and Carrie glared at it. If he gave her any more lip, she was going to pluck it out.

"Of course not," she huffed.

He waited.

"I gave him the bracelet, so it can't count as burglary to take it back," Carrie said.

Finn crossed his arms, and she tried to ignore his flinty judgment.

"I'll get my kit," he finally said.

The town was dead and dark. Frognot's tourists, who tended to get up early for wholesome activities like sunrise mountain biking, were wisely asleep. Carrie made a wide detour around the diner, which was the only place in town where someone might recognize her blue truck in the middle of the night.

A light was on in the sheriff's office when they drove past, and Carrie cursed. She parked two streets away and pulled out her phone. A few taps informed her that the office was, as of this spring, open twenty-four hours a day.

"Well, we're not doing a burglary," she said quietly.

"Good. Let's get pie."

"Apparently, we're doing a *robbery.*"

Finn sighed. "What's the difference?"

"A robbery is much more prison time."

This elicited a snort. "I'd like to see a prison try and hold me."

"You may be in luck."

She climbed out of the truck. Finn was right behind her, a bandolier of delicate tools slung across his chest. A practical outfit for a burglary, but out in the open he looked sinister. Carrie wasn't used to seeing him in all-black; the politest possible way to describe his usual style was eclectic.

Just before they walked into view of the bright office window, Carrie pulled Finn under an elm tree. "We need a plan," she said.

"Locks on these old buildings aren't likely to put up a fight," Finn said, stroking the silvery lockpicks on his bandolier.

"You don't know what you're looking for," said Carrie.

"Mmm. How will I possibly choose the right cursed silver bracelet from the vast piles of magic jewelry in this small-town sheriff's office?"

Carrie glared at him. "I don't appreciate the sarcasm."

"I don't appreciate being dragged out of bed in the middle of the night to commit crimes."

Carrie snorted. "You weren't asleep. You weren't even in bed."

"I might have been."

"Here's the plan," Carrie said. "I distract whoever's in the office, you steal the bracelet."

"Should we go over it again? The complexity may overwhelm me."

"Watch it, mister, or I'm going to start charging you rent," Carrie said. She turned before he could fire off whatever smart response he had in the chamber. "And no tunneling through the floors! We don't need to raise that kind of suspicion."

From somewhere in the darkness, a voice whispered, "You're no fun."

CHAPTER EIGHT

Carrie leaned across the front desk towards the young sheriff's deputy, whose scrupulously polished badge identified her as Dahlia Macintosh. "I need to report a crime," Carrie said.

This cheered the young woman up considerably. "Yes, ma'am! That's what we're here for." The deputy snatched a stack of blank reports from a corner of the desk and popped open a fresh ballpoint pen, her hand quivering with excitement at the prospect of fighting crime. Freckles dappled the young woman's nose and cheeks, and her light brown hair was pulled back in two French braids at the sides of her head, a style that made her look twelve.

"You're new," Carrie said.

"Yes, ma'am. Dahlia Macintosh. People call me Mac."

Carrie had an inappropriate impulse to shout that she'd found a dead body. It would probably send the overeager young lawwoman into ecstatic fits. After a moment, Mac cleared her throat, interrupting this daydream.

"What kind of crime?" Mac asked.

What a good question. The kind of question Carrie should have thought about before marching through the front door of the Sheriff's department. Behind the front desk, Sheriff Thorne's office was dark and locked. A whisper of snowy white beard appeared behind the glass as a window in the far back slid open.

She slammed her hands dramatically onto the desk to cover the sound. Mac jumped, her enthusiasm abating. Tut, tut. If she was going to work the night shift in Frognot, she was going to have to juggle a lot more crazy than this.

"Don't write any of this down! It could be dangerous. For both of us," Carrie improvised, snatching the ballpoint pen from Mac's hand. A faint scrape of wood on wood from the sheriff's office almost made the young deputy turn her head, and Carrie tapped the ballpoint hard against the desk to recapture her attention.

"I'm supposed to write everything down," Mac said warily.

"Of course you are. That's what *they* want."

"What *who* wants?"

"If I knew that, I wouldn't be here," Carrie stretched her eyes wide, pushing her face slowly towards the increasingly unsettled young deputy. When Mac flinched away, she stopped. "What are you going to do about this?"

"About what?" Mac asked, hand creeping toward another pen.

"The people following me. Wherever I go, there's always a car behind me."

This brought Mac cheerfully back onto solid ground. "A

car! That's good. Do you have a license plate? Make? Model?"

Carrie shook her head. "It's a different car every time," she said, punctuating each word with a stab of the pen. As she straightened up, something in the corner of the ceiling caught her eye. The shiny black dome of a security camera, watching over the reception area. *Shit.* She should have thought of that. Well, maybe it wouldn't matter. Crazy people must pass through the station all the time. The report might not attract attention.

Mac's face fell. "Oh."

Carrie felt a twinge of guilt about dampening the young woman's rookie enthusiasm. Tonight, it couldn't be helped. Sooner or later, Mac would get a taste of a real crime, and then she'd daydream about being bored and handing out traffic tickets. For the next quarter of an hour, Carrie fabricated diverse paranoid complaints. The drinking water tasted like metal. Squirrels staked out her house on Tuesdays and Thursdays. Strange trails of smoke in the sky spelled out her initials.

Mac, to her credit, listened carefully to Carrie's fictions. When Carrie saw the window in Sheriff Thorne's office close again, she announced that she was done. "Are you sure you don't want me to make a report?" Mac asked doubtfully. "Um, I have a card here, for someone who might be able to help you." She rummaged through her desk and retrieved a business card for Mountain Mental Health Care. "If you tell them we referred you, you can get a free consultation. It's a new program," Mac said gently.

Bless her heart. Guilt plucked at Carrie's guts again, for this last in a lengthening line of offenses. "I'll do that.

Thank you very much," Carrie said. Mac, having fulfilled her civic duty, beamed.

"You have a good night," Mac said.

Carrie smiled indulgently. If Finn's robbery had been successful, she would have a good night.

CHAPTER NINE

When Carrie saw Finn's face in the window of her truck, she knew something was very wrong. "What is it?" she asked, climbing into the driver's seat. "Did you find it?"

He held up the bracelet. The dangling charms clinked together as the silver spun in the moonlight. "You shouldn't touch that." Carrie yanked the cursed bracelet away from him and deposited it in the empty travel mug in her cupholder, slamming the lid on tight.

"It's a baby curse. Barely a papercut," Finn scoffed.

Carrie shook her head. "You didn't spend much time with Emily. She was really ill. And anyway, if it's a baby curse why do you look so worried?"

"Because that's not the only thing I found in Thorne's office," Finn said. He held up a water-bottle-sized cylinder. It looked very similar to the iron container he'd used to contain the debt-stone last night. This cylinder, however, was silver. Which wasn't a good sign. Iron was proof against most magic, good or bad. Finn breaking out the good silver meant he'd found something really foul. They had collaborated on the cylinder's production—he did the metalwork, and she did the protective magic. It was a containment device for particularly dangerous magical artifacts.

Carrie flipped on the overhead light. Finn twisted off the lid of the silver canister and held the open end towards her. She recoiled as a corrosive cloud of evil magic washed towards her. A thread-wrapped tuft of hair peeked out amid the evil overwhelming smell. It was a tiny human figurine, knotted from black hair. A manikin. Carrie couldn't bring herself to wonder where the hair had come from. A small sound emanated from the doll. Carrie didn't want to get too close to it, but she managed to lean in until she heard a small pulsing noise. It was a heartbeat, faint but unmistakable.

"Close that thing," she coughed. Finn screwed the lid on as she started the engine and opened the window, coughing madly. It was lucky he had the cylinder with him.

The object inside had conveyed an impression of powerful evil. "What is it?" Carrie asked.

"Bad news, that's what. Come on, we gotta ditch this thing as quickly as possible."

Carrie drove fast, rolling through stop signs and taking corners hard as she made her way back up the highway along the Santa Sangre. She had judged the sheriff as meddling and rude, but not evil.

"Do you think Thorne made that thing?" she asked. She hadn't detected a magical aura around him. But if he was powerful enough to make the foul thing in the canister, he might be powerful enough to cloak his magic. Maybe his little visit hadn't been about Alethea Murrow's roses at all. Maybe he had been sizing her up as a witch, figuring out what he could get away with. And she had sent him home with a cursed bracelet. Stupid.

"I don't care who made it. As long as we destroy it. We've got to get it to the tower," Finn said tersely. Carrie's anxiety climbed when he leapt out of the still-moving truck to tug open the oxbow's wrought iron gate. Before she'd turned the engine off, he snatched the cylinder out of the truck and took off towards the house at a jog.

Carrie moved more deliberately, taking a detour to deposit the travel mug on her kitchen counter, under the watchful eye of a bundle of sage that dangled from a hook above the window. It was more than enough to keep the minor spell contained.

She found him at the door to the tower stairs. No surprise there. The tower was Carrie's magical retreat, where she worked her most powerful spells. Carrie retrieved a key from a leather thong around her neck and opened the door's intricate iron lock. Finn prodded her up the steps, which he took two at a time, and only relaxed once he had deposited the cylinder in the protective circle carved into the smooth mahogany floor. He pulled a large container of table salt off a nearby shelf and sloshed it into the grooves, reinforcing the spells. Carrie fiddled with a silver mirror on a small stand until it cast a beam of moonlight from the west window over the lines of salt, adding an additional layer of protection.

Salt offered powerful protection against magic, and it didn't matter what kind it was. Five years ago, Carrie had met a witch in Venice Beach who only worked with black lava salt imported from Hawaii. It was so expensive that she was stingy with it, practically lining up individual grains for her protective lines. This extravagant carelessness still irritated Carrie, who would never stand for such posturing. She bought iodized table salt in bulk from the Costco in Farmington, and she didn't skimp on her wards.

When their preparations were finished, Finn reached for the cylinder, and Carrie saw for the first time a blackened wound on his palm. She grabbed his wrist to inspect it.

"Did this happen in the sheriff's office?" she asked.

He nodded tersely and tugged his hand back. "When I touched the manikin. I've got some salve in the basement. Quartz paste, good stuff. I'll be all right."

"If there's anything I can do, you know I will. I don't care how tired I am."

Finn shook his head, face unreadable. The healing magic she normally used didn't work on him. Or at least, it didn't work in the same way. She'd tried asking him about it, but Finn was secretive about all things gnomish. Outside of his hatred of ceramic lawn gnomes, he was remarkably tight-lipped. They'd established a solid working relationship during their time living together, but sometimes, he still seemed like a stranger.

"All I want is to figure out what we're dealing with," Finn said. Wincing slightly, he unscrewed the threaded lid of the cylinder. Noxious smoke belched out as he tipped its contents into the circle. The acrid wisps couldn't cross the salt lines, but Carrie could guess how it smelled. Finn inspected the silver cylinder, eyes narrowing at an etched rune where the curse had eaten into the silver. Grumbling, he placed it inside the circle next to the twisted doll.

"We'll have to make a new containment cylinder," he said.

"Is it that bad? What was it doing in Thorne's office? And why couldn't he *smell* it?"

"Those are the questions," Finn agreed.

Carrie selected a long silver pick from a nearby glass jar and poked at the twisted manikin. The jointed model of the human body hissed where Carrie touched it, and when she probed the interior of the bundle, the pick banged against a hard object in the interior.

"Have you seen anything like this before?" she asked.

Finn shook his head.

Carrie pursed her lips. Looking directly at the manikin made her nauseous, but when she directed her attention elsewhere, the loops of hair coiled and writhed in her peripheral vision.

"It's hard to imagine the sheriff making this."

Finn shrugged. Carrie imagined Thorne hunched over a table somewhere, rubbing dark-magic imbued grease into strands of dark hair. The picture didn't fit the frame.

"Open the windows," Carrie finally said. "I want to get rid of this before it does whatever it does." She didn't know what that was, but based on the magical burn on Finn's hand, it couldn't be good. If they couldn't destroy the manikin, something terrible was going to happen. She was sure of it.

Finn opened the windows, and a cool cross-breeze ruffled Carrie's hair, airing out the thickening rot that had collected in the room. Carrie went to a tall, carefully labeled apothecary chest, and pulled a sprig of sage from a larger bundle. She crushed the sprig between her fingers, smelling the savory, vegetal aroma. After a moment's hesitation, she grabbed the rest of the bundle. She was due for a foraging trip, anyways.

Sage was a powerful cleansing herb. Carrie hoped it would be powerful enough. She confirmed that the fire extinguisher was by the door before grabbing a squeeze bottle of lighter fluid. She and Finn had worked hard to fireproof the tower, but it was worth being careful, especially when curses were involved. She dropped the bundle of sage on top of the manikin and doused the whole thing with lighter fluid. When she was done, she whispered a short magical incantation. The tip of her finger turned red hot as Carrie released the small fire spell.

A cylinder of orange fire roared to life. The protective circle contained the licking flames, but not the heat. Carrie's cheeks turned red at the sudden change in temperature. This wasn't fancy, but it ought to work on a bunch of greasy hair. As the manikin caught fire, the flames twisted and darkened, the oranges and reds turning a bruised purple. Smoke rose from the circle in a dense column, and Carrie peered through it, trying to catch sight of the burning manikin. All she could see was sage, twisting and turning to ash in the fire.

The smoke should have died down after a minute, but instead it flared up with a loud *crack*! New orange flames shot to eye-height. *Shit.* The manikin packed quite a combustive punch. What was happening? Looking closer, she noticed a strange shadow around the inside edge of the salt ring.

"Shit, Finn, it's burning through the floor," she said. With the overkill of protective wards in the tower, the floorboards should have been able to resist a firebombing. This was bad. Very, very bad. *Your house should have flooded today, but here we are.*

The corner of a floorboard collapsed inwards with a thundering *crack*, taking a part of the salt circle with it. Black smoke streamed from the opening, pushing through the protective wards. Carrie tried to swear, but her throat had closed against the thickening corrosion. Beads of sweat evaporated in the heat as soon as they formed on her face, and she could barely see through the fog as she fumbled for the fire extinguisher.

Every year, the fire chief held a two-hour training on how to use an extinguisher. A big part of that training was on how to avoid fires in the first place. And today, Carrie had broken every single one of his rules. Although to be fair, he hadn't warned the class against dousing their floorboards in lighter fluid. Presumably, he considered that common sense. Fernandez would disapprove of her approach to breaking curses. But it was too late for that now.

Carrie pulled the extinguisher's pin. When she squeezed the lever, it let out a satisfying hiss, and Carrie swept the cloud of powder back and forth through the room.

"Grab the salt!" She choked out the words as the flames died down. The instant the smoke cleared, Finn was there with a full box, refreshing the protective lines with thick layers of salt that turned gray–black as they hit the charred wood. The cross-breeze picked up, giving Carrie a sudden clear view of the circle.

It was a wretched black pit. The fire, constrained by the wards, had burned half an inch through the floorboards. The sage had been reduced to ash, along with a good chunk of the wood.

The only thing that hadn't burned was the manikin. It stared up at them, the twisted hair and greasy string unchanged. A chunk of wood crumbled beneath it, and one of the 'arms' twisted in the heat, like it was waving at them. Below the manikin, the floor started to smoke again.

"It's still burning!" Carrie said.

She looked for Finn, but he was already on the stairs. A faucet turned on downstairs, and a moment later, he was back in the tower with a cup of water, which he drizzled over the manikin. It hissed and steamed.

Carrie took the glass from him and gulped down half the water left inside. By the time she was done, the floor had started to smoke again. If the house burned down, Alethea Murrow would lose her mind. What a twist! That was about it for silver linings.

"Shit," she said, and dribbled water into the protective circle again. Fortunately, the refreshed ward kept the steam inside. She didn't want to think about what the acrid manikin-rot-laced steam would do to human lungs.

"Make that water last," Finn barked, and sprinted back down the stairs. This time, he returned with a large, full bucket. Sitting beside the circle, he carefully ladled water onto the manikin, like an attendant at the world's worst sauna. Carrie refreshed the circled salt wards, glad she was using the cheap stuff.

It took six buckets to put the fire out. By the time they were finished, the sun was rising. Carrie glared out the east window, but the sight only made her feel emptier. She had had enough fiery orange glows for one day. Collapsed against the curved wall of the tower next to Finn, she chugged their remaining water straight from the bucket. It tasted like ash and death.

"What the hell do we do with this thing? We can't leave it here." Carrie eyed the manikin, suspicious that it might reignite.

"We could put it in a thick box and ship it to Ouagadougou," Finn said.

"Ouagadougou is a real place, and they don't deserve to have their post office cursed," Carrie muttered.

"Then we treat it like a toddler. We watch it carefully, and if it tries to burn down the house, we stop it."

Carrie wondered if Finn had done much babysitting. As always, it was hard to tell. She sighed. "I'll try to find out more about how to destroy curses." She was exhausted, and a headache was threatening to crush her skull from the inside. But it was clear that they couldn't leave the manikin alone. "Flip you for first watch?" she asked, fishing in her pocket for a coin.

Finn shook his head and pointed stubbornly at the door. "You go to sleep. I'll wake you up if my will falters." His face brooked no disagreement.

Carrie lacked the energy to argue. The walk to her bedroom was a blur, and she fell asleep with her clothes on.

CHAPTER TEN

Carrie slept until mid-morning, then climbed into the tower to relieve Finn of his watch. To her dismay, the round room was empty. A full bucket of water sat on the far side of the room, but Finn was nowhere to be seen. Throat tightening, Carrie inspected the protective circle. The manikin was there, at least, topping the pile of ashes like a cherry on a demonic sundae. Looking at the twisted black doll sapped all the energy she had recovered during her scant four hours of sleep, and when Finn's voice spoke from the empty air in front of her, she jumped half out of her skin.

"Carrie!" the voice exclaimed. It was coming from an unfamiliar object on her bookshelf—a dark metal sphere about the size of a golf ball, propped on a gold stand.

Carrie gasped. She never should have left Finn alone. "Oh my god, did the manikin turn you into a marble?"

The marble sighed. "Come downstairs. I'm in the kitchen."

She almost cried in relief when she saw Finn's shock of

wavy white hair. He was hunched over a frying pan on the stove. When he turned, his appearance startled her. Finn was wearing a strange device over his left eye. It looked like the offspring of an eyepatch and a telescope. The polished brass gleamed in the morning sun.

Carrie collapsed at the kitchen table. "You're alive. I thought the manikin had turned you into a metal ball."

He shook his head. "I've survived worse. But that thing was making me nauseous, so I set up an Iron Iris." He tapped the dark lens over his left eye. "It lets me keep an eye on things. And I can be up there in fifteen seconds from anywhere on the property. I tested it."

That must have made a lot of noise, but Carrie had slept through it. Finn slid a plate of toast and eggs in front of her and loomed over her until she started in on it.

"We need to know what that thing is, and how to destroy it," Carrie said.

"And who made it," Finn said darkly.

Carrie agreed. "That's a whole other can of worms. Except, that's not really the right metaphor. I *like* worms. Unlike that cursed manikin, worms provide valuable ecological services."

"What are you going to do?" Finn asked.

Carrie chewed her last bite of toast. She guessed Finn had baked this bread himself. "I'm going to do some research," she said.

CHAPTER ELEVEN

Maggie Lane inspected the drawing Carrie had sketched on a piece of torn-out notebook paper. "It looks terrible," she said.

"Sorry about that. I'm not a very good artist."

"I wasn't talking about your drawing. I was talking about…that *thing*."

"I couldn't bring myself to take a photo," Carrie admitted. In fact, she hadn't made it all the way up the tower stairs. Just standing in front of the door made her light-headed. A crazy idea had crossed her mind that taking a photo of the manikin might transmit its curse. She couldn't afford to walk around with a curse in her pocket, and she couldn't afford a new phone. Thus: bad art.

"Do you recognize it?" Carrie asked.

"Definitely not."

Carrie reached for the paper, but Maggie put her hand down on it. An ostentatious gold ring with purple rhinestones glittered on her index finger. It was a nice match for the purple wool dress she was wearing, which had a peter pan collar and big fabric buttons. "Cute ring," said Carrie.

"Marcus got it for me," Maggie said, struggling to contain a smile. "It's not real, obviously. That would be crazy."

"He's giving you jewelry! Maggie Lane, have you bagged a romantic?"

Her smile widened, then stretched into a yawn. "We were up late last night."

"Oh, really?" Carrie leaned over the circulation desk and waggled her eyebrows.

"He came over to my place for the first time last night. You know, with Reg being gone for a few weeks." Maggie suddenly seemed to remember she was sad. "I miss Reg massively, of course I do, but he was so excited to see his dad. You should have seen him with his suitcase—such a little gentleman, even though it's almost as big as he is. But boy howdy, it's been so long since I got to live that single life. I had a nap before our date, Carrie. A nap! And then Marcus cooked me dinner. This sun-dried tomato chicken. I kept raving about it and he sent me the recipe. Guess what? The New York Times calls it 'marry me' chicken."

Carrie's eyebrows climbed. Maggie smacked her lightly and said "Don't look at me like that! *This* is costume jewelry." She waggled the purple ring, which refracted the light into a pretty pattern on the desk. "It's very pretty though. Very, very pretty." A little sigh escaped her lips.

"I'm sorry to pull you out of your hazy romance. A fucked-up hairball doll is way less fun than a shiny ring." Carrie traced the outline of the manikin with her finger.

Maggie's spirits were too high for one lousy cursed doll to bring down. She tapped her pen against the paper, right in the middle of the manikin's chest. "Here's what we're going to do," she said. "You're going to get us both large mochas with extra whipped cream, and I'm going to go see what I can find in the reserve stacks."

Maggie found someone to take over at the circulation desk, and Carrie went off to Blacktree Perk across the street. The shop roasted its own coffee beans and bought its pastries from a local bakery. The lower level was full of people working on computers, and the loft had comfortable sofas and chairs. When Carrie ordered the mochas, the young woman behind the counter asked, "Is this for Maggie?" Apparently, she had a standing order. Carrie said that it was, and when the barista handed over the cardboard carrier with the drinks, she added a bag with two scones in it. Blueberry, by the looks of it, their tops dotted with chunky sugar crystals.

"The scones are on the house. Tell Maggie I say hi," the barista said. Unlike Carrie, Maggie was popular in Frognot.

Carrie paid for the drinks and went back over to the library. Maggie was still downstairs, and after a minute of slurping whipped cream through the hole in the plastic lid, Carrie went to find her. She headed downstairs, pausing briefly in front of a door marked 'Employees Only'. Carrie tried the handle. It wasn't locked. Would Maggie mind her poking around?

When she pushed through the door, the rich, papery smell of old books slapped her across the face. Carrie's eyes widened in amazement at the size of the basement. The library was already a rambling expanse, but this place was *huge.* Two six-foot mountains of stacked books guarded the door she'd just come through like sentries. Just behind them was a groaning shelf.

"Maggie!" Carrie said softly and turned left. To her left, books were stacked in loose, high piles. To her right, the shelf ran at least eighty feet into the distance. At the end, it split in two directions.

Just how big was this place? Carrie had heard of other western towns riddled with secret underground levels. Havre, Montana, where she'd completed a year-long apprenticeship with an ancient and unfriendly witch named Faye Eccleston, had a tunnel that ran from the mayor's house to the apartment building that had once been a brothel. That had been little more than a hallway, however. This was a labyrinth.

Carrie turned left at the end of the row and ran up against a dead end. She found herself breathing a little easier at the sight of the stone wall. She had half-expected the book-lined passageways to go on forever.

Carrie returned the way she'd come, taking the next right back to the entrance. Only this time, she walked the whole length of the row without finding a doorway. Somewhere, she had taken a wrong turn. She doubled back to the dead end, but she had gotten mixed up. This was a corner, turning towards another section of the basement stacks.

"You shouldn't be down here!" Carrie jumped out of her skin when a heavy hand fell on her shoulder, half-expecting to see a minotaur. But it was only Maggie. The librarian's face was pink, and her eyes blazed with an emotion Carrie had never seen before. "There's a sign on the door, and I know you can read," Maggie said sharply. Maggie was angry.

"I'm sorry." Now that she knew how upset it had made Maggie, she really was. By way of apology, Carrie extended the white paper bag. "The barista gave me free scones!"

"Come on," Maggie said, fingers digging in deep when she tugged on Carrie's arm.

"The exit's the other way!" Carrie protested, as Maggie led them back towards the dead end.

Except it wasn't. The sentry book stacks rose up to their right, alongside the plain gray stairwell door. "It's easy to get lost down here," Maggie said, pushing Carrie ahead of her through the door.

By the time they were back in the main library, Maggie had thawed back into her cheerful self. She plucked the mocha from Carrie's cardboard carrier and slurped it eagerly as she led them to a picnic table in the small garden behind the library.

Carrie couldn't shake off the basement's disorienting size so easily. "What's going on down there?" she asked suspiciously.

"Alphabetization. Occasional brave sorties into the Dewey decimal system. Eat your scone." Maggie's face was implacable. Carrie could run into that wall headfirst all she wanted, but Maggie wasn't going to budge.

They enjoyed their snack in silence. When they were done, Carrie brushed scone crumbs off her black pants.

"Did you learn anything about the manikin?" Her brief visit to the basement made her simultaneously more and less optimistic. On the one hand, there were a *lot* of books down there, and one of them might have answers. On the other hand, if such a book existed, it would be impossible to find it amid the stacks. Additionally, Maggie was empty-handed, and Carrie doubted the pockets of her vintage purple dress were big enough to hide a book. *Maybe the answers aren't in a book. Maybe they're in a nice short pamphlet. With a title like 'Super evil curses for beginners.'*

"I think I found something," Maggie said.

"What?"

Maggie took a smug bite of her scone, chewing slowly. Maybe she *was* still annoyed at Carrie's basement intrusion. As Maggie washed down the pastry with a sip of mocha, the back door to the library opened, and the young man they'd left at the circulation desk rushed out.

"The sheriff's here for you," he said breathlessly. Carrie was pretty sure this was Archie, the kid who had refused to let Kaylee have her Whartons.

Maggie leapt to her feet, hands shaking so badly that a little mocha leapt out of the lid of her drink and splattered across her purple wool dress. "What's wrong? Is Reg okay?"

"Sorry, I was talking to *her.*" Archie pointed at Carrie. "He seemed pretty insistent."

Carrie froze, glancing at the woods that bordered the library garden. If she ran, Maggie wouldn't stop her. Even if she was annoyed with Carrie. But no, that was ridiculous. If she was really in trouble, Thorne wouldn't have sent a lackey to fetch her. He would have come himself. Possibly with a gun.

Carrie finished the last of her mocha, glad she'd splurged on something fancy instead of her usual black coffee. She was going to need the energy.

"I'll call you later," she told Maggie.

"You'd better," Maggie said, face still worried.

Sighing, Carrie went to meet the sheriff.

CHAPTER TWELVE

S heriff Thorne had been incredulous when Mac told him about her late-night visitor, but when he checked the security camera footage, sure enough, there was Carrie Moonshadow on the screen, her long dark hair streaming down her back. The footage was too low-resolution to capture her piercing green eyes, but she was nonetheless unmistakable.

"Welcome back to the station," he said lightly, sitting down at his desk across from her.

She folded her hands on the dented wood. Long black sleeves hid most of her intricate tattoos. For a doubtful moment he wondered if they could be gang signs. But Frognot wasn't exactly a hub of gang activity. Disorganized crime was the order of the day. He had a fleeting thought that a coven was sort of a gang.

Carrie's expression was unreadable. "More complaints from Alethea? Or has there been a spree of botanical crimes? Someone poaching petunias from the window boxes at Town Hall? Chopping down Ponderosa pines to improve the view from their cabin?"

"You came to the station under false pretenses," Thorne said.

"Why do you say that?" she asked.

"I can drag Mac out of bed to identify you, if I have to. She won't be happy about it after working the night shift, and I'll be considerably less friendly after shelling out for unnecessary overtime." He reached dramatically for his phone, which only elicited an eye roll.

"You could just play the security footage," Carrie said dryly, glancing pointedly at the black dome of a camera in the corner of the reception area ceiling.

Thorne sighed. He was a straightforward man, not built to play bad cop.

"A few things disappeared from my office last night," Thorne said.

"If you've watched the footage, you'll know I didn't go anywhere near your office."

"You could have come back later," he pointed out.

"I didn't. Anyways, why would I steal back a bracelet I gave you?"

Thorne grinned, suddenly back on track. "I didn't say anything about a bracelet." Fleeting self-recrimination crossed Carrie's face. *Got her.*

The expression passed, however, replaced with a bland smile. "What else would someone possibly steal?" Her lip curled as she glanced at his ten-year-old desktop computer, with its even older monitor. "Does that dinosaur even work?"

He'd caught her in a lie, but what she'd said held true. Why *would* she steal a bracelet she'd given him? It was time to change tactics. "I'm not worried about the bracelet. What do you know about the fire out at the Beckermeir cabin?"

"I saw smoke the other day. *The Daily Croaker* published something about a fire, but I didn't read the article. What do *you* know about it?" A mixture of suspicion and a second, less readable emotion flashed in her eyes. Her irises were green and glinting, like mica sparkling through lichen. After a moment, it hit him. She was afraid. It was a shocking realization. Surely she couldn't think he would rough her up over a foul-smelling cooler and her own bracelet?

"If the items that were removed from my office were to reappear by, say, Saturday, then we wouldn't have to take this any further."

"I'd like to show you something," Carrie said softly.

Thorne sat expectantly back as she retrieved a small object from her pocket. It was a tiny figurine, smaller than a thumbnail. A gold frog, with green gems for eyes. Carrie twisted it so that it sparkled in the light.

The world around Thorne slowed as the frog's green eyes shifted kaleidoscopically. They were captivating, better than television or any of the time-wasting games on his phone. The green hoops pulsed before him, and time seemed to slow as Carrie rolled up her right sleeve, revealing a tattooed ladder of interlocking triangles. The beautiful design looked vaguely like a human spine.

Carrie's gaze recaptured his attention. He fell into those green eyes, swimming in the algal depths. She was doing something with her finger. Tracing the outline of the tattoo, maybe? But he couldn't look away. The motion was hypnotic. Everything around him slowed, the light in the room turning a pale green. A distant voice said, "That won't be necessary." The frog twisted again, the gold glint catching his attention.

"That won't be necessary," Thorne repeated.

"What's gone is gone," Carrie repeated.

She was right. There was no point in rehashing the past. It was better to move on. The frog stared at him, solemn agreement in its gemstone eyes.

"Is that all?" Carrie asked.

Thorne must have said yes, because several minutes later, he was alone in his office. Theo knocked on his door, shielding himself with a chocolate muffin.

"Are you okay, Sheriff?" he asked. Thorne took the muffin without argument. He didn't know the answer to the question. Was he okay? His conversation with Carrie had been perfectly run of the mill. Only, when he tried to think too hard about what they discussed, his mind slid off the edges. The thoughts turned slippery.

They had come to a satisfactory resolution, and that was all that mattered. The fact that he could see those glittering green irises when he closed his eyes made him stop for a moment. No, they were striking eyes in a striking woman, and that was all. The muffin tasted like cardboard, and he threw half of it in the trash.

Carrie sat on the brick retaining wall outside the sheriff's department breathing hard. The frog figurine dug painfully into her palm. She had only done a light mesmerizing spell, a mesmer, on Thorne, a small redirect. Eroding someone's will was big magic, and she couldn't have kept it up for long if she'd wanted to. Guilt pounded in her temples. Of course, if he was some all-powerful sorcerer who had created the twisted manikin, she'd just shown her hand.

Mesmeric magic was tricky. For one thing, it was ethically dubious. You could slice the bread any way you wanted, but at the end of the day you were altering someone's wants and needs. But people got manipulated all the time, though not usually with magic. A little mesmer was no worse than advertising, right? She wasn't trying to convince people that top shelf vodka would make their problems go away, or that the newest video game system would make their kids love them. All she had sold was one tiny get-out-of-jail-free card. That she deserved. And Thorne would have let her go if he'd known the whole story. Right?

Still, she'd further depleted her energy. Pain rushed in behind the guilt in Carrie's temples, and she fumbled in her bag for an Advil, dropping the frog and remembering Thorne's comment about her willow bark tea. As she gripped the bottle, she realized that two of the nails on her right hand had turned black. The magic was extracting its price from her. *Shit.* She hoped it wasn't so bad that the nails fell off. It would make gardening difficult. Maybe Finn would have an idea. He burrowed through bedrock on a regular basis. Surely his nails were fairly sturdy.

She had planned to return to the library, but Carrie was too tired for anything but sitting on an IKEA Kivik sofa and watching bad reality television. If she hadn't had that mocha, she'd fall asleep on the drive home.

Where had that manikin come from?

CHAPTER THIRTEEN

On Saturday, Thorne finally got around to visiting Emily. He'd been so preoccupied with the robbery of his office that he hadn't found the time to investigate the cow problem. He met her sister at the door of their apartment.

"If you're looking for James, he and my sister broke up," she said without preamble.

"I'm not looking for James." Thorne wondered who she was talking about. "I'm here to talk to Emily. I need to ask her some questions about the Menkin ranch."

A few minutes later, he was seated across from Emily at one of the picnic tables on the lawn outside the apartment. Maybe he should have tried to talk his way inside, look around her apartment for weird test tubes or Petri dishes or burlap sacks labeled "cow poison," but he seriously doubted she was building bioweapons in a two-bedroom condo. And his appearance had upset the sister.

"Paul Menkin and Doc Kelley tell me you're interested

in veterinary school." He hoped starting with chitchat would soften her up, but her eyes narrowed. The colorless gray irises were sunken into her face, somehow shadowy under full sun.

"Is the sheriff's department doing college counseling now? New program?" Emily drawled.

Maybe he wasn't cut out for good cop, either. "No. No, we're not. I'm here about Menkin's cattle."

"Did someone steal a cow or something? I thought cattle rustling was a thing of the past. This isn't the old west. But in any case, I haven't been there in weeks," Emily said. "I've been sick."

More bad news. Thorne resisted an urge to scoot away from her, and any contagious illness she might have. What if she'd contracted the same disease as the cattle? He scrutinized her eyes for any signs of redness. After a moment of this prolonged eye contact, she blinked in discomfort and picked at her nails.

Thorne softened his face. "Can I ask what you're sick with? I promise you it's relevant, I'm not just being nosy."

"What's going on?" she demanded. Her voice was soft, but insistent.

"Paul Menkin's having trouble with a mysterious bovine illness. He says the cattle got sick right after you started. I told him I would talk to you. Ask if you knew anything."

She sniffled, picking a chip of blue paint off the edge of the picnic table. "He thinks I did something?" Her eyes were glassy, and she looked intensely distressed.

"I can't tell. But he's not a big believer in coincidences."

"*You* think I did something?"

His meeting with the rancher and vet had certainly made him wonder. Now he was developing a different theory. What if Emily was infected with some new disease, and it had jumped species to the cattle?

"Did you do something to the cattle?" he asked.

Her face, which to this point had been the color of old paper, reddened. She tried to say something angry, but choked up, and wiped a tear away before pulling it together. "I loved those cows. Well, not all of them. A few were assholes. But I loved the work. I liked Paul, too. Luke can come on a little strong, but he's mostly harmless. I'm a hard worker. Or I was before I got sick. And those cows are valuable. Poisoning them isn't like stealing a stapler from work. Not that I've ever done that. Do you know how much beef cattle are worth?"

Thorne nodded. "That's why I'm here. How long have you been sick? Do you think you could have caught something?"

"You mean the disease that's making the cows sick?" she asked.

"Yes. That's what I'm asking. I'm sorry to press you on this when you're clearly ill, but this could be a public health emergency."

Emily frowned, redirecting her attention back to chipping paint. A troubled expression crossed her face. Whatever its source, she chose not to share it.

"Am I under arrest?" she asked.

The prospect of putting a woman with a mystery illness in a crowded lockup did not appeal to him. "No. But I hope you'll help me anyway. Have you seen a doctor?"

She was already halfway to her feet, shaking her head. "I'm sorry. I can't help you."

"Wait! Emily!" He called after her, but she was already halfway up the stairs to her apartment. A moment later, the door slammed. *So much for that.*

CHAPTER FOURTEEN

Carrie waited to go into her greenhouse until the sun dropped below the western peaks. It would still be hot and muggy, but the worst of the glare would have faded by then. When her whole garden turned gold-tipped blue, she approached the glass door and touched the heavy padlock holding it shut, tracing the symbols on the silver plating with her right index finger in a specific and intricate pattern. The tattoo that ran all the way to her nail hummed like a live wire. When the protective spells on the metal had faded, Carrie slid an ornate silver key into the padlock.

A hot wave of vegetal smells hit Carrie in the face as she stepped inside. She breathed in the scent, eyeing the tables of greenery with the cautious appreciation of a zookeeper staring at her biggest predators. Leafy plants flourished on every surface, shooting up from terra cotta pots and climbing trellises with wild abandon. In a few places, mesh cabinets held back leaves that were either painful or poisonous to the touch. Her mischievous belladonna had—

alarmingly—pushed a full leafy stem out of the corner of its cabinet. *Naughty plant.* Black berries dangled delinquently in the open air. One more thing to take care of.

Carrie armored herself with heavy leather gloves, plastic glasses, and a protective lab coat, then grabbed a pair of shears and moved carefully towards a terrarium containing a two-foot-tall plant with spiky, scalloped leaves and threadlike needles along its spine. The glass enclosure had two functions: one, it kept the native Sonoran Desert plant dry, and two, it prevented her from accidentally brushing against the sharp spines, which oozed a painful toxic sap. The plant's common name was *mala mujer,* but Carrie called it Bitch Weed. When she had transplanted it into the terrarium, her wrist had carelessly grazed the fine hairs on the plant's stem. The next day, her arm felt like she'd been whipped with a red-hot coat hanger. The rash that bubbled up had been so painful she'd spent half the day by the Santa Sangre with her arm in the icy spring runoff. Keeping it around was a stupid move. But Carrie was inexplicably drawn to the shrub's pretty white flowers and vindictive spirit and couldn't bring herself to dump it.

"You're not going to get me today, bitch," Carrie said affectionately, pulling the terrarium's lid off. She had had some trouble with fungus around the roots. The plant was already looking better, but she sprayed it with extra fungicide to be safe. It was still too damp in the terrarium, but it would have to do for now.

Bitch Weed tending finished, Carrie checked the escaping belladonna, also known as deadly nightshade. The mesh covering the corner of the cabinet had come loose, and the deadly plant had pushed its way out. Carrie trimmed the stem mercilessly and stapled the mesh shut, tutting at the oval leaves and the deceptively innocent-looking black berries tucked within. The whole plant contained atropine, which would turn anyone who consumed it into a red-faced, hallucinating madwoman. Way back in the day, Italian women had used diluted nightshade to dilate their eyes for cosmetic reasons. Going for that wide-eyed doe look. Carrie, who could barely be bothered to put on lipstick, doubted she would take up the practice any time soon.

With the belladonna safely locked up, Carrie made a final circuit of the greenhouse, passing stinging nettles, hallucinogenic salvia, and stalks of shiny red rosary pea seeds. The garden of poisonous plants was her pet project —not exactly safe, of course—but tending to it made her blood pump and turned the rest of the world brighter. Some witches had black cats, she had bitch weed. Frognot was full of extreme sports nuts. People who climbed sheer cliffs and chucked themselves down class five rapids. Carrie's extreme sport just happened to be gardening. And of course, the plants were useful for more powerful spells. She wondered if something in here could be used to manage her manikin problem.

There was a tap on the glass behind her. Finn stood back from the door, waving her out. He looked worried. Carrie hung her gardening armor carefully back on its hooks and went to see what he wanted.

"Emily's here. She's in pretty bad shape."

Carrie rushed into the house. The young woman leapt up from the sofa as she walked in, rushing over to Carrie.

"There's another problem," she said. The young woman looked like she'd been on a poorly supplied backpacking trip through hell. She spoke rapidly, her thoughts tumbling out in fragments. "It's the cows," she said.

"What?" Carrie coached her through the story about her encounter with Thorne. *Uh oh. I guess we're both on the sheriff's radar.*

"Could the bracelet have made the cows sick?" Emily asked, nails digging into Carrie's tattoos. Carrie carefully extracted her wrists.

A minor siphoning curse couldn't make a cow sick unless the cow managed to swallow it—a difficult feat for a ruminant. Truthfully, she was surprised Emily had gotten as sick as she was. Tired and run-down, sure. But maybe the bracelet had had a dark synergistic effect with an existing illness.

"You didn't make the cows sick," Carrie said. She was almost totally sure of it. Still, it was quite a coincidence.

"Will you go make sure? Like, will you check on the cows?" Emily asked. "I...I like them. I know they're gonna be food, but I don't like to think of them suffering."

Carrie grabbed the young woman's shoulders and directed her onto the sofa. Emily's shoulder bones stuck out sharply below her cotton shirt.

"I don't know the Menkins that well. I don't know how thrilled they'd be to find me in their cow yards."

Emily snorted. "Pasture," she whispered. "It's called a pasture."

"Yeah. Their pastures. Okay. I can tell you care about them. But, forget about the cows for a minute. Are you feeling any better now that the bracelet's gone?" Carrie asked.

Emily forced a smile. "Yes. Yes, of course. I really appreciate what you did." She sat up straighter on the sofa, putting on a show.

Carrie was reluctant to get involved. The people of Frognot kept her at arms' length, unless, like Emily, they were desperate. And there was a serious imbalance of power here. Paul Menkin was successful and well-liked, whereas Carrie had recently burgled the sheriff. *But I did not burgle the dep-u-tyyy,* she hummed in her head. This cursed bracelet situation was tugging her into deeper, darker waters. And she still didn't know how to destroy the manikin in the tower.

"It's generally unwise for witches to mess around with people who own literal pitchforks," Carrie said.

Emily's pained smile turned briefly genuine. "At night all the pitchforks are locked up in the barn," she said. There was a sparkle of enthusiasm in her eyes.

CHAPTER FIFTEEN

S everal hours later, when Carrie's right heel slid into a warm cow patty as she leapt over the front gate, she decided that the pitchforks weren't her biggest problem. Her biggest problem—literally—was the cows. Despite being the size of station wagons, their black hides made them nigh invisible in the dark.

Carrie stared at the imprint of her shoe in the cow manure, which had perfectly captured the distinctive ridges on the soles of her hiking boots. Could this foot-print be used as evidence against her? In some kind of tres-passing or cow interference case? She had a long malodorous think about it and decided she'd rather go to jail than stomp it out.

Worse than the cow manure was the fact that Carrie didn't know what she was looking for. She didn't know any spells that could take out a whole herd of cattle, and as far as she knew, she was the strongest witch in Frognot. *Aside from whoever made that manikin.* Maybe the cattle disease was unrelated. Maybe the cows and Emily were both sick with a virus that the cursed bracelet had made worse. If either of those things was true, her field trip would be pointless. But Emily had seemed distraught about the cows. As distraught as Carrie might have been if someone put herbicide in her *mala mujer*.

She had exactly one tool at her disposal for situations like this: a dowsing pendulum, attuned to find lost objects. Whatever was causing the problem with the cattle was more mysterious than lost, but she hoped it would work anyways. Dowsing was an ancient magical tradition. Some witches used silver rods, but they wound up looking like baton twirlers or heavy metal drummers.

Carrie's dowsing pendulum was a polished amethyst marble in a long crochet sack. Compared to some of the pendulums she'd seen, which had, say, fire opals dangling from solid gold chains, Carrie's wasn't much to look at. But none of the expensive pendulums she'd used had worked to her liking, so she'd made her own. The project had cost her more time than money. The amethyst in the pendulum was pretty but not valuable. The real trick had been weaving magical knots into the crocheted tube that held it. Frognot didn't have a yarn store, but she was on a first-name basis with the women who ran the one down in Farmington. Several sheep's worth of wool later, she had her pendulum.

Letting it dangle from her hand in the cool night air, she focused in on the sensation of weight. The amethyst swung back and forth as Carrie circled the pasture, alert for any unusual movement. It was an instinctual process, and she flung her senses wide open. The cold air. The moonlight against black hides. The smell of grass and manure. The soft earth under her feet.

Carrie had created a few different dowsing pendulums, one of which she used exclusively for finding her car keys. She had built this one to find magical objects after losing her favorite protective amulet. The chain had broken while she was bushwhacking through BLM land foraging for hawk's wing mushrooms. The solid gold amulet was one of Carrie's few really valuable possessions, and she hadn't held out much hope of finding it. Sure enough, however, when she'd gone back to the area, the pendulum had tugged her to a scrub oak bush, where dappled sunlight had reflected off a gleaming chain in the branches. The amulet had fallen into the middle of the leaves.

She knew it could work. But she'd known what her amulet looked like. She understood its heft, and the feel of the metal in her hand. Now, she was looking for a big dark question mark. She made one circuit of the pasture, then two. Fear and frustration wouldn't help her here, so she pushed it down.

Just as Carrie was about to give up, the crocheted yarn twitched in her hand. Amazing. She loved magic, and joy sparked through her as the amethyst marble tugged faintly in the direction of the cow shed. Carrie took two steps forward, dry grass crunching under her feet, a breeze blowing moist summer air across her skin.

The dowsing pendulum was pointing her straight at a massive cow.

Shit.

Maybe one of these things *had* swallowed a cursed charm.

If that was the case, she was out of luck. Pasture skulking was one thing. Digging around in a cow's guts was another. An animal rights movement in the 1980s had largely put a stop to witches using entrails for divination. Faye, the crusty old witch Carrie had done her apprenticeship with, was the only haruspex she knew. She had called the animal rights people 'politically correct pansies', but she hadn't put up a fight when Carrie had declined to learn chicken gut fortunetelling.

The amethyst tugged again. She took another step forward, pulled towards a massive cow with a scar on its nose standing in front of a round aluminum trough. It mooed loudly, and when she moved closer, it trotted away. The amethyst tugged again, not following the retreating cow, but pointing Carrie straight towards the aluminum trough. The other cows collected around it split in two directions and headed out towards the further reaches of the pasture. Good. The curse wasn't hidden inside a cow. *Faye would be disappointed.*

The next twitch of the amethyst pulled her right up against the trough, a round metal cistern a few feet deep. There was nothing obviously magical about it. But as Carrie approached it, the dowsing pendulum swung forward. Carrie peered at the silvery reflection of moonlight on the dark surface. The amethyst vibrated, tugging on the yarn. There was something in the water. Gripping the metal with her left hand, she reached into the trough, trying not to think about how many cow tongues had been in there. Goosebumps rose on her skin as her hand brushed the bottom. The water was much colder down there than it was on the surface, which was weird for this shallow a depth. Her hand ached with the cold, and Carrie leaned in, reaching until the water was practically up to her armpit. The tattoo on her hand buzzed with energy. She was so close. She stretched, extending her hips over the side.

Her right foot slipped on a thin layer of hay covering the hard ground. Carrie yelped as dark water enveloped her.

When scientists wanted to test people's pain tolerances, they used cold water immersion. As Carrie sank into the uncanny icy underlayer, she understood why. Yelping, she scrambled to her feet, her body one big ache, ice water draining out of her ears.

The grass rustled from the direction of the farmhouse, and a figure stepped forward, backlit by the ranch house's lights.

"Are you a siren?" a man's voice asked. Her heart beat faster as visions of vampires, or bat creatures, or vampire manbats flashed through her mind. She forced herself to breathe slower.

"I'm not a siren. No tail," she said through chattering teeth. Spears of icy pain sent her slogging to the side of the trough. At least she had rinsed a little of the cow pie off her feet.

The man stepped closer, and she could see his face. It was one of the Menkin boys—Luke, she thought—wearing a cowboy hat with elaborate silver decorations on the band. He would have been handsome, but his skin was a dull gray everywhere but his nose. Carrie guessed he'd closed down one too many bars this week.

"You're pretty. Prettier than the McKellen's bartender," he said.

He swayed on his feet. Carrie guessed he had seen that bartender recently. A whiff of whiskey breath hit her in the face. *Very recently.*

Inebriation that deep could turn dangerous fast, and Carrie knew she should book it. She wished the two-ton cows would come back to cover her exit. But she had dropped her dowsing pendulum in the cow trough, and she still didn't know what it had tried to lead her to.

"Is there a way to empty the trough?" she asked.

Luke pointed. At the bottom, a small spigot hovered over a ravine. Keeping an eye on Luke, she turned it on. Water rushed out, and soon the level in the trough was noticeably lower. It was cool at night in the summer, and Carrie wrapped her arms around herself. The long-sleeved black t-shirt she'd selected in an effort to stay incognito was plastered to her skin. Also, she smelled faintly of cow. *Perfumiers take note of this hot new mountain trend.*

When the water drained, she reached for her phone and turned on the flashlight, grateful that she'd gotten a waterproof case for it so she could bring it on occasional tubing trips down the Santa Sangre. The only thing inside was the heaped mess of her pendulum. Carrie stepped over the side to retrieve it, but when she bent down and grabbed the casing, the pendulum remained firmly attached to the metal. Pulling only stretched the crochet.

She felt around to see if the yarn was stuck on something, then grabbed the stone and pulled. This time, the amethyst came loose, although it felt like it weighed twenty pounds. She had found the spot, alright.

"Help me move this trough," she said, circling the aluminum and pointing at Luke. He blearily obeyed her orders, and with some effort, they were able to move the trough over three feet. It clattered onto the hardpacked soil, and Carrie wiped her hands off on her wet jeans.

There was a shallow pit below the circle of dirt where the trough had been. Nausea washed over Carrie as the light on her phone illuminated the interior of the muddy hole. It was caked with wet earth, but the shape was unmistakable. Another manikin, braided from rough black hair and tied with greasy string. A different color this time—an oil-slick blue-black.

The cows had been infected by something much, much worse than Emily's bracelet. Although it still wasn't clear how the manikins worked or even what they did. Carrie cursed inwardly, wishing she could get more information from Sheriff Thorne about the story behind the one in his office. What black magician was going around making these things—and worse, using them? It didn't make any sense. The curse on the bracelet was minor. It might even have been a mistake, produced by a good witch with bad skills who had mixed up her protective symbols. The manikins, on the other hand, were more than just bad. They were actively malevolent, twisted pieces of magic meant to—what? Maggie hadn't come through with more information, and Carrie was treading dark water without a life jacket.

She wished she'd brought the silver containment cylinder, even in its current state of disrepair. Carrie reached for the manikin. When her left finger touched it, a bright, hot blossom of pain sizzled on the tip.

"What is that?" Luke asked, looming over her back.

"Get back!" Carrie barked. She didn't need a plastered

125

man knocking her face-first into a radioactively cursed doll.

Luke stumbled back a step and fell, landing on the hard dirt with an *oof*. Carrie left him on the ground as she paced around the empty aluminum trough. She couldn't leave the manikin here. She imagined Luke passing out on top of the thing. Carrie couldn't be sure, but she didn't think a human would survive prolonged skin contact with the curse.

The iconic shape of a barn loomed fifty feet away. It was even painted red. Totally retro.

"Is the barn locked?" Luke didn't reply until Carrie walked over and shook him. He jumped back, eyes shooting open as he realized she was only a foot from his face.

"Vampire!" he shouted.

"For heaven's sake. Or hell's sake, I guess, if we're talking about vampires. I'm not a mermaid or a vampire. Why stop there, though? If you're wondering, I'm also not a harpy, succubus, lamia or medusa." Although Medusa probably also had plenty of experience with men staring at her with frozen, slack-jawed expressions. "If you must know, I'm a bigfoot," she said sardonically.

To her great relief, Luke took a large step back, appraising her doubtfully. "I don't think so," he said.

Carrie sighed. "Open the barn, Luke."

A minute later, she was brandishing a pitchfork across the packed dirt. She felt ridiculous. The next thing she knew, angry villagers would be shaking their torches at her. When she reached the trough, she raised the pitchfork and skewered the manikin. The wooden shaft vibrated as the central prong slid along something hard and abrasive at the center of the twisting hair.

Carrie raised the pitchfork, waving it gently back and forth to make sure the manikin stayed put. The bones in her hands ached and the light nausea she'd felt since uncovering the monstrous thing continued to roil her guts. But this was the best she was going to do tonight. A faint heartbeat echoed in her ears, and she could feel the same vibration through the wooden pitchfork handle. Carrie shivered at the sound.

Luke watched this procedure uncomprehendingly, and when she headed towards the fence, he waved.

"Goodbye, bigfoot!" he slurred.

The pitchfork and its evil prong passenger went in the bed of her truck, which was parked on a small pull-off along the shoulder of the road a quarter mile from the Menkins' front gate. Her knuckles ached, and she was eager to get home and rub one of her herbal salves into them. But less than half a mile down the road, there was a pop from the undercarriage, and Carrie's truck tilted to one side, vibrating wildly.

She had gotten a flat. The rim of her rear right wheel was flush against the pavement, and she didn't have a spare. Peeking over her open truck bed, she glared at the manikin. She'd put the pitchfork diagonally in the bed. She didn't think it was a coincidence that the manikin was in the same corner as the flat tire.

"You asshole," Carrie said. The manikin's featureless head stared back at her. She flipped it off and grabbed her phone. But it was after two in the morning, and there was no one for her to call. Finn didn't have a car, Emily would be asleep by now, and even if Reggie wasn't still visiting his dad, there was no way Maggie would leave him alone in the house in the middle of the night. Her contacts list took up less than one phone screen. Thorne's phone number was still in there, and for one moment, her finger hovered over the button. Late-night curse-dialing a man she'd burgled while he was actively investigating her would be catastrophically stupid. But she couldn't discard the notion that if she called, he would show up to help. She put her phone away and set off on foot. It was only a few miles back to the house.

Only one car passed her as she trudged along the side of the highway. A dented black camper van with a peeling paint job. The van slowed, and a suspicious face turned towards her. And then it was gone, accelerating nervously away. What was the world coming to that strangers wouldn't stop to help a soaking wet woman carrying a menacing doll on a pitchfork along a desolate country road in the middle of the night?

Finn was almost less happy to see her than the person in the camper van. "What happened to you?"

"This stupid doll happened, that's what." Carrie waved the pitchfork in his direction, and he darted away with an alarmed grunt. She apologized, but didn't drop the pitchfork. She didn't want it to touch anything in the house.

Finn crossed his arms over his white beard, stance wide. "What are we gonna do now that we've got twins?" he asked.

Carrie twirled the pitchfork like it was a marshmallow skewer. "Put it in the protective circle with the other one?"

The line between Finn's eyes turned abyssal. "What if it's like getting two rabbits? What if they breed?"

Carrie hadn't thought of that. A year ago, Finn had found a pregnant feral cat under their porch. It had been hard enough finding foster homes for a litter of adorable kittens. Putting a cardboard box saying "free cursed dolls" on the side of the road would produce disastrous results.

"Maybe they won't breed. Maybe it'll be worse," she said. "Maybe they'll take up evil doubles tennis. Or evil swing dancing." Finn frowned. Carrie wasn't convinced he knew what swing dancing was. "I couldn't leave it with those cows," she said, remembering the sickly red eyes staring at her through the darkness.

"You could have," Finn said. "Better a few sick cows than burning your house down."

"Not for the cows, it's not," Carrie said.

The problem was the protective circle upstairs had taken them almost a full week to lay out and activate. What kind of havoc could a loose manikin wreak in that time? It was a good thing she'd pulled that cooler out of Thorne's office, no matter what he said. His silver eyes with their shining topaz rims wouldn't be nearly as attractive blood red.

Finn looked suspicious. "Why are you smiling?"

Carrie shook her head to clear the image of Thorne's eyes. "This is a serious problem. But I won't be able to think of a better option until I get some sleep. Unless you have something to contribute, I'm going to bed."

Outside, a light wind blew through the garden. The protective windchime outside the greenhouse jingled eerily, and an owl hooted from the trees on the other side of the river. The sound of the Santa Sangre underscored everything.

"No ideas here," Finn admitted.

"Okay, then. Ginger here goes in the tower."

"Ginger?"

"I had a lot of time on my walk home to think of a name. The other one's Fred."

"It's a bad idea to name them," Finn said darkly.

"It's a joke, Finn. I'm exhausted. I'm trying to keep my shit together."

He pried the wooden handle of the pitchfork from her hands. "It's a bad, bad idea," he muttered, voice fading as he climbed the steps up to the tower. "Bad, bad, bad. Isn't it, Ginger?"

CHAPTER SIXTEEN

Sheriff Thorne watched the grainy footage again, this time at one-quarter speed in case he had missed something. When Carrie walked into the frame, he shivered. Her long hair and calm stride were already eerie—in slow motion she looked like she'd been transported through a portal from a different Earth. She leapt gracefully over the fence and disappeared off frame. The video cut automatically to another image, this one of a car dropping an unsteady Luke Menkin off at the end of the road. After a lengthy struggle with the gate lock, he surrendered and lay down on the road, motionless for long enough that the sensor cut the video. It started back up again when he climbed to his feet. This time, he fumbled the gate open with a heroic if wobbly effort. To his credit and Thorne's surprise, he got it latched and locked again before he weaved offscreen toward the ranch house.

The video cut to Carrie again, only this time she was leaping over the fence in the other direction. With a pitchfork. One of its prongs was uneven, but the resolution was too low to see why.

Thorne ticked off Carrie Moonshadow's petty crimes. Minor floricide, illicit bracelet retrieval, and now pitchfork theft. Weird offenses that didn't pay. As a criminal mastermind, she was totally inscrutable. She was also really bad at avoiding security cameras. Inexplicably, he found himself wanting to give her this helpful feedback.

He dialed up Paul Menkin.

"You watched it?" the old rancher asked.

"I watched it."

"It's weird as hell. Gave me the creeps to know that she was skulking around outside our windows with a pitchfork."

"You heard noises outside the house?"

"Well– no. Just Luke coming in."

"He didn't see her?"

"From the shape he was in, I doubt Luke could have seen the end of his own nose. Got a hundred-and-fifty-six-dollar charge for puking in Ken Takata's Lexus."

Ken was one of Frognot's two rideshare drivers. Sheriff Thorne hoped, for the town's sake, that he wouldn't stop picking Luke up. He didn't want Luke driving again. He'd give Ken a call when he was done, to try and smooth things over. He had a minuscule budget for confidential informants, but keeping Luke off the roads would be worth a few hundred bucks a month.

"Do you have any idea what she wanted on your property?"

"I do not. To be honest, I'd feel better about this thing if she had robbed us. It would at least be comprehensible behavior. You know what folks say about her."

Alethea Murrow had certainly had plenty to say. "I know, Paul. Are you absolutely, one hundred percent sure nothing went missing?"

"Just the pitchfork," he said. There was something about the way he paused before he spoke that set off Thorne's alarm bells.

"What aren't you telling me?" Thorne asked.

"Luke musta opened the barn for her."

"It was locked?"

"Yeah. I oughta take away his keys to the building, but he's a grown man—in theory—and I don't need him doing any *less* work than he already does."

"Have you looked over the barn? Checked to see if she stole anything else?"

"Yeah. Nothing's missing. Not so far as I can tell." Menkin said. "Didn't touch the power tools, which are the only valuables she could've carried out on foot. She drained my trough, though."

Thorne paused, puzzling out what Menkin meant. "Sorry, is that a metaphor?"

"Nope. She literally drained the water out of my cattle trough."

"Why?"

"Not a sliver of an idea, Sheriff."

Thorne added 'random cattle dehydration' to Carrie's bizarre rap sheet. "Do you want to press trespassing charges? I could tack on the pitchfork as a misdemeanor. And I can walk you through filing a restraining order." With the video as evidence, he didn't really need Paul's buy-in. But he wasn't sure how he wanted to handle this himself.

"What I want is to not wake up to my security system sending me unsettling videos of unearthly lady skulkers."

"Don't we all, Paul."

"I don't know about the trespassing situation, Sheriff. Maybe not. In my experience, it's never wise to antagonize a crazy person."

"I can appreciate that," Caleb said. They chatted for a few minutes, enough for Paul to calm down a little. When they were done, Thorne called up Ken Takata.

Ken ran a small but wildly successful IT consulting firm. He was single, and as far as Thorne could tell, incapable of relaxation. He had never found a hobby he liked, so he drove Uber on nights and weekends to save for an early retirement that he would almost certainly find intolerable.

"How's your car, Ken?" Thorne asked.

"Smells like Luke Menkin's last three rounds at McKellen's," Ken said.

"So I hear. Look, Ken. If that happens again, you bring your car to the station. I'll have the guy who details our fleet take care of it. On the house."

"What's the catch?" Ken asked.

"I don't want Luke driving home from the bar. Or biking drunk on that road. Or walking. You understand?"

Ken's sigh was so loud and so long that Thorne could have knocked off several emails before it was over.

"I'm gonna hold you to that free detailing, Sheriff," he said.

"That's why I called. Thanks, Ken." Ken hung up the phone.

In a town the size of Frognot, drunks were Thorne's bread and butter. Not an easy problem, exactly, but a straightforward one. Most of the crime in town was straightforward. Once a year or so, a backpacker would get lost or a climber would get injured, and he'd have to support search and rescue operations. But that was as exciting as things got. This thing with the forest fires and sick cows was much weirder, and Carrie Moonshadow was at the heart of all of it. He wanted to know why.

He grabbed his ticket book. Before heading to Carrie's, he got two lattes from the drive-through window of the tiny coffee hut across the street. Armed with both carrot and stick, he headed to the oxbow.

CHAPTER SEVENTEEN

Carrie flung open the front door to find Sheriff Thorne standing on her porch, coffees in hand. He looked nervous. *Oh my god, is he going to ask me out?* Irritation and pleasure dueled inside her. She smiled despite herself. He smiled back, but quickly reformed his expression into something sterner, holding the paper cup out.

She recognized the cup sleeve. The drive-through hut wasn't as good as Blacktree Perk, but they opened an hour earlier, and they made a great cider donut. "I don't know how you take it, so I got you a latte. With two espresso shots. I thought you might need it. After your late night." He held the cup out. *Late night. What the hell?* Still, Carrie took the cup eagerly, draining half the life-saving caffeine in one go. Small-town sheriffs weren't always known for their upstanding behavior, but poisoned coffee wasn't Thorne's style.

His eyes scanned the living room behind her. "May I come in, ma'am?"

Revulsion washed over her at the sound of Caleb

Thorne's pleasant, deep voice calling her 'ma'am.' His face twitched in regret.

"I appreciate the coffee, but unless there's a double shot of warrant at the bottom of this cup, we'd better stay on the porch."

He put his hand on the door. "I could get a warrant if I needed to. To recover stolen property."

"Is this about the bracelet again? I thought we resolved that."

"No. Something new. I'm here to get Paul Menkin's pitchfork back."

He could waste as much time as he wanted to ogling her IKEA furniture. The pitchfork wasn't in the house. Hopefully, he wouldn't look too closely at the greenhouse on his way out. The pitchfork was inside, under her potting table. She'd kept it as an ironic souvenir. Plus, it had spent a few hours in contact with the manikin, and she was worried the metal might be cursed. The Frognot County waste collection division didn't have a "cursed disposables" program.

"Are you here to arrest me?" she asked curiously. He probably wouldn't go to the trouble over a pitchfork, but if he was still pissed off about the bracelet, he might do it.

He frowned, tracking a pine jay as it scared two robins away from the birdfeeder on her porch. *Oh shit, he's considering it.* His eyes traveled toward the greenhouse.

"The pitchfork was a gift," Carrie blurted.

Thorne's eyebrows climbed until they were nestled against his hairline. "Really?"

"Luke Menkin gave it to me. He invited me out to the

ranch." There was a hesitation, barely noticeable. "He said I was prettier than the bartender at McKellen's."

Thorne's deepening discomfort reddened his face.

"If he invited you, how come you hopped his fence fifteen minutes before he got home?"

"How do you know that?" she asked.

"Paul has a security camera."

Shit. Of course he did. This was starting to get embarrassing. "I didn't want to leave my car in town," Carrie lied.

"You drove out to the Menkin ranch--at Luke's invitation--but you didn't give him a ride?" Thorne asked. He was enjoying himself, which annoyed her.

Carrie cursed inwardly, scrambling for a logical response. "He said he never lets women drive. And I *obviously* couldn't give him my keys."

Menkin's eyes narrowed. He didn't believe her, but surely he believed this was a thing Luke might say.

"Okay, so... at Luke's invitation, you beat him to his ranch, hopped the fence, waited for him by the barn, and eventually accepted a pitchfork as a gift."

"What can I say? I'm a romantic." Carrie smiled at the flash of jealousy in his eyes.

"Why'd you drain the trough?" Thorne asked. His previous questions had been meant to needle her, but now he seemed genuinely curious.

She grinned. "It seemed fun?"

"We're in a drought," Thorne said, open exasperation on his face.

"Well then, send the EPA after me."

"Maybe I will."

"Maybe you should," Carrie said.

Thorne glared at her coffee cup, looking like he regretted bringing it to her. She took a smug sip. "I wouldn't have thought you and Luke Menkin would have had much in common," Thorne said gruffly.

"Why's that, Sheriff?"

"Because he's a drunk whose most recent experience of personal growth was puberty."

Carrie encouraged him with a smile. "And?" *What about me, Sheriff?*

"Do you know why Menkin's cows have been getting sick?"

She bristled. "Why would you think I'm involved in that? Why would I want to make a bunch of cows sick?"

"I don't know. But they've got a mysterious illness, and you're the mysterious star of some spooky-as-shit security camera pitchfork footage. I'm trying to put the pieces together." He was as frustrated as she was, and Carrie almost broke down and told him about Emily. But she still didn't trust him. Why had he been keeping a cursed manikin in his office? Was this a ruse to get it back? Was he trying to intimidate her into letting him search her place?

"I'm sorry I can't help you," she said. "Unless you're going to arrest me, I'm closing this door."

CHAPTER EIGHTEEN

The knock on the door two hours later made Carrie furious. Thorne couldn't bother her all day, every day. The sun had gone down, and as she stomped downstairs, she hoped the Sheriff had brought decaf this time. When she flung open the door, however, her jaw dropped.

Luke Menkin was on her steps with a bouquet. She blinked rapidly, trying to make sense of the picture. For one thing, he wasn't holding flowers. No, the man had ten zucchinis wrapped in a cone fashioned from today's edition of *The Daily Croaker*. He held them out proudly.

"Good evening, Miss Moonshadow," he said formally, struggling to tip his hat while holding the zucchini. Carrie resisted the urge to laugh.

Pulling herself together, Carrie spoke warily. "Hello, Luke. Are you here for your pitchfork?"

To her surprise, he looked genuinely wounded. "A gentleman never takes back a gift," he said.

Carrie scrutinized his face. Was he making fun of her? But no, he looked painfully earnest. "Good. I wouldn't give it back anyways. It's my new favorite." She felt her cheeks warm just a little.

Luke was confused. "Your favorite what?"

"Pitchfork," Carrie said quickly.

"You have a favorite pitchfork?" he asked.

"I do now."

She felt sorry when his smile widened. When he was put together and sober—or mostly sober, anyways—Luke Menkin was an attractive man.

"These are for you," he said, holding the zucchini out. Carrie accepted the bundle awkwardly.

"Why don't you come in," she said, against her better judgment. She led him to the kitchen and got the zucchini settled in the colander by her sink.

Luke cleared his throat. He was actually nervous. "I'd have brought flowers, but the gardens are mostly veggies at this point. I can send you my best zucchini recipe if you need. I call it Luke's zukes. But I guess I would need your cell number." He smiled shyly as he said this. *Uh oh.* She hadn't really thought through the consequences of the lie she'd told Thorne.

"Um, to what do I owe this pleasure, Luke?" Carrie asked tentatively.

"Well, Dad says he talked to the sheriff, who says he talked to you, and that you told him we had an amorous encounter."

Oh, god. What, exactly, did Luke Menkin think had happened between them? Worse, what did *Thorne* think had happened? Technically, yes, they had gone to the hayloft together. But not in the *biblical* sense. Only for pitchfork retrieval!

"I gotta confess, Miss Moonshadow, that I don't remember the particulars of the evening." Luke leaned in close and lowered his voice. "Did we go skinny dipping in the cow trough?"

Now Carrie actually laughed out loud. She stopped when she saw Luke's pained face. She sensed a lot of guilt and no malice. "We did not go skinny dipping in the cow trough," she said. Desperately hoping to reverse his hangdog look, she grabbed her phone and held it out. "Why don't you put your number in there. I'd love to whip up some Luke's zukes."

A loud thud echoed out from the hallway, and Finn strode into the room. He was wearing a loose pink women's robe over a pair of checkered pants, and he made a beeline for the zucchini.

"You buy vegetables for once?" he asked, barely nodding at Luke. "Nice change from frozen taquitos."

Luke was already climbing to his feet.

"I'm sorry. I'm just here get to know the neighbors," he sputtered, his tongue tripping on his words. He looked desperately at Carrie. "I didn't know that you were. Uh. That you had a–"

"Oh. No! Finn is my–"

"Butler," Finn said, as Carrie said "roommate."

Luke looked cautiously between them, trying to decide if this was some kind of perverse role play.

"Luke brought us the zucchini as a thank you," Carrie said.

"Is that so? A thank you for what?"

Because he thinks I polished his pitchfork in a cow trough.

"For a wonderful evening," Carrie said. It was her turn to look pained.

Finn was completely confused by this exchange, and so he decided to ignore it. Finn plucked a zucchini from the basket, rinsed it off, covered it in salt, saluted them both, and began eating his prize raw as he walked from the room.

"Weird guy," Luke said.

Carrie sighed. "He's a terrible butler."

Remembering social convention, Luke snatched his cowboy hat off his head and held it over his heart. The young rancher was mustering his courage. As he cleared his throat, Carrie was resigned to finding out why.

"I guess we had a pretty good time last night," he said. "Seeing as how I sent you home with my best pitchfork."

Carrie wondered, briefly, what made a pitchfork good or bad. The one she'd come home with hadn't seemed particularly notable. She'd have to inspect it later. Dread mounting, she waited. "I feel awful ashamed that I don't remember the evening, and I'd like to take you out for a do-over. A proper one, this time," he said.

His eyes were wide and hopeful.

"I'll text you about that zucchini recipe, and maybe we can find a time," she said, cursing her own politeness. She should have just told him no. She had his pitchfork, so even if he got angry, what could he do?

Then again, she rarely got asked. The Frognot locals kept their distance, and she only encountered tourists in passing.

Luke was staring at a piece of stained glass in her kitchen

window. It was a blue glass eye, an ancient protective symbol. She had seen it at Frognot's annual Christmas craft fair, and thought it was pretty. She had waved some sage over it, but other than that it wasn't terribly magical. It was prettier during the day, but Luke still seemed drawn to it.

"Is it true you're a witch?" he asked.

"What makes you ask?"

"My brother said you were. But he's got some weird ideas. I dunno. Dad said I'd better stay away from you."

"What do you think?" Carrie asked.

"I think it would be nice if you were a witch," he said morosely.

The response surprised her. She was used to visceral reactions. Luke was actually *winsome.*

"Why is that?"

"Then you could do cool stuff. You could make potions, that kind of thing. I'd like to have a love potion, if I could."

There was a sharp edge to his voice, and Carrie wondered if inviting him inside had been a mistake. People desperate enough to seek out love spells were usually in bad shape. They were trying to fill a hole that couldn't be filled. Most 'love spells' Carrie had seen in her years of witchcraft weren't really love spells, anyways. They were mesmerizers, like the one she'd cast on Thorne. Only more powerful, and more corrosive. To keep someone under your spell long-term, you had to erode their personality. That could actually cause brain damage.

"Who would you give a love spell to?" Carrie kept her tone light. *Please don't say me.*

She was startled when Luke immediately responded, "I'd find a good woman and give it to myself. All my best friends are married now. The guys who are left at McKellen's are angry or sad."

That was a new one. Carrie guessed Luke was the kind of guy who lost interest in a relationship easily. He looked embarrassed, like she'd tricked him into a moment of vulnerability. He grinned, "Can you turn someone into a frog? There are a lot of assholes out there who would make way better frogs than people."

"I can't turn people into frogs," Carrie said with a winsome sigh. At least, she didn't think she could. A spell that size would produce a debt-stone that would take out way more than one prize-winning rose bush. A big forest, maybe.

Luke climbed to his feet, nodding chivalrously. "Well, I hope to hear from you, Miss Moonshadow. You've got my number. Come say hi to the cows any time you like."

Paul Menkin wouldn't like that. Maybe she'd do it, just to piss him off. That would show him for ratting her out to the cops. "Maybe I will," she said, and showed Luke to the door.

"How are you getting home?" she asked, hoping she wouldn't be called upon to provide a solution. He pointed into the dark, toward the cast iron gate. Just inside, a rusty blue bike was chained to a post.

"Doesn't your hat fall off?" She frowned at the wide brim.

"I do the strap up real tight," he called over his shoulder, as he headed to the driveway.

Carrie lingered in the cool night air as Luke turned on a single bright headlight, gravel crunching under his tires as he made his way up the road. As she went to fix herself a cup of willow bark tea, she mulled over the lies she'd told to Caleb Thorne. If you told the universe enough lies it might find a way to make them true. She would have to be more careful the next time she was lying to the handsome sheriff. *A girl can always use another latte.*

Finn poked his head back into the living room. He was wearing the Iron Eye, which he had previously removed in deference to Carrie's guest. "You didn't give him a love potion, did you?"

"You were eavesdropping!" Carrie complained.

"That's a butler's job."

"You're not my butler."

Finn scratched his beard. "Hmm. Are you going to savor his zukes?"

"Am I *what?*"

Finn pointed at the colander. "Are you going to get the recipe for Luke's zucchini dish?"

Carrie considered the question. Texting Luke would open a can of worms. On the other hand, she liked worms. They were good for the garden. "I'm admittedly curious about Luke Menkin's recipe drawer." Finn waggled his eyebrows. "Knock it off!" Carrie said.

"Alright. But I need you to come take a look at something in the tower."

Her anxiety spiked. "Oh god. Did the manikins breed?"

They hadn't, but the situation still wasn't good. Up in the tower, Finn directed Carrie's attention to the protective circle. He had placed the manikins on a terra cotta plate commandeered from the garden. "That's there to protect the floor. The wood below it was going bad. Some kind of dry rot problem."

"I thought the orange-string manikin was a fire spell. And the red one was for sickness."

"I'm not sure they're that specific. Anyways. Terra cotta's pretty sturdy. This should hold for a bit. There's a reason archaeologists still dig up pottery. But even this isn't a long-term solution. Have you heard anything from your librarian friend?

"No," Carrie said. "I think Maggie's mad at me. And being escorted out of the library by a sheriff's deputy isn't a great way to win people over."

"Maybe keep trying. For the house's sake, if not yours."

Carrie liked Maggie. She liked the library, too. But maybe it was better not to get people she liked involved in this wicked business.

CHAPTER NINETEEN

When Maggie Lane called her the next day, Carrie decided she couldn't afford to worry. The phone rang while Carrie was in the middle of furiously googling "ugly evil hair doll reddit." She found some gruesome art on r/creepy, but nothing that would help her solve the problem.

"Maggie! Tell me you found something."

"I'm sorry. I haven't yet." Despite this, she sounded excited.

"Oh. Alright."

"I'll keep looking, I promise. In the meantime, I wanted to invite you to dinner."

"Girls' night?" Carrie asked.

"Not exactly. More of a dinner party situation," Maggie gushed. "I want you to meet Marcus. I can't introduce him to Reg yet, of course. But I thought I'd surprise him. That we could all meet up tonight for my famous fondue."

Maggie was not a great cook. Work and raising her son had left her little time for the finer culinary arts. She and

Reggie ate a lot of turkey burgers and steamed vegetables. But fondue, Maggie insisted, was basically just French queso, and queso was basically just dropping cheese into a crock pot.

"When?" Carrie asked.

"Tonight, if you're not doing anything?" Maggie's voice suddenly sounded lighter.

Carrie was exhausted, but Maggie sounded so hopeful that she couldn't refuse. It didn't take her long to get ready. But she stopped suddenly on her way out the door. "Finn, can you watch the twins?"

"Is that our nickname for them now? Sure, I've got it," he said with a weary smile.

"I can be back by seven. You know what, I don't have to go."

"You need a break," he said, waving his hands at her. "Come home refreshed. That's my order. As your friend."

"Then I suppose I have to now."

"And prod Maggie about her research. We need all the help we can get."

"Will do," Carrie said.

CHAPTER TWENTY

An unfamiliar camper van was parked in Maggie's driveway. Marcus must already be here. Carrie was excited to meet this mystery beau.

Maggie greeted her at the door with a nice cabernet. She was glowing, wearing a shiny green bias-cut dress that cascaded over her curvy frame. And she looked taller than Carrie remembered.

"Something's different," Carrie said.

Maggie pointed at her toes. She was wearing cute and dramatically high vintage heels. The purple ring glittered on her finger.

"Ooh la la," Carrie said. "I'm underdressed."

"Don't be silly. You can wear whatever you want. I was just feeling festive. Marcus bought me this dress. Or he picked it out for me, anyways. I've never had a man go shopping with me. He said it made me look like Lana Turner." She spun, sending the emerald fabric flying in a wide hoop.

"If I knew who that was, I'm sure I would agree with

him," said Carrie.

"He's really into old films. He wants to educate me. I guess I can do the same for him with books."

"You're so cute when you go into librarian mode," a man said, emerging from the kitchen with a skewer. A cube of bread was speared on the end.

"You must be Marcus!" said Carrie.

He was gazing at Maggie, and didn't seem to hear her. After a moment, however, he looked over.

"Pleased to meet you." He juggled the skewer and stuck out his hand.

Marcus had sandy, wavy hair and a handsome peppering of stubble. He was fit, but more wiry than muscular. He was also younger than Carrie had expected, maybe in his late twenties. He snaked a hand around Maggie's waist, leaning in for a kiss.

"If you want to finish putting on your makeup, I can entertain our guest," he said.

Maggie's face pinched slightly, but she pecked Marcus on the cheek and disappeared into the house. She already looked great, but maybe she was attempting some kind of fancy YouTube tutorial for their grown-up dinner party.

"Maggie says you live out at the oxbow," Marcus said, pouring himself a large glass of wine.

"I do. I bought it about a decade ago."

He nodded. "You ever get lonely out there?" His light brown eyes flashed. She was suddenly uneasy.

"I have a butler!" Carrie blurted. Some deep part of her didn't want him thinking she was alone out at the house.

Marcus's face radiated disbelief. "A butler?"

Carrie straightened, taking another sip of wine. This

MARTHA CARR & MICHAEL ANDERLE

young man was throwing her off-kilter. "Yes. For a few years now. He works for room and board."

"Does he wear a tuxedo?" Marcus asked.

Carrie thought back to the pink velour women's tracksuit Finn had been wearing when she left. "He wears whatever he wants," she said. It didn't comprehensively cover Finn's fashion anarchy, but it was true enough.

"Are you some kind of secret heiress?" Marcus asked.

Carrie almost snorted a mouthful of cabernet. What she had inherited from her upbringing in the Oregon woods was a little magic, and a lot of trouble. Carrie cracked an ironic smile. "That's right, Marcus. I'm actually descended from the Cape Cod Moonshadows. I rode here on my favorite polo pony, and I brought us all diamond tiaras to wear at dinner."

A brief, intense emotion flashed in Marcus's eyes. Maybe he was a sensitive person, and the quip had hurt his feelings. "How's the surveying business?"

Marcus took a long sip of wine. "I'm off work for a few days. Projects shuffling around. That's alright, though, gives me more time to spend with my best girl."

"My ears are burning," Maggie said, hustling back into the room. She had applied thick cat-eye liner to her lids and swapped her usual lipstick out for one the color of a brand-new fire engine. She looked different, but good.

"There's that beautiful face," Marcus said approvingly.

Maggie smiled and cracked open the lid of the crockpot on the kitchen counter. "I think we're ready!" she said. Marcus carried the fondue to the dining room, and Carrie grabbed the wine. Golden evening light streamed through the western windows, which looked out on the Blacktree range.

Stuffing herself with melted cheese and good, crusty French bread significantly boosted Carrie's spirits. So much so that she began to muse over whether cheese might be an effective ingredient in a healing spell. She would have to try it out at some point, once she'd resolved the manikin problem.

"This is amazing," Carrie said, drowning a chunk of apple in melted Gruyère.

"What kind of wine is in here?" Marcus asked, taking a nibble of bread off his skewer.

Maggie grinned. "The cheapest Chardonnay Albertsons sells."

"You should get something nicer next time," Marcus said, leaving the bread half-eaten on his plate. "I'll get it for you. I want my girl to have the best of everything." He gazed at Maggie with a smitten expression, which brightened her sadness about his assessment of the fondue.

"I think it's flawless," Carrie said pointedly.

"Maggie is flawless," Marcus countered, wrapping his hand around her waist and pulling her in for a kiss.

"He's taking me to Pagosa tomorrow for a romantic hot springs outing," Maggie said, beaming.

Pagosa Springs was a few hours' drive. A small town bisected by the San Juan River, its primary attraction was the Hot Springs Resort, a collection of natural springs that clung to the steep banks of the river in the center of town. The pools were fed by the Mother Spring, which was located less-than-idyllically in the hotel's parking lot. It was the deepest hot spring in the world. When the Guinness Book of World Records tried to measure it, their 1002-foot plumb line never hit the bottom. "You'll have to bring me back some springwater," Carrie said. It was rich in minerals and useful in a number of spells.

Maggie, who understood exactly what Carrie meant, grinned. "I'll pack my gallon jugs, don't you worry."

"What do you mean?" Marcus asked.

They paused. As in love as Maggie seemed, Carrie wasn't ready for the "Hi, I'm Carrie Moonshadow and I'm a powerful witch" conversation. It had a way of sending people running for the hills, and Maggie was way too happy for her to risk it.

"It's, uh, all the zinc and magnesium. It's supposed to be good for you," Carrie said.

"It's cute when a girl's into all that woo-woo crystal stuff," Marcus said, squeezing Maggie again. "Who knows, maybe you're right about the water."

Maggie leaned conspiratorially across the table. "I think he just wants to see me in a bikini."

Marcus grinned. "What can I say? I'm a simple man of simple pleasures. I personally am excited to lie back in a nice warm pool with my best gal and suck down margaritas. I definitely need a break."

"You've been working so hard," Maggie agreed.

They finished their fondue and took their wine out onto Maggie's back porch to enjoy the last rays of evening light. Carrie was surprised to see this much PDA from Maggie, but the two lovebirds were so giggly and affectionate that she endured it stoically. She tried to imagine Luke Menkin whisking her away for a romantic hot springs getaway. She couldn't imagine him thinking of it.

Although he certainly wouldn't object to poolside margaritas.

When the affectionate giggling got more intense, and Carrie began to feel like she was at serious risk of watching the conception of her friend's second child, she excused herself. "Nice to meet you, Carrie," Marcus said, waving at her lazily from his lawn chair. Maggie extracted herself from his embrace to walk Carrie to the door.

"I didn't want to say anything in front of Marcus, but how's your research on the manikins coming along?" Carrie asked. "There have been...developments."

Maggie adjusted her silky dress. "I'm sorry for letting the ball drop. I've been a little distracted."

Carrie was annoyed. Which wasn't entirely fair. Maggie didn't know that the manikins had almost burned down her house. Or that she and Finn were losing sleep babysitting them. And her friend deserved some joy in life after so many hard years. "Don't worry about it, Mags. I'll stop by the library when you get back from Pagosa. In the meantime, enjoy the hot springs with your handsome new beau. He seems very taken with you."

Maggie smiled bashfully, then flung her arms around Carrie. "I'm going to bring you enough spring water to bathe in!"

"I might not need *that* much," Carrie said. She said goodnight to her friend and made her way back north to the oxbow.

Carrie tried to feel happy for Maggie, but the next day, she was restless. She spent the morning pacing around the house, drinking buckets of coffee, tidying and straightening up the house where she could. Finally, Finn demanded she leave. "You're getting on my nerves. A butler needs his space."

Carrie needed to clear her head, and she also needed to replenish her stores of a few wild herbs. She laced up her hiking boots and put on an old t-shirt and a pair of black wool cutoffs. You weren't supposed to wear cotton outdoors. The fibers didn't retain warmth when they got wet. But Carrie had never warmed to the all-Patagonia uniform popular in town. She bought a lot of her outdoors gear from the military surplus store. When she and Maggie went hiking, which was an infrequent occurrence, usually at Reg's request, Maggie would say that Carrie looked like she'd walked straight out of a 1950s L.L. Bean catalog. Her backpack was a genuine antique, an old canvas number that she'd inherited from her grandfather. The woman who ran the outdoors store downtown was always trying to convince Carrie to trade it in for a lightweight, modern model, but Carrie couldn't give this one up. Call her sentimental. She drew the line at heavy old metal canteens, however. Filling her Nalgenes and throwing a few granola bars into the bag with a chunky sweatshirt, Carrie tossed her backpack in the truck and headed out.

The Beckermeir Canyon trail had been closed since the fire, and the parking lot was cordoned off with orange cones and caution tape. Carrie slowed as she passed the turnoff. The fire had spread in the opposite direction, and the burn front was plenty far away by now. It was her favorite hiking spot, and there was a hillside full of sage just a few hundred yards off the main trail. And she was curious about the fire.

She pulled onto a gravel road a quarter mile from the

trailhead. The turnoff led out to an old USDA research station and a fancy fishing ranch. Carrie parked on the shoulder just behind some trees and got her bag out of the car. The talented witch had helped the ranch owner with a bear problem a few years back, and he wouldn't have her car towed if he saw it on the road. Or at least, not without calling her first. And she wasn't planning on being gone for more than a few hours.

It took only a few minutes to walk back to the trail-head. The lot was empty at the moment—if the Bureau of Land Management was planning to send trail cleanup crews, they weren't here today. Ducking under the yellow caution tape, Carrie headed up the singletrack path.

She wasn't fast, but once she found a steady pace, she could go forever. The trail climbed steeply in its first stretch, splitting an aspen grove in half until it leveled off into a gentle pine basin. There, the trail switchbacked through the forest onto a ridge. That's where Carrie's sage was, behind a distinctive cluster of boulders near the final switchback before the saddle. There, two granite slabs leaned together over a round boulder, forming a rough pyramid. When she reached it, however, she still felt antsy. Wanting to burn more energy, she continued up the trail to check out the burn area. She could get the sage on her way back.

The forest around her still smelled like a campfire, and as she approached the actual burn area, the overhead branches darkened with residual smoke. A thin black coating of ash blanketed the green pine needles.

And then, the trail dead-ended at a charred black waste. The ground was still warm from the fire, and Carrie wondered if this had been a stupid mistake. Trees could burn for a long time, and the area might still be smoldering. The Forest Service hadn't blocked off the trail capriciously. Carrie laid a palm against the ground. It was warm but not hot, and so she marched out into the ash.

The branches of the pines had burned, but their trunks still stood, eerie upright sentinels that looked like wiry hairs covering scarred gray skin. This must be what mites felt like walking across an elephant.

Carrie would have to come back in the spring, when the place would be choked with wildflowers. With the seeds exposed to sunlight after years of lying dormant, extremely rare plant species might bloom from the ashes. These were sources of powerful magic, particularly for spells involving renewal.

According to *The Daily Croaker,* the fire had started at the Beckermeir cabin. Given that, Carrie had expected the structure to be gone. But the frame was still there, a blackened line drawing of a structure at the base of a boulder field. The charred skeleton of the building made Carrie shudder.

It had been a mistake to come here. She stumbled away, back to where the trail met the charred waste. Back under the trees, she found herself actually jogging. What was it that had scared her? Carrie's heart rate didn't start to slow until she was nearly back at the pyramid boulders on the ridge. There, she veered off trail, picking her way through the scrub along the ridge to her beloved patch of sunny sagebrush. She collected the plants carefully, making sure to leave enough behind that the bushes could regrow. She secured her harvest in burlap bags and deposited them in the canvas backpack. She had brought a book with her, another Hercule Poirot novel by Agatha Christie, and had intended to spend a pleasant hour on a flat rock, sunning herself like a rattlesnake. But the burn area had left a bad taste in her mouth, and a surprise bank of gray clouds had poured in over the mountains. Carrie sat on her selected rock for a scant minute before her legs got cold. The wind blowing down the mountain carried small particles of ash with it, and a low sense of dread rose in her guts. Glad she had some sage on her, she fled the mountain.

The downhill bit was the best part of any hike, but Carrie couldn't enjoy it. She was antsy, eager to get back to her car, and the smell of smoke nipped at her heels. Later, when she rinsed the herbs she'd collected, the water in her sink ran black.

"You smell like a cigarette butt," Finn said.

"You smell like a regular butt," Carrie shot back. The burn area had rattled her, and she wasn't sure why.

CHAPTER TWENTY-ONE

Carrie didn't hear from Maggie for another week and a half. By that time, the afternoon monsoons had dried up, and the aspens had started to turn. Big patches of the hillsides were golden yellow, and when the wind ran through them, they rustled like paper coins. She spent a lot of time in the tower, refreshing the protective wards and glaring at the manikin twins. Her texts to Maggie went unanswered, until one day at two in the afternoon, she got a call.

"Tell me you have something about the manikin," Carrie said. Did she sound as desperate as she felt?

There was a creaking noise, and a coughing jag on the other end of the line. Maggie sounded like her nose had been stuffed with wet cotton. "Sorry, bud I'm nod feeling well," she said, some of her words rounding into a sluggish 'd' at the end.

Carrie felt a surge of uncharitable disappointment. The tower wards wouldn't hold out forever. But Maggie was in no shape for archival research. "I have a favor to ask," her friend said limply. All the bubbly energy had drained out of her. "Can you pick up Reggie ad the airpod?"

"Of course," Carrie said. "Are you okay? How's everything going? How was his trip?"

There was a long hesitation. "It hasn't been a great twenty-four hours. Marcus and I had a big fight."

Carrie's heart sank for her friend, who had been so enthusiastic about her new squeeze. "What's going on?"

"His new land surveying project keeps getting pushed back. Anyways, he wanted to stay with me for a few more days. He's got his camper van, but he said he wanted to be a part of my life. He really wanted to meet Reg."

"Ah."

"That's a hard limit for me, you know? I promised myself I would wait at least a year before bringing any new person around. I don't want Reggie's life to be a chaos of revolving uncles. Bud Marcus wasn't happy aboud it. He went off in a huff, and the stress must've got to me. I feel like someone nailed my sinuses shut."

Carrie spent a few minutes comforting her friend and assured her that she would pick Reggie up at Frognot's tiny airstrip at six. Maggie sounded incredibly relieved.

"Thanks, Carrie. Oh! I forgot to mention. I think I found a book for you."

"More Agatha Christie?" Carrie asked.

"No. Something I dug out of the archives. A book about the ugly little doll drawing. I'll give it to you when you drop Reggie off."

Relief surged through Carrie. She prayed that the book

would contain a solution. She found the prospect so relaxing that when she sat down on the couch to read, she fell asleep.

Carrie woke up several hours later with a sinking feeling clutching at her guts. When she looked at the time on her phone, she was so horrified that she almost physically flung it away from her. It was six fifteen, and she was late to pick up Reggie.

Maggie was going to kill her. Reg, who was a sweet kid, would forgive her, but that almost made it worse. Carrie dove into her car and sped down the highway.

The airport was little more than a long building, so small that even during the winter you had to go outside and board the plane from zig-zagging ramps. It was, unfortunately, somewhat out of the way, way out in the farmland at the southeastern corner of the county. She gunned her old truck as much as she could, but she was going to be at least half an hour late. At the first red light that stopped her, she texted Reggie to apologize and let him know she was on her way.

There was more traffic than usual at the airport. Its tiny size meant that a scant dozen cars could cause a bottleneck, and with two full flights coming in this afternoon, it took Carrie a long time to get through the roundabout. She idled in the car, listening to pop music on the radio and tapping her fingers on the wheel. Reggie still hadn't called, and Carrie was starting to freak out. But maybe he'd run his phone down on the plane playing video games.

Carrie finally pulled up to the curb at arrivals, searching for Reg's face. She hoped it was buried behind the lines of frustrated adults. She laid on her horn twice, then put the car into park and hopped out. "Reg!" she shouted.

A rent-a-cop in a golf cart in front of her backed up, making an aggravating beeping noise that drowned out her screaming. "No idling," the man inside said. "Active loading and unloading only."

"I'm picking up my friend's twelve-year-old son," Carrie explained, assuming this would garner some sympathy. Yet again, she underestimated the capacity for callousness of airport employees.

"No idling. If your kid's not here in the next ten seconds I give you a ticket."

Carrie cursed, wishing she really could turn people into frogs. The security guard already had the beady eyes and squashed face for it. She scanned the crowd for any sign of a Spiderman suitcase, then got back in her car and pulled forward. Reluctantly, she picked up her phone. She dreaded worrying Maggie, but she didn't have a choice here.

"Have you heard from Reg? I'm at the airport, but I don't see him."

A car behind her honked, and Carrie leaned on her own horn in response, drowning out Maggie's words.

"Say that again?" Carrie said.

"He's not with you?"

"Not yet. And he hasn't texted."

Maggie made a strangled noise. When she spoke again, she sounded terrified. "I–but–he's on his way home."

"What do you mean?" Carrie gripped the wheel.

MARTHA CARR & MICHAEL ANDERLE

"There's an app on his phone that lets me see his location. He left the airport about ten minutes ago. He's on highway 221. I thought he was headed back to the house."

Fear gripped Carrie's guts. She cursed herself for falling asleep and letting this happen.

"Where is he?" Maggie was almost shouting now. She was apoplectic, and Carrie wasn't far behind.

"He didn't text you?"

"No!"

Had someone kidnapped him? Seen a lone kid idling in front of the airport and grabbed him? Surely Reggie wouldn't have gotten in the car with a stranger. But you never knew. Reggie was barely old enough to fly by himself.

"Shit. Call 911. In the meantime, I'll go after him," Carrie said. "Where is he?"

"On the highway, headed back into town."

Two cars blocked the exit from the roundabout. Carrie leaned her full weight on her horn, but all it got her was responding horns and a middle finger stuck out of a rolled-down window.

"Maybe he saw a friend at the airport," Carrie said. It sounded stupid, even to her, but she was racing to find an explanation. A gap opened up between cars, and she gunned it onto the shoulder, her left mirror collapsing back against the truck as it scraped against a blue sedan. More honking. Her wheel jolted onto a low curve, then dropped with a jarring thump, and she zoomed along the highway.

"I made it out of the roundabout," Carrie said. "Where is he?"

"Still going along the highway," Maggie said. "I'm hanging up to call the cops."

Carrie pushed the gas pedal all the way into the floor, not easing off until the steering wheel began shaking in her hands. The phone rang a minute later.

"He stopped," Maggie shouted. She sounded panicked. "Oh my God, Carrie, he stopped. What if they dumped his body? Or threw his phone out the window."

"No one dumped his body," Carrie said, almost as panicked as her friend. "Where is he?"

"He's at that one gas station just before you get into town. With the pizza parlor and the dog grooming place."

Carrie drove as fast as her ancient truck would let her. A stoplight turned yellow in the distance, and instead of slowing down, she hit the gas. Rubber screeched on the asphalt as a car turning left at the intersection braked, narrowly avoiding slamming into her rear doors.

"Are you okay?" Maggie asked, hearing the noise through the phone.

Carrie panted a weak "yeah". The gas station was at the bottom of the Santa Sangre valley, visible for almost two miles before you actually reached it. The drive was torture. When the speed limit went from seventy to forty, she slowed, but still kicked up gravel as she careened into the parking lot. She parked her car outside the gas station and snatched her phone from the cupholder.

At the sight of the black camper van in the parking lot by the gas station, Carrie froze. Marcus was here. And there was no way it was a coincidence.

Carrie sucked in her breath, suddenly unsteady. Everything felt like it was collapsing. Was Marcus trying to kidnap Reggie? To what possible end? Maggie didn't have any money. Other motivations were too horrible to think about. With pounding panic, she ran towards the van, pulling up her sleeves and tracing the outline of a tattoo. If Marcus really had kidnapped Reggie, Carrie wanted to be battle-ready.

But there was no one in the van.

"Aunt Carrie?" a timid voice said. A small figure with curly brown hair was seated at a metal table in the gas station's shaded picnic area. It was Reggie. Relief flooded her body as her field of vision narrowed to that beautiful brown mop. Reggie, alive and blissfully unaware of any danger, was juggling a Mexican Coke and a rapidly melting Cornetto ice cream cone. He was trying to eat the chocolate off the side without pushing the ice cream onto the table.

Carrie sprinted towards him. "He's here. Maggie, he's fine!" Carrie screamed into her phone. Maggie said something, but Carrie couldn't hear her over her own shouting. "Reggie! Reggie," she said. As Reggie spun, the glass gas station door flew open, admitting Marcus onto the patio. He was carrying a packet of cigarettes and several kinds of chips.

Carrie stepped between them. "What the fuck do you think you're doing?" she demanded. The exhaustion of the last few days was gone. Or at least, her surging adrenaline had pushed a big old pause button on it.

Normally, Carrie's magic was ritualistic. She cast her spells carefully, ushering magic into meticulously planned runes or exacting potions. Her tattoos gave her a few ready-to-use spells. But she rarely winged it. Right now, however, she wanted to shoot fireballs out of her hands straight into this asshole's face.

Carrie had known exactly one witch who could shoot fireballs out of his hands. His name was Yuri, and he had been one of Faye's other apprentices, who had shown up around halfway through her own time in Havre. Yuri had used the fireball trick to pick up women at bars, even though it left him too exhausted to fight off their angry boyfriends. He only lasted a few months before Faye sent him away.

"It's a pointless waste to shoot fireballs out of your hands when there are three perfectly good gun stores in town," Faye had said. "You might as well exhaust yourself using magic to boil water." Sometimes she punctuated this lesson by shooting one of her many guns into the air over Yuri's head. On such occasions, Carrie would wonder if any apprenticeship could be worth this kind of trouble. Fortunately, Yuri left town before Faye missed. Or before she stopped aiming for the air. Faye frequently reminded Carrie that when she died, her estate would be divided between the Sierra Club and the NRA. Completely inscrutable politics. Carrie pitied the executor.

Carrie rarely wished she was Yuri, but today she had an intense desire to burn the placating smile off of Marcus's face with a super-nuclear fireball.

"Hey, Carrie." He took a step towards the picnic table, but Carrie flashed forward to stay between him and Reggie.

"Take a big step back," Carrie said.

He didn't move. His eyes widened, a cold question burning in the pupils: *or what?*

Carrie tossed her keys to Reggie. "Go get in my truck, hon," she said.

"There's been a misunderstanding," Marcus said. By this point, Carrie's lizard brain was standing at full attention, getting her ready for a physical altercation. The same internal alarms that went off when she saw a rattlesnake— or once, on the bluffs by Fort Clark, a mountain lion— were sounding now, so forcefully that she could actually hear the whine. Wait, no, those were actual sirens, attached to a pair of flashing lights coming up from the valley.

"Do you know Marcus?" Reggie asked, not moving from the table.

"Listen to me, Reggie! Get in the truck!" Carrie shouted. It startled Reggie, and the already-unstable ball of ice cream on the end of his cone plopped onto the asphalt.

"Shit!" he cursed at himself.

"I'll buy you a new one on the way home, sweetie, but please get in the truck." She had clearly scared him, and he scrambled to his feet. But he still wasn't moving away.

"It's okay, he's friends with my mom," Reggie said. "He showed me some pictures of them going hiking. She texted me and said he was coming to pick me up."

"What?" Carrie demanded. *What the hell was Reggie talking about?*

"I think there's been a misunderstanding," Marcus said with a creamy smile.

"Am I in trouble?" Reggie asked.

"No, honey. But please go get in the truck."

"My suitcase is in the van."

"I'll get it for you," Carrie said. Reggie still didn't move.

Marcus raised his hands in supplication. Carrie knew

he was dangerous. Every hair on her body tugged at her skin, telling her so. But he wasn't acting like a kidnapper. He looked more annoyed than afraid, sneering at Carrie as he said, "I can't let Maggie's kid go off with some crazy bitch."

Reggie sucked in his breath. "You said the b-word." As a librarian and lover of the English language in all its colorful forms, his mother was not averse to profanity, although she encouraged Reggie to avoid four-letter clichés. But she had definitely drilled the word "bitch" out of Reggie's vocabulary a long time ago.

"I don't know what your problem is, Carrie, but I'm going to take Reggie home," Marcus said. He took another step forward.

"You're not," Carrie said, anger burning so hotly and cleanly inside her that she debated trying to lob one teeny, tiny fireball at his face. *I wonder if he prefers his left or his right eye.*

"Maggie has a hard time trusting men," Marcus said lazily. "I'm showing her that she can rely on me. That she has someone in her corner, even when she's sick."

"You and Maggie are done. Trust me," Carrie said. "You're a lunatic if you think she'll forgive you for kidnapping her kid."

"What?" Reggie yelped.

"Please get in the truck, sweetheart," Carrie repeated, mentally urging the sirens and lights closer.

"She asked me to pick him up," Marcus said.

"No, she didn't. That's a lie," Carrie said.

"Her fever's off the thermometer. Maybe she made a mistake."

"Mom's sick?" Reggie asked. He sounded worried.

"Just with the flu," Carrie said, hoping Maggie wasn't sicker than either of them had realized.

A small sniffle reached her ear. Carrie glanced over and realized that Reggie had started to cry.

"C'mon, kid, big boys don't cry," Marcus said, giving Reggie an encouraging smile.

"Don't listen to him, Reg. Real men cry all the time. Which Marcus will demonstrate for you shortly if he doesn't take a few fucking steps back."

"You said the f-word," Reggie said, so startled that the sniffling stopped.

"You know what your mom says about the f-word," Carrie said encouragingly, advancing on Marcus. Her quarry was wary now, and actually backed away.

"It's not very original, but sometimes it's the right tool for the job," Reggie recited.

And then the sirens and lights reached them. It was just two cars. Carrie recognized Sheriff Thorne's Chevy Tahoe, and one of his deputies was right behind him in a Crown Victoria cruiser.

"Carrie?" Thorne half-shouted. Car doors opened and closed, and she thought with alarm that she heard Thorne's deputy unholster her gun. The sheriff shouted her name again. Even with his smug ah-I-see-you're-involved-in-criminal-activity-again tone—the one with the little sigh at the end—she liked hearing Thorne say it.

Marcus didn't miss a beat, striding up to Thorne with brash unconcern. "Hey, Sheriff, there's been a misunder-standing here."

"You stay right where you are," Thorne said. Unlike

when Carrie spoke to him, Marcus complied immediately. This only deepened Carrie's irritation.

"You're Reggie Lane?" Thorne turned to Reggie, who froze in the middle of a sip of Coke. He looked slightly panicked.

"Yes," Carrie and Reggie said at the same time.

"Your mom called us. She's worried about you," Thorne said. Mac was a few feet behind him now, gun out but at her side.

Carrie and Mac locked eyes. Mac had good reason to be suspicious of Carrie after the stunt she'd pulled at the station, but she still didn't like being treated like a deviant kidnapper.

"I'm Maggie Lane's boyfriend," Marcus said cheerfully. "She got sick and asked me to pick her son up from the airport. There's nothing weird about it."

Anger sparked inside Carrie. He was lying with total conviction, confident that Thorne would take his side. So confident, in fact, that Carrie was afraid Thorne might fall for it.

"He's lying!" Carrie said. "Maggie didn't want to introduce him to Reggie. She called me and asked me to pick him up from the airport. There's no way in hell she would ever send a stranger."

"She had a pretty high fever when I left." Reggie's tone was appeasing. "If it got so bad that she forgot she asked me to pick up her kid, I'd better get Reggie back to her. Maybe take her to the urgent care."

"You are *not* leaving with Reggie!" Carrie shouted so forcefully that Thorne gave her a hard look.

"Carrie Moonshadow. Nice to see you again," he said,

tipping his hat. Carrie wasn't going to fall for his sheriffy charms. Not today.

"Here, look," Marcus said, pulling his phone out of his pocket and walking up to the sheriff. "These are her texts." He proffered the screen.

Thorne squinted while he read.

"He faked it," Carrie insisted, although she was starting to doubt herself. Maggie hadn't seemed *that* out of it when they had talked today. But maybe she had sunk into a fever and forgotten? It was barely this side of possible. Thorne looked up and clocked her uncertainty.

"Hey, Reggie," Thorne said. "There seems to be some confusion here. How would you like to ride home in Mac's squad car? If you ask nice, she'll put the lights and sirens on."

Reggie was twelve, not six, and he fidgeted in response, unmotivated. "Am I in trouble?" he asked.

Marcus was pissed off and Carrie was anxious. There was a good chance Maggie was both. Thorne sighed and said, "That I can't tell you. I don't know your mom too well. You'll have to be a little brave."

Reggie nodded solemnly and went to Mac with such suffering dignity that Carrie half-expected to hear someone shout "Dead man walking!" Mac holstered her gun as Reggie reached her. Some of the anxiety eased out of Carrie's spine. Whatever else happened here, Mac would keep Reggie safe. Mac spoke to Reggie in a low, cheerful voice as she led him to her cruiser.

The second the cruiser pulled away, Marcus turned back to his camper van. "I'll follow 'em back to Maggie's, we can get this sorted out. What?" He hit the ground with an *oof* as Thorne tackled him onto the pavement. "What the fuck, man!" he shouted, his silky calm evaporated by rage. He let out a stream of cursing that would have impressed even Maggie. The bitter transformation was so rapid that Carrie felt vindicated.

Marcus was a scrappy fighter. In a bar fight, he would have pulled dirty tricks, but after his initial burst of anger, he pretty quickly realized that tricks wouldn't get him out of trouble with the sheriff. Going limp, he allowed Thorne to stuff him in the back of his Tahoe.

When Thorne was done, he turned to Carrie. He was sweaty from the fight, and the small muscles on his neck twitched as he caught his breath. She had thought he would come through in a pinch and was pleased to be proven right. As he picked up his hat from where Marcus had knocked it off his head, he looked a little sad. Pulling a pair of disposable plastic handcuffs from his pocket, he slapped them against his hand.

"Please don't make me tackle you," he said, taking a tentative step forward.

"Why? Because you'd like it?" Carrie snapped. Thorne froze, then held out the cuffs.

"Carrie, please."

Oh my god, he was actually going to arrest her. "I just saved my best friend's son from a kidnapping, and you're handcuffing me?"

Fireballs. Fireballs for everyone. She had a sudden desire to burn down every stupid square inch of Frognot county.

"You're a known criminal element at the scene of a

kidnapping," Thorne said, pronouncing *known criminal element* like the words were red hot irons.

"What the fuck? *Criminal element?* Jesus, Caleb. I'm not a mafioso. This is Frognot, Colorado."

He blinked at the sound of his own name. Maybe he liked hearing her say it. Despite the circumstances. He coughed. "Technically you'd be a mafiosa."

Carrie rolled her eyes. "Can't you cut me a break?"

Thorne shook his head. "I can't give every woman who bats her eyes at me special treatment," he said.

Carrie's anger flared through her spine and pressed against the top of her skull. "Excuse me?" Her quietly murderous tone made him flinch.

A muscle in his jaw clenched, and he doubled down. "I mean I can't let friendship interfere with my professional judgment."

"Oh, I wouldn't worry about that," Carrie shot back murderously. "We're not friends. I don't make friends with assholes."

His expression as he secured the cuffs around her wrists was so somber and professional that Carrie was tempted to do a Hannibal Lecter and try to bite a chunk out of his nose. "Good luck ever getting me in handcuffs again," she growled. That muscle in his jaw twitched again, but all he did was lead her to his Chevy Tahoe.

The physical proximity of Marcus disgusted her. She didn't want to be associated with him. She couldn't believe that Thorne would consider them criminal equals. She was spitting with rage when she turned to him, but his posture was already relaxed.

"Maggie really botched this one," said Marcus. "She'll have to do another fondue night to make it up to us."

His jarringly warm smile invited Carrie to join forces with him against her friend. Carrie inched away on the back seat; her hands twisted behind her. "You're never eating Maggie's fondue again. Not with cheap chardonnay. Not with nice chardonnay. I've got your number, dickbag," she said.

He looked surprised. His schtick must work on most people, or he wouldn't deploy it with such confidence. The friendly smile turned cruel. "Friendship can't compete with love. I always win," he said.

Carrie had a vision of being trapped with Marcus in one small cell in the Frognot County jail. But in the end, they didn't go to jail at all. Thorne let them languish on plastic shell chairs in the back hallway of the sheriff's department, then took them each to his office to make brief statements. Carrie wished she and Maggie had texted about the airport pickup, but at least he could see in her call log that they'd spoken on the phone that morning. Back in the plastic chairs, she shifted uncomfortably.

She had been in the building for less than an hour when Thorne emerged from his office with a grim look on his face.

"What's going on?" Carrie asked. "Did you talk to Maggie? Are you going to arrest this premium sack of dicks?" She pointed at Marcus. She wished they could go somewhere outside of Marcus's hearing.

Thorne scratched his stubble awkwardly and released Marcus's cuffs.

"I'm not detaining you," he said.

"Great. Who do I talk to about my chiropractic bill?" Carrie demanded, waggling her fingers at him from where her arms remained cuffed behind her back. His face was worried.

"Maggie's pretty sick," he said. At Carrie's panicked expression, he put out a reassuring hand. "Mac took her and Reggie to urgent care. High fever. I'm sure she'll be okay. She seemed kind of confused."

Maggie hadn't been confused when Carrie had talked to her on the phone. Sick, but not confused. No, Maggie had been crystal clear about her wishes.

"What did Maggie tell you?" Carrie asked.

Thorne shrugged. "Not much."

Carrie needed to get to her friend more than she needed to dress Thorne down. "Are you going to give me a ride back to my car?"

"I had it towed." Carrie opened her mouth to protest when he said, "I had it towed *here*."

He fished her keys out of his pocket, pausing to admire her keychain. It was a silver sphere with a protective symbol etched into it. Marcus noticed it immediately and looked at Carrie with a new appreciation. Carrie snatched the keys out of Thorne's hand, shooting darts of poisoned loathing into his skull with her eyes. *Last chance for fireballs.*

A long string of creative profanity formed in her throat. Carrie pressed her lips shut against the mounting temptation to give Thorne a piece of her mind.

She rubbed her wrist. "Are you sure you don't need anything else? I can give you a statement to support your kidnapping case," she said, turning her radiant hatred on Marcus.

Thorne scratched his stubble. "There is no kidnapping case. Look, I really think there's been a misunderstanding here. Maggie pretty clearly asked you both to pick her son up. We have the texts. I'm sorry about the confusion," he said. "Reggie is lucky to have so many caring adults in his life."

He went to release Marcus.

"What! You can't let him go!" Carrie resisted the urge to try and physically restrain Thorne. A twinge of guilt glittered in his eyes, but he pointed Marcus to the door. "There's a deputy outside who can give you a ride back to your car."

Marcus nodded pleasantly.

"I hope you feel less stressed," he said to Carrie. And then he actually had the gall to wink. Carrie's jaw dropped open.

"There's something wrong with that guy," she told Thorne. "How can you just let him go?"

"There are texts from Maggie to him asking him to pick up Reggie."

"He must have forged them."

"She's pretty sick, Carrie. She seemed confused about whether she sent them. They've gotten close."

"He's bad, Caleb. Are you really this incompetent at your job?"

His head jerked towards her. That arrow had hit a sore spot. "It's not illegal to be an asshole, Carrie. If it was, you'd be able to see the Frognot County jail from space."

"Maggie would never put Reggie in danger," Carrie said, a little desperate.

"For both their sakes, I hope that's true," Thorne said.

She stormed out, tempted to drive straight to the urgent care to demand answers. She hoped Maggie was okay. She wondered if Maggie was losing her mind. In the end, Carrie settled for texting Reggie.

I know today went haywire, kiddo, but you did great. XOXO

In typical tween fashion, he didn't text back. Carrie sighed. If Maggie had information about the manikins, Carrie needed it soon. But it could wait one night.

CHAPTER TWENTY-TWO

Carrie Moonshadow's accusing eyes stayed in Thorne's head for a long time. He felt fairly tortured about having to arrest her. Logically, it had been the correct choice. But he wasn't in logic-land anymore. What she'd said to him hurt, because a lot of it was right. There was definitely something wrong with Marcus Alvers, age thirty-two, resident of New Mexico. But whatever it was, it didn't show up in a police database search.

He'd basically called Carrie a criminal. Which, to be fair, she was. A trespasser, at least. But Carrie's crimes were weird, not malicious. This Marcus guy was the kind of unfiltered bad news that revolved in and out of correctional facilities in every county in the state. When they'd run his ID, the system hadn't kicked up anything of note. A few speeding tickets in Frognot and a few in New Mexico. Marcus's younger brother had a more serious rap sheet, but that wasn't a chargeable offense.

Thorne stayed at the department late. His body hadn't let go of the high-alert nerves he'd brought to the gas station. He'd thought he might have to actually use his gun. He found paperwork to fill his time, settling into the tedium of employee evaluations. When that was done, he double-checked a few of Mac's reports. Sometimes new deputies needed coaching when they started, but Mac seemed to be running on rocket fuel. Her reports might actually be better than his own.

At loose ends, he went to make coffee in the break room, where Theo caught him. "I can do that for you, Sheriff," the young admin said.

Thorne shook his head. "I'm killing time until Mac gets back."

Just when he was considering hopping in his Tahoe and tracking her down, she came back into the office. Poking her head in the door, she said "Theo said you waited for me?" Noticing one of her reports on his desk, she straightened. "Is that report okay, sir? I wasn't sure how to handle the bit about the dog outside."

"You handled it fine. In fact, there's a few veteran deputies who could learn a lesson or two from this. I should have you teach a seminar." He waved the paper in the air.

Mac beamed and gave him a sharp nod.

"How'd things go with Maggie Lane?" he asked.

"She was thrilled to see Reggie, no surprise there. But she had a pretty high fever. The urgent care said it's a virus. Prescribed fluids and rest. I hope it's okay I stayed with them for a while. I didn't want to send her home in an Uber."

"It's fine, Mac. What was your impression of the situation? What did she say about Marcus and Carrie?"

"She was very clear that she called Carrie to ask her to pick up Reg. But she seemed confused about Marcus."

"Confused how?"

"I don't know. Like, she'd say his name, and she'd look really angry. But then she'd go blank. Like she was rebooting, or something. It was weird. I guess it's the fever? And she showed me the texts she sent, but she didn't remember sending them."

"Hmm."

"Did I handle it right?"

"I think so, yeah."

"Should we call social services to check on the kid?"

"I don't think this rises to that level. Maybe I'll stop by tomorrow, though. Check and make sure everyone's okay."

"Alright."

That night, he went to sleep with the image of Carrie's furious green eyes burning in his brain.

CHAPTER TWENTY-THREE

The next morning dawned light and cool. It was the first whisper of fall. Carrie made coffee and brought it in a mug to Finn, who was in the backyard etching protective spells on a piece of plywood.

While Carrie had been down at the Sheriff's department, the rot in the tower floor had worsened to the point that the manikins had almost broken through the planks. The wards on the tower itself were still providing some protection, but Finn had had to reinforce the floor with some plywood from the greenhouse. Without Carrie to add protective magic, however, the plywood had warped and cracked within a few hours, and the rot had gotten worse. They were barely holding back the evil, and Carrie didn't want to think about what would happen when the dam broke.

"Maggie said she found a book that could help. But we got, uh, caught up before she could give it to me."

"Was that before or after you were arrested for kidnapping her kid?"

"I wasn't arrested for kidnapping!" Carrie protested. "I was *detained* on *suspicion* of kidnapping."

"Uh huh."

"They're completely different things. But I'm sorry I wasn't here to help you with the twins."

Today, they were busy making backup plywood boards that they could slide under the manikins as the old ones wore out. Finn drew the protective symbols with a sharpie while Carrie prepared two different herbal pastes for anointing and sealing. When they were done, she helped Finn carry the jerry-rigged protective circle up to the tower. Her feet began to hurt as she walked up the steps, and her teeth clenched together at the threshold of the tower. The dark aura in the tower made her molars ache where they met her jaw, like they'd been covered in acid.

The manikins hadn't changed or moved, but the atmosphere up here was increasingly foul. A lot of witch-craft was straightforward work—memorizing symbols, identifying herbs and learning their properties, following recipes to decoctions and poultices. But sometimes, you had to rely on intuition. The tower had always helped free Carrie's mind for such insights. Bathed in moonlight, high over the river, she'd done some of her best work.

Now, the energy was awful. The overhead lighting was harsh, throwing shadows with knife-blade edges, blinding her to the view over the Santa Sangre. The sunlight that made it in the windows was a sickly yellow. Carrie tapped a crack in the glass. "What's going on here?" she asked.

Finn's chin quavered, shaking his snowy beard. "Birds keep hitting it," he said. "It's happened a few times while I was here. The one that cracked it was a big raven." Carrie

MARTHA CARR & MICHAEL ANDERLE

peered out the window. A few dark, unmoving shapes were clustered by the gutter. The corpses of birds. A dark shadow roiled across the jade orb on her bookshelf but disappeared whenever she looked at it directly. Carrie felt sick, a sensation worsened by a twist of movement in her peripheral vision. This, too, was a trick of the light.

Down on the floor, a line of ants marched out of a crack in the wall. Carrie watched in horror as individual insects removed salt grains from the protective circle, carrying them back to a growing pile along the wall.

"What the fuck?" she said. "They're destroying the protective lines."

Finn brought his soft-soled leather shoe down on the ants with a sickening crunch. "They're not very fast. But that's about the size of it. I keep putting out poison, but they find their way in." He grabbed a cylinder of salt from the bookshelf and refreshed the protective line. "I can do this all day, assholes," he said to the ants. They marched over the squashed bodies of their comrades and grabbed more salt.

The plywood beneath the manikins had a hairline crack in it, although the salt circle remained unbroken. Finn scrutinized the board.

"Should we swap it out?" Carrie asked.

He shook his head. "Nah. We can get a few more hours out of this one. I can manage on my own. You go see Maggie. Find out more about that book."

"Will you be okay on your own?" Carrie asked.

"If you find out what these things are, I will be," Finn said.

"Can you feel what I feel? The horrible atmosphere?" Carrie asked, staring at the line of suicidal ants.

"The sickness here? Oh yes," Finn said. He was gripping the salt container very tightly.

Relief washed over Carrie as she fled the tower. She took the stairs two at a time, knowing Finn would hear her panicked retreat. There was something very wrong upstairs, something that gripped her spine with tiny, needle-like claws. The evil loosened its grip when she went outside and released her completely once she was on the highway. At the turnoff for I-60, her fingers twitched on the wheel. If she started driving now, she could be five hundred miles away from the manikins by tomorrow morning. She forced her hands to stay on the wheel and keep herself on the road to Maggie's.

Her heart sank when she saw Marcus's camper van parked in Maggie's driveway. The asshole was still here. Carrie wondered as she climbed Maggie's steps if she should have brought some kind of weapon. She had a shiny new pitchfork that wasn't seeing much use.

Knocking on the door with trepidation, Carrie prepared for the worst.

Marcus opened the door. Anger flashed across his face, then cooled into a smirk. "Carrie Moonshadow," he said. "Run out of kids to kidnap?"

Carrie tried to sidestep him. When he moved into her path, she put out a hand and shoved him aside. As she did, her index finger—the one with the tattoo—grazed his collarbone under his open shirt collar. At the skin-to-skin contact, a flash of white-hot hatred shot into Carrie's body, like an icicle ramming through her chin and into her skull.

185

Carrie shrieked and stumbled away. Normally, she had to activate her empathic powers to use them. It didn't just happen. Had Marcus made it happen?

Carrie had felt many different emotions when using her empathic touch. Grief. Guilt. Good old-fashioned horniness. This was something different. Marcus's raw hatred burned white-hot, bright enough to blind. As Carrie tried to regain her balance, she crashed into Maggie's hat rack. It clattered onto the floor, spilling backpacks and beanies and a canvas bag of granola bars across the floor.

"Whoa, Nelly," Marcus said casually. He offered her a hand up, but his eyes burned with pinprick embers of rage. *What the fuck is that?* Carrie scrambled to her feet on her own, just as Maggie came out of the kitchen.

"What are you doing here?" Maggie asked. Her voice was weak and distant.

For a woman incapacitated by a fever less than twenty-four hours earlier, Maggie looked good. Too good, in fact. Maggie should be wearing sweatpants on the couch, but instead she had donned a curve-hugging gold silk dress. Lots of makeup, too, although Carrie guessed that her bright red cheeks were a lingering symptom of fever and not the result of too much blush. Something was wrong. Maggie was *off.*

As Maggie walked towards Marcus, she swayed unsteadily. Maybe she was still very sick, after all. But then Carrie looked down and realized that Maggie was wearing six-inch stripper heels.

"What the fuck?" slipped out of Carrie's mouth at the sight of the two-inch rhinestone platforms.

Marcus wrapped a stabilizing arm around Maggie's waist, and Carrie hated him for it.

"You should be in bed," Carrie said.

Maggie starcd at her blankly. Marcus's fingers tightened around a piece of Maggie's waist, and she smiled in response. It was a strange smile, blank and unblinking. "I feel good," she said, admiring the glittering purple ring on her finger.

"Where's Reggie?" Carrie looked down the hallway towards his bedroom.

"He's at school. Marcus dropped him off."

"Can I talk to you for a minute? Alone?" Carrie asked.

Maggie stared right through her, the smile on her face wavering. "We're talking right now," she said. Her voice was slower than normal.

"Don't you usually work on Mondays?" Carrie asked.

Maggie didn't respond at all. It was like she was a porcelain doll. Or worse, a ventriloquist dummy, with Marcus's grip on her waist moving her mouth. This was wrong. It was very wrong. Could he be threatening her? It was possible, just barely. But Carrie suspected that the truth was much worse. She stared again into Maggie's eyes. Beneath the glaze of ambivalence was the tiniest pinprick of fear.

Maggie hadn't been blinded by love. Not exactly, anyways. It might have been that way at first, but her original affection had been twisted into something different.

Marcus was using a fucking mesmer. No wonder her friend was so out of it. As Maggie gazed at her sparkly ring again, Carrie saw the truth of it. The purple stone was a mesmeric focus. When Maggie looked at it, the spell would refresh itself. Marcus was a powerful witch, and he was eroding Maggie's will. It was possible, if you didn't have a conscience. You could use magic to make their personality pliable, like wet clay. As Faye had once told her, "Mesmers can be useful, but keeping one up on a permanent basis is pure evil and it would be kinder to put a fucking ice pick in someone's eye."

To destroy the mesmer, she would need to get Maggie away from Marcus and to take that ring off her finger. She didn't think she could do either of those things without help.

Worse, Carrie really, really needed the information Maggie had discovered about the manikins. They couldn't keep shoring up the tower floor with plywood—they needed a real solution, fast. But she couldn't stand the thought of her friend being tethered to a brainwashing asshole, either. Maybe Finn would know something that could help.

With sickening clarity, Carrie remembered Marcus handing her a glass of wine at fondue night. She had drunk it thoughtlessly. Marcus could have put something in it. If he was a powerful enough witch to enchant Maggie like this, then he would have recognized Carrie's tattoos for what they were. He knew she was a witch.

"I want to talk to Maggie alone," she announced, widening her stance a little bit, showing Marcus she wouldn't back down.

Marcus's hand squeezed again, ragged nails catching on the gold silk at Maggie's waist. "Anything you can say to me, you can say to Marcus," Maggie recited.

"This is private," Carrie said. "Girl talk. I can't talk about it in front of Marcus."

Maggie blinked twice, like a doll with articulated eyelids. "Anything you can say to me, you can say to Marcus," she repeated. Carrie wanted to throw Marcus through the window.

Fuck. Fuck-fuck-fuck. *Like Maggie says, sometimes it's the only word for the job.*

"We have a big day planned, so I think you should leave," Marcus said, smirk widening.

CHAPTER TWENTY-FOUR

C arrie slammed the door to her truck, fuming. She connected her Bluetooth to her phone and played her favorite heavy metal album, but there weren't enough screaming men with eyeliner in the world for how she was feeling right now. She pulled up Sheriff Thorne's contact information, trying to divine from the flat digital numbers whether a call would produce anything useful. What crime could he possibly charge Marcus with? Not harassment, not if Maggie said she wanted him there. Same with trespassing. She didn't think *violation of human dignity via mesmeric ensorcellment* was in the county laws anywhere. Plus, if she explained the concept of a mesmer to him, he might start thinking about what had happened in his office when she'd waved her gold frog at him. He might start asking questions. And her answers would ruin their relationship forever.

What relationship? He arrested you!

The thought of Reggie finding his brainwashed mom dolled up in stripper heels made Carrie sick. Even if

Marcus didn't have nefarious intentions toward the boy, it wasn't a healthy environment for a kid. Somewhere beneath the makeup and the new clothes, a locked-up piece of Maggie's brain must be screaming warnings at her son.

Carrie couldn't leave Reggie in that house. The terrible certainty gripped her heart. Her brain kicked up logical objections, *kidnapping a child is a federal crime that could get you into prison* being chief among them. But there were no nearby exits from the cold, hard truth. Maggie would have wanted Reggie protected at any cost. Even if Carrie wound up in real legal trouble.

Reggie was a seventh grader at Bates Middle School, which was up on the bluff next to Fort Clark. It was a steep uphill walk to the school, so Maggie drove Reggie in the mornings before she went to work. But he walked home by himself afterwards. Maggie wavered between pride in her son's independence and fear that she was damaging him by not observing every last second of his childhood.

In any case, it gave Carrie an opportunity.

She texted Finn to say she wouldn't be home for a few more hours. Then she drove up the bluff to wait. She parked on a long, steep section of road just below the middle school and rolled down her windows. The following ninety minutes went by in an interminable jumble of Google searches on the subject of "love spells." She thought she was dealing with a simple if powerful mesmer. But she had to be sure. Most of what she found was barely legible garbage. Ad-clogged listicles with titles like "Top 10 love spell moments in film" jockeyed for positions with half-baked essays about the history of witchcraft. Many sites promised her immediate results from the man of her dreams for a low, low, down payment. Carrie swore, wishing for the return of the useful witchcraft blogs from the early aughts.

She was wading with increasing despair through the twenty-eighth page of Google results when a distant school bell rang. A few minutes later, kids began trickling down the road. Carrie waited anxiously for Reggie's curly brown mop to appear.

She finally spotted him at the top of the hill. He was walking with two other kids. Although he was participating in the conversation, an incomprehensible discussion about a YouTuber named Mr. Monster, he seemed distracted. Carrie stuck her hand out the window and waved.

"Hey, Reggie!" she shouted.

Reggie was surprised to see her. The boy on his left, who was as thin as a fencepost but four inches taller, elbowed Reggie in the gut and shouted, "stranger danger."

"That's not a stranger, that's Aunt Carrie," Reggie said.

"She's got tattoos," the boy said, half disgusted and half awed.

"Can I talk to you for a minute, Reggie?" Carrie asked. "I'll give you a ride home."

Reluctantly, he waved goodbye to his friends. He didn't get in the car but lingered beside the open window.

"Hey, Reggie. How are you doing?" Carrie asked.

Reggie shrugged.

"I went by your house this afternoon," Carrie said.

Reggie nodded.

"The thing is, I think your mom is sick."

Reggie looked worried. "Her fever went down," was all he offered.

"Yeah, but she's still not feeling well. In a different way."

Reggie's nod was short and suspicious.

"What do you think about Marcus?" Carrie asked.

"He called me sport and bought me a drone, but I think he used Mom's credit card," Reggie mumbled.

"Are you scared of him?" Carrie asked.

Reggie pressed his lips together and fiddled with the waist strap on his backpack.

"I'm more scared of Mom," he said. Carrie understood his perspective. The rapid personality shift after his vacation must have been jarring. His voice grew quiet. "I think she's angry at me. For going to see Dad?"

"What? Honey, no. She missed you, that's all," Carrie said. Maggie tried her best to make sure that Reggie didn't pick up on her anger at her ex. Carrie wished she could explain the situation to Reggie. But telling the kid that Maggie was being puppeteered by an evil witch wouldn't soothe Reggie's worries.

A knot of girls was coming down the hill. They stared at Carrie and Reggie. They could see her face, and they might remember it. There was nothing to be done about that, now.

"How would you like to come spend a few days with me at the oxbow?" Carrie asked.

Reggie cheered up considerably. The banks of the Santa Sangre were rich with opportunities for observing frogs and finding nice smooth stones to throw into the river. "What about Mom?" he asked warily.

Carrie's mind raced. She couldn't just disappear with

Reggie. For one, she didn't think she'd get away with it. The kids would recognize her. They had already commented on her tattoos. And while Marcus might not care whether Reggie was around, he had a vindictive streak and would love to see Carrie arrested. If she could buy herself some time, she could work it out.

"Why don't you come over for the afternoon. And I'll go talk to your mom about a sleepover," she said.

She was agitated all the way back to the house, but she tried to make conversation. Talking to a twelve-year-old boy could be like pulling teeth at the best of times. One who was worried and withdrawn was a locked vault. She abandoned the effort to get more than one-word answers out of him and flicked on the radio.

In the short time Carrie had been gone, conditions at the house had worsened. The evil atmosphere, which had previously been confined to the tower, had infiltrated the whole property. As she drove through the gate, rotten anxiety tugged at her guts. Reggie's mood darkened noticeably. *Shit.* Maybe she had been wrong to bring him here. Maybe he'd be safer at his mom's. But the image of a blank-faced Maggie Lane swam in Carrie's mind. She couldn't let him see his mom like this. Still, she had to destroy the manikins, and soon. Before what was happening at the house wrecked the town.

Reggie squirmed and frowned in the front seat, and Carrie wondered if he could feel the dark energy. The second she parked, Reggie begged Carrie for permission to play by the river. Carrie happily sent him off, promising to bring him a cheese and mayo sandwich. His favorite. After she'd fed him, she assembled a two-person war cabinet at her kitchen table.

"We need to kidnap Maggie Lane," she told Finn. "We've got to get her away from that asshole Marcus. Reverse the mesmer and help her kick him out of her house."

Finn absentmindedly braided a strand of his beard. "Okay," he said.

"Okay? That's it?"

"I can think of a thousand ways it could go wrong. I'll write you a list if you want, but I'd need a forest of paper and by the time I'm done Maggie might be gone."

By 'gone' he didn't mean that Maggie might leave town. He meant that her personality might be erased by whatever spell Marcus was casting.

Finn added, "I support this plan, but we can't leave the house alone with those *things* in the tower." He eyed the ceiling with a scowl. "And we *really* can't leave Reggie alone in the house with the twins."

"No," Carrie agreed.

"You're going to need some help," Finn said.

Before she could stop herself, Carrie pulled up Thorne's number on her phone. Having an actual sheriff on her side would make kidnapping a breeze. She imagined walking him through the problem. *I need to kidnap my best friend so that I can reverse the mesmeric spell an asshole cast on her, but I can't leave her son—who I have also kidnapped—alone in a house with cursed dolls in the attic.* For some reason, Thorne wasn't wearing a shirt as she told him this. Carrie shook her head until he was back in his sheriff's uniform.

Carrie spent a minute lost in thought, trying to work

out the problem. A minute later, she picked the phone up and sighed. Reluctantly, she dialed. "I need your help," she said.

CHAPTER TWENTY-FIVE

The beady black eye of the motion-activated security camera stared Carrie down when she went to pick up Luke Menkin from the gate of the ranch. "Is your dad going to make a stink about me coming by?" she asked, glancing at the camera. Luke took it as an insult to his independence.

"I'm grown. I can have whatever woman I want drop by."

"Oh *really*," Carrie said, grinning. "Any woman you want? Anyone at all?"

"I mean I run my own life." This was not the right moment to point out that he relied on his dates for rides. But Luke's cheerful mood was infectious. "And anyway, the prettiest girl in town has already got me in her front seat."

"This isn't exactly a date," Carrie pointed out, blushing slightly.

Luke glanced over his shoulder at the pitchfork in the bed of her truck. "You don't normally bring your favorite pitchfork on dates? City girl, huh?"

"I'm a mountain girl now," Carrie said. Luke fiddled with the radio restlessly, settling on SUNN 98.9, the county's solar-powered country music station. They were playing old Emmylou Harris today. Carrie approved.

"This okay? Too country for you? We can put in one of your Enya CDs if you prefer," Luke said.

"I don't have Enya *CDs*," Carrie said. Then admitted disgruntledly, "All my Enya's on my phone." She was so distracted by a massive Range Rover from Texas swerving around her that she almost missed Luke's widening smile.

Realization dawned. "You're making fun of me," she said.

"I never make fun of a woman with a pitchfork," he said earnestly. He fished a silver flask out of his denim jacket, took a swig, and offered it to Carrie. She shook her head.

"C'mon. Don't leave me drinking by my lonesome."

"It's illegal," Carrie said.

"So's kidnapping," Luke pointed out.

"This is benevolent kidnapping. There's no such thing as benevolent drunk driving." She said it sharply, and Luke's easygoing smile dissolved, replaced with blankness.

"When a lady in distress calls me, I'll show up. But I dunno if we can help your friend. You can't talk sense into a woman who's got her heart set on a fuckup," Luke said. "Ask my exes' mothers."

Carrie coasted to a gentle stop at a red light. "Talking's not part of the plan."

"Right," Luke agreed. "Pitchforking, on the other hand…"

"Only if things go very badly," Carrie said.

"If you don't want to talk to Maggie, what *is* the plan?"

"She's dating this guy. Marcus Alvers."

"*Marcus?*" Luke asked. He sounded shocked.

"You know him?"

"Hell yeah, I know him. We went to school together. He used to be a regular part of the McKellen's gang. Up until his first kid was born. Four or five years ago, now? Afterwards, he and his wife moved to New Mexico to be closer to his wife's family. *That's* who your friend's having trouble with? *Marcus Alvers?*" Luke was incredulous.

"Yeah. He has a wife?" Carrie couldn't imagine the asshole who had ensnared her friend having a wife. And the thought of him having kids was even more distressing. But maybe Maggie wasn't his first target. Marcus seemed young for a midlife crisis, but maybe he was ahead of the curve.

"Yeah. Nice girl. Cute kids, too. I see them on Facebook."

"Something's off," Carrie said. "I don't think we're talking about the same person."

Marcus had been with her down at the sheriff's department. Surely they'd checked his ID. As she pulled onto Maggie's street and parked, Luke handed her his phone. He had opened Facebook to the profile for Marcus Alvers.

"Is this him?"

Looking at the photo on his phone, Carrie was about to say yes. Sandy hair? Check. Wiry frame? Check. And the face in the picture looked very similar. But the man in the photo was wearing sunglasses. She swiped to the next picture, this one a family portrait.

The man in the photo looked so similar to the man staying in Maggie's house that she had to stare at the photo for ten seconds before she could confirm it wasn't him. The eyes were the same color. The nose had the same bump just below the bridge. But it wasn't the same guy. For one thing, this man didn't look like a fucking evil brainwasher. His smile was genuine.

"Marcus—your Marcus—doesn't have a twin, does he?" Carrie asked. She was half serious.

Luke's expression shifted. Carrie had been joking, but she had reminded Luke of something. "Well, kinda," he admitted.

"Oh my god, do *not* tell me we're looking at evil twins."

"No. But Marcus has a brother. Four, five years younger? When we were in high school he was just a kid, and I barely noticed him. But now that they're older they look really similar. A couple of years ago, the younger brother showed up at McKellen's. The first time I saw him, I thought Marcus was back in town." Luke looked even more uneasy now.

"What is it?" Carrie asked.

"For one, James got permanently banned from McKellen's for fighting. Even back in high school, the kid was troubled. Marcus wouldn't really talk about him. To be honest, I think part of why he went to New Mexico was to get away from the whole situation."

"The brother's name is James?" Carrie asked, her heart sinking. Her ears rang with the name of Emily's bad exboyfriend. The one who wouldn't let her go. *Shit.* That made a lot more sense than a family man from New Mexico blowing up his life to mesmerize a single mom.

"Do you know James?" Luke asked. He took another swig from his flask. This time, when he offered it to her, she accepted. The bourbon inside was surprisingly good, and the burn fueled her anger.

"I think James stole his older brother's ID. He told Maggie he was a land surveyor," Carrie said. The brothers looked so much alike that Thorne hadn't caught it when he ran the name.

Luke shook his head. "A land surveyor? That kid never did an honest day's work in his life. He was always stealing from their mom. And don't look at me like that, I realize you could drive a tractor through the holes in my resume."

"We've got to take him down. Maggie's not the first person he's done this to," she said. Emily had gotten sick, but she hadn't lost her mind. Clearly, this guy—James or Marcus—was refining his methods.

"Well, at least we have a little leverage if we need it, now. Threaten to turn him in for impersonation if he doesn't leave your friend alone." Luke was over-fortified with whiskey at this point, but Carrie took another sip and grabbed the pitchfork. Let James call the cops if he wanted to.

"Wait! What are we doing?" Luke called after her.

Carrie tightened her grip around the pitchfork handle. "Storming the castle," she said. She would worry about the intricacies of reversing the love spell later. Luke couldn't help with that, anyways. He might be open-minded, but magic would never be in his wheelhouse.

"Help me get Maggie back to my place, and I'll take care of it," Carrie said over her shoulder. Luke trotted loyally behind her.

She slammed her fist on the door. The blinds on the front windows were down, blocking her view of the interior, but a second after she knocked, the wooden floors creaked. "Maggie? Marcus? James!" At this last name, someone inside knocked into a piece of heavy furniture, stumbled, and swore.

Carrie tried the door, but it was locked.

"Can you kick it down?" she asked Luke.

He stared, glassy-eyed, at the brass handle. "I have no idea," he said honestly. Then he straightened and puffed out his chest, his masculine pride overtaking his tipsy uncertainty. "But I can try."

Luke backed up and ran towards the door. Just as his shoulder was about to make contact with the wood, it swung open, and he barreled straight into the man they now knew to be James. The men tumbled into an antique hutch that faced the door. A blue vase fell from the top shelf and shattered, and old paperbacks fell open on their spines amid the tumble of hats and coats. Carrie ran for the hutch as it teetered, and barely stopped it from collapsing onto the grappling men below.

Maggie appeared at the end of the entrance hallway. She stood, unspeaking, still wearing that gold dress and purple ring. A blank ghost. Carrie shouted her name, but it wasn't enough to pull her back into the world.

Luke had made it onto his knees with James pinned below him. James searched the floor with a frantic hand and found a hand-sized shard of vase, slashing it up towards Luke, who swayed out of reach. James screamed as the sharp edge of the glass bit into his own hand instead, draining blood out of his palm.

"Maggie!" James shouted in a panic. "Maggie! Help me!"

Maggie disappeared into the house. Carrie sprinted

after her, pitchfork in hand, praying she could convince her friend to leave of her own volition. She sent a silent thanks to Maggie's newfound penchant for platform heels, which slowed her down considerably.

Carrie caught up to Maggie in the bedroom, just as Maggie pulled an object from under her pillow and spun. Carrie froze at the sight of the pistol. "Maggie..." her voice was barely a squeak. Her vision narrowed to the barrel of the gun. Of course, James had a gun. And of course that degenerate left it unsecured.

Maggie's eyes were so empty it made Carrie want to scream.

"Maggie. It's me. Carrie. Your friend."

It was like talking to a badly painted portrait. Everything was wrong. "Help. Help," Maggie muttered. Was it an entreaty, or was she just repeating James's last words to her?

"I'm here, Maggie," she said. Magic had done this to Maggie, and it made Carrie furious. "Please. Please tell me that you're in there somewhere. I want to help you."

More glass shattered at the front of the house. Maggie's head swiveled languidly towards the sound, and Carrie took her chance. Leaping forward, she brought the wooden handle of the pitchfork up and swung it down with all her strength on Maggie's wrist. The crack of wood and bone grated on Carrie's ears, but the gun fell from Maggie's hand. As it hit the carpet, it discharged with a burst of light and a flash of heat by her right foot. She forced herself to look down, relieved to find she was still whole. The bullet had ripped a channel across the carpet and embedded itself in the molding along the far floor.

Carrie grabbed the gun. As she did, Maggie kicked her. The rhinestones on the heavy shoe dug into the soft area just under Carrie's ribs, knocking her against the bed. "Stop! Maggie! It's me, your friend Carrie. The guy out there? He lied to you. His name's not even Marcus." She rasped the words, praying Maggie was somewhere in there, listening.

Their eyes locked for an instant, and the glaze in Maggie's eyes ebbed, revealing raw panic. "Carrie?" she mumbled.

"I'm here," Carrie said. Maggie looked at her broken wrist, face constricting with pain. Carrie nearly screamed as the glittering purple ring caught Maggie's eye. The momentary spark of awareness was washed away by the mesmer, and Maggie's face went blank. She raised her foot for another blow, careless of her own broken bones. Carrie spun away and the kick went into the bed frame. When Maggie raised her foot again, Carrie drove her boot into Maggie's heel. Maggie, already unsteady, toppled to the floor, her head so close to the corner of her dresser that a splinter in the wood yanked out a strand of her curly brown hair. Close call.

A spell that destroyed the human will was easiest to cast when the target was blandly content. But the will to survive was strong, and hard to override. Controlling magic sometimes lost its foothold when the subject was in pain.

"I'm so sorry," Carrie said as she scrambled forwards. Maggie's right wrist was already starting to swell, and Carrie reached for the red flesh like it was a bullseye, fending off wan kicks and slaps. Grabbing the wrist, Carrie pressed down.

Maggie screamed. The noise was horrible but human, and Carrie started to cry as she pulled her friend closer. "Maggie. Please... are you there?"

Maggie's pupils went dinner-plate wide. "Carrie!" she said, recognition and agony on her face.

"I'm here," Carrie said.

As Maggie opened her mouth, another wave of pain washed over her. Her eyes went blank again. For a moment, Carrie thought the mesmer had regained control. But no, Maggie was in shock, her limp body sinking to the floor. Carrie brought her down as gently as she could. "Shit," Carrie said, leaning over her friend. Maggie's pulse was strong, and she was breathing fine.

Yanking the sheets off Maggie's bed, Carrie ripped them into strips and bound Maggie's ankles, murmuring apologies under her breath. Before she bound Maggie's wrists, she yanked the purple ring off her friend's finger, tucking it in her pocket. She hated having to tie Maggie up, but she didn't want to have to repeat this fight if Maggie lost lucidity. When Maggie was secure, Carrie picked up the gun from where it lay on the floor.

Carrie had shot rifles with Faye a few times, but the old witch was often drunk and hazardously laissez-faire about gun safety, so she had mostly tried to stay out of range and hoped she wouldn't have to find a spell that could patch up a bullet hole. But Carrie had never fired a handgun. She spent a second trying to ascertain where the safety was, and if it was on or off, but a shout from the front of the house spurred her to more immediate action. Opening

Maggie's window, Carrie dropped the gun into a bush. This time, it fell into the branches without firing. Carrie picked up her pitchfork and went to help Luke.

Luke and James had burned through their first wave of brawling energy and were circling each other warily. James was accustomed to starting bar fights, but Luke was accustomed to finishing them. Blood ran from his nose as he feinted two jabs.

Carrie didn't appreciate having to break bones to snap a friend out of a mesmer. This time, when she rushed James with the pitchfork, she used the pointy end. James wasn't prepared for the prongs to pierce his denim jacket. He fell away from the blow with an *oof*, blood spreading across his white tank-top from a pencil-sized hole in the chest.

"You bitch," James screamed, heedless with rage. When he rushed towards Carrie a minute later, he almost speared himself on her pitchfork. Before he got there, however, Luke dropped him with a haymaker, the blow connecting with a crunch. From the way Luke's face immediately went white, she guessed the punch had broken his hand.

Before James could squirm to his feet, Carrie lowered the pitchfork to his neck. He froze, the only movement his pulse fluttering in his throat below the metal point.

"What did you do to Maggie?" Carrie demanded.

"I wooed her," James rasped. His face was very still, but a cruel smirk glittered in his eyes. "She was lonely and now she's not."

"She's not anything anymore. You erased her." James was quiet, but his pulse beat faster.

"I know about you," Carrie said. "You're throwing

powerful magic around like it's Halloween candy. You've been keeping her under a constant mesmer. I don't particularly care if it comes back to bite you in the ass, but other people are going to get hurt."

"I don't know what you're talking about." Jame's voice was soft.

"Tell me what you did to Maggie and tell me how to fix it." Carrie demanded.

Luke coughed into the silence. His lungs made a wet, worrying noise, which told Carrie they needed to get out of here soon.

"Tell me!" she said and pressed the pitchfork down. The metal point made a dent in James's skin, just below the Adam's apple. He made a strangled noise, and she let up.

"I'll show you," James said. "There's a totem in my pocket."

His hand inched towards his jeans, and Carrie pressed the pitchfork in again. "No. Luke will get it," she said. "Luke?"

Luke bent down, keeping a watchful eye out as he reached into the front pocket of James's jeans with his left hand. His back blocked Carrie's view, but she could tell from his posture that he'd found something.

"What is it?"

"Show it to her," James said beneath her. His voice was honey smooth, and Carrie pulled the pitchfork back as Luke showed her. A purple gemstone nestled in his palm. The size of a marble, but faceted, sparkling with inclusions. "Look inside," James instructed.

"Not a chance." She took a half step back.

It wasn't necessary anyway. A starburst float out of the

gem, creating a small firework. Carrie followed a line of glitter falling back into the gem.

It was working despite her efforts to keep her distance. Outside sounds faded, blending together into a matte white noise so complete that she heard only the first peal of sirens. But that faded, too, as she fell into the galaxy inside the marble. Everything in the physical world disappeared, except for that purple starburst, and Carrie dropped into a deep well of fractal light.

CHAPTER TWENTY-SIX

Later, she would discover that she'd lost about fifteen minutes of time. When Carrie came back to herself, the first thing she felt was the grain of the hardwood floor pressing hard into her face. Someone was holding her down. A harsh voice barked in her ear, making incoherent demands that she couldn't have complied with even if she understood, because she still didn't have control of her body. Finally, the deadened sensation in her limbs turned into prickles, and then pain, and the voice at her back became coherent. She'd assumed it was James, but her stomach twisted when she heard the tone. "Do you understand me?"

It was Caleb Thorne. Now she understood why her wrists were so warm. He had them secured in one of his strong hands. Carrie cursed.

"Whoa, there you are," Thorne said.

"I wasn't cursing at you," Carrie mumbled, words garbled by the floor pressing against her jaw. She wasn't angry at Sheriff Thorne at all. She was angry at herself. She had fallen for a mesmer. Something she should have seen coming a goddamn mile away. She had been so focused on helping Maggie that she had forgotten to guard herself against James's magic.

"Where's James?" she asked.

"Who?" Thorne sounded confused.

"The guy you arrested the other day. His name's not Marcus. It's James. He was using his brother's ID."

This took Thorne by surprise, and the pressure on her cheek let up. "Can I sit up?" Carrie asked.

"Don't try anything," Thorne said. Grumbling, Carrie slid into a sitting position, her back against the hutch.

"How did you miss that he's a whole different person?" she demanded. The brothers looked so similar that she would have missed it, too, but she was pissed.

"There wasn't an alert on the ID. Either Marcus didn't know his brother took it, or he knew and didn't want to report it."

Released from her mesmeric trance, Carrie looked around. Her neck craned to the point of aching. She hoped he was already outside in a squad car. "Where is he?"

"He's gone. We think he took Maggie's car."

"How is she?" Carrie asked.

Thorne went pale. "I probably shouldn't tell you this. The ambulance just took her away."

"Was she– how did she seem? Was she alert?"

"Not really. She was pretty out of it."

"Shit."

"Are you going to tell me what the hell happened?" Thorne asked.

Well, Caleb, sometimes when a man has an unhealthy obsession with a woman, he casts an evil love spell on her.

"Have someone you loved ever gotten involved with a bad dude?" Carrie asked.

"Yeah," Thorne said.

"She was sick, and I was worried. Luke and I came to check on her. He knew James's brother and we figured out what was going on," Lies were easiest when they hewed closely to the truth. "We told Maggie, and she asked James to leave. He freaked out about it."

"Did you see the physical altercation? Between Luke and James?"

Carrie shrugged.

"What, exactly, are you doing with Luke Menkin?" Thorne asked.

Carrie's anger spiked. "We're on a date," she announced.

"What? We are?" a voice said from across the room. Luke, also in handcuffs, looked at her hopefully from the floor. He even managed a winsome smile.

Carrie cursed inwardly. But Thorne was transparently stricken, and her heart soared. "Yes. Luke and I are dating," she said. Thorne coughed spasmodically. Luke, on the other hand, beamed, his smile fuzzy but genuine. She was causing herself more trouble down the road, but all she could do was keep going.

"Are you on drugs?" Thorne asked, back to being a gruff sheriff. His face was now entirely unreadable.

"Hey, a lot of women who aren't on drugs wanna date me," Luke interjected.

"It wasn't a judgment. I found you two passed out on the floor. And Maggie, she's *really* out of it."

Carrie opened her mouth to argue when Luke shouted "Lawyer!" from across the room.

"But–." Carrie said.

"She wants a lawyer, too," Luke said. Carrie appreciated his effort to take care of her, now that they were dating—or at least, now that he thought they were—but she didn't have daddy's beef money to fund her legal expenses.

"Is that true, Carrie? You want a lawyer?" Thorne asked. His voice softened again, mellow and low. The kind of voice she would like to hear ask about her day. Or ask how she wanted her coffee in the morning.

"Am I under arrest?" she asked.

Thorne sighed loudly, making it clear this was a question he struggled with himself.

"Where's the kid?" he asked.

She wanted, badly, to tell him everything. To explain the protective bracelet, and the manikins, and the mesmers. To ask for his help. But if she announced she was a witch, there was a good chance she might wind up in Frognot Hospital on a mental health hold.

"I don't know where Reggie is," she lied. "He wasn't here when we showed up. Maybe they got a babysitter."

"If you're not arresting us, can you get me out of these cuffs?" Luke shouted.

"I said I wasn't arresting *her.*" Thorne spun on Luke. "You're going in the tank for brawling. And if you puke on my truck, I'll add a property damage charge."

"I told Ken I was sorry," Luke muttered. Carrie wondered who Ken was, but she had more important things to think about.

"Are you looking for James?" Carrie demanded.

"We are," Thorne said. "We've got an APB out. If it's really James Alvers, he's got warrants."

No surprise there. Thorne helped Carrie up. "We'll run a tox screen, but do you know *anything* about any drugs Maggie might be on?"

"I can't help you," Carrie said. Given a chance, however, she might be able to help Maggie. "If I'm free to go, I'll go pack up some of her things and meet her at the hospital."

"I was hoping you could wait here in case Reggie gets back."

"Can't you post a deputy?" she asked. Thorne looked annoyed. Carrie understood, a little. Frognot was a small county, and he didn't have limitless resources.

"Just this once, I will post a deputy," he said softly. The warmth was back in his eyes, and she felt guilty. "Now if you'll excuse me, I've got to take your boyfriend to jail."

Carrie grinned at the edge in his voice. She blew a kiss to Luke. "Have fun in jail, boyfriend," she said. Luke's hands were cuffed behind his back, but he turned his cheek in the direction of the kiss. Thorne hauled him to his feet, saying brightly, "Every time you dry out in lockup, I hope it'll stick. Today could be your day."

She didn't hear Luke's response, but from the way he yelped when Thorne yanked on his hands, she guessed it wasn't nice.

Now that she thought about it, going to the hospital to see Maggie wasn't the worst idea. Carrie picked through the clothes piles in Maggie's bedroom, looking for something clean and hospital appropriate. Now that there wasn't a gun in her face, she could appreciate how out-of-character the mess was. Most of the discarded clothes looked new. A few of the dresses on the floor still had tags attached. Carrie ogled the prices. Mesmerizing someone was bad, but running up credit card debt in their name might actually be worse. And now James had Maggie's car, too. Carrie grabbed a nearby dress that looked clean, but it turned out to be a strapless cocktail dress with a thigh-high slit. Not something she could bring to a hospital.

Carrie dug through the closets until she found sweats, yoga pants, and two clean cotton t-shirts from the library's annual 5K fundraiser. *Let your imagination run wild,* the shirt said. Maggie had left her zip-up canvas work bag on the floor, and Carrie unzipped it, intending to stuff the clothes inside. When she saw the stained red book nestled at the bottom of the bag, Carrie froze. Its leather cover was unmarked, but Carrie could tell it was old. Was it the book Maggie had meant to give her? Did it have information about the manikins? Breathing fast, Carrie opened the cover.

It was a grimoire. From the early nineteen hundreds, she guessed. Not so old that it was hand written. Maggie must have found it in the library, before she'd been engulfed by James's mesmer.

Carrie deposited her armful of clothes on top of the nearest pile, then sank to the floor and threw open the book. There was no title page or index, and a quick flip through the pages revealed that most of the book comprised dense blocks of unillustrated text. Distressing, but at least it was written in English. She guessed from the spelling that it had been printed in London.

The book would take hours to read and parse—maybe even days. Carrie didn't have that kind of time, not with

Maggie in the hospital and James on the loose. She flipped through the pages randomly looking for illustrations, but nothing caught her attention. After a minute, she decided to try something different. Reaching into her pocket, she retrieved her amethyst dowsing pendulum. She wasn't sure if it would work, but it was worth a shot.

When the dangling pendulum settled, Carrie opened the book. Letting her gaze drift across the page, she focused on the stone's pulling weight and formed an image in her mind of the manikin. The sickening twist of hair and limbs made her shiver, rocking the pendulum, and she took deep breaths until her anxiety calmed. Flipping through the pages, she let the manikin loom large in her mind as her fingers slid soothingly across the paper.

Two things happened at once. The pendulum in her left hand twitched, and the edge of a page sliced through her right finger. Pricks of blood rose up from the papercut, smudging the page. Sucking on her finger, Carrie scanned the text until her eyes settled on the words starting with 'd'. The section breaks in the book were noted by small dots, sometimes in the middle of lines, and she paged back to find the start of the section. She read slowly, and a few times had to stop to Google a word on her phone.

She read it three times, and with each read, her unease mounted. According to the book, the "devil's helper" was a kind of a cursed magnifying glass. Just one of the manikins could dramatically increase the power of a curse or destructive spell, which explained how Carrie had almost burned her house down with what was supposed to be a small fire spell.

Left to their own devices, however, the manikins—

according to the book—had a way of amplifying negative events. Even relatively normal ones, like flat tires. In effect, the dolls turned molehills into mountains. In the absence of malignant magic, the twisted dolls latched onto things like illness, or conflict, or loneliness, and amplified them, growing local evil until the manikin's surroundings were choked with dark energy. That's why it had been eating through her floorboards—the manikin was amplifying the rot, not causing it.

There was a noise at Carrie's feet, a scrape of stone on wood that made her jump. Had someone come in while she was engrossed in the book? But there was no one in the room. A mouse, or rat? A twitch of movement caught her eye.

It was the pendulum. She had abandoned it on the floor while she was reading, and now she watched in amazement as it inched towards the bed of its own volition. Where was it going? Carrie reached for the yarn tail, but an invisible force tugged it out of her grasp before her fingers could close around it. She scrambled onto her knees as the knitted casing disappeared under the bed. *What the hell?*

Carrie flattened herself to look under the bed, turning on the flashlight on her phone so that she could see into the dark space beneath. The dowsing pendulum banged frantically against an opaque plastic container. It turned out to be a lunchbox, and when Carrie undid the clasp, she sucked her breath through her teeth in dismay. She wasn't surprised by the contents, but the worry in her stomach tightened into a hard knot. She could practically feel an ulcer forming.

Finn was going to be pissed, but there was no getting around this. He picked up on the third ring.

"Are you in jail?" he asked.

"No. Worse."

He made a low, reluctant noise, clearly not eager to discover what was worse than jail. "What is going on?" he finally asked.

Carrie peered at the manikin inside the lunchbox, at two gaps in the twisted hair of its head that looked like eyes. "We've got triplets," she said.

CHAPTER TWENTY-SEVEN

Finn re-read the section of the book that described the "devil's helper".

"New information is not going to appear," Carrie said. "We'll have to work with what we have."

They were speaking in low voices so that Reggie wouldn't hear them.

"The first thing we need to do is get the kid out of our house," Finn said.

"He needs our help. We can't abandon him."

Finn shook his head. "You misunderstand me. It's not that I mind having a houseguest. But it was barely safe before, and it's certainly not safe now." His gray eyes drifted to the tower.

Carrie and Finn's housekeeping had taken a hit amid the recent chaos, and they were out of coffee. Carrie angrily plunged a year-old tea bag into a mug, watching the boiling water turn inky. That's how the atmosphere at the oxbow house felt. Everything was turning black and bitter. Finn was right. This wasn't a safe place for Reggie.

But if she turned Reggie over to Thorne, he would put her in jail. And she didn't know anyone else who could help Maggie. She felt like a fly in tar, flapping her wings without going anywhere. James was more powerful than she'd realized, and now he was on the loose. He wasn't the type to let go of a slight, and she hadn't seen the last of him.

At least she understood the problem now. James had used the manikins to amplify small curses. Carrie felt sick when she thought about what he'd had to do to create the twisted dolls. The grimoire wasn't exactly a recipe book, but it outlined the construction process for creating the manikins. It wasn't pretty. The heartbeats the manikins emitted weren't a magical effect. There were real hearts inside the dolls—the book didn't specify what kind, but it must be some kind of small animal. There were teeth in there, too. Carrie was reluctant to go toe-to-toe against a person willing to go to such disturbing lengths. At least she understood why the manikins had produced such disparate effects.

Unfortunately, the grimoire didn't say anything about destroying the dolls. Carrie would kill for a nice clean "dunk it in holy water and stab it with a silver knife under the full moon" instructional. Not that she had a silver knife budget.

"We've got to get Maggie back on her feet as quickly as possible," Carrie said. "The manikins amplify curses. We know that now. It explains how Maggie's will was overcome so quickly. The manikin was making the mesmer much worse than it should have been. And it explains how James was able to pull one over on me."

"We should go over to the hospital and do a magical cleansing," Finn said.

"That might not be enough. You didn't see her, Finn. She was in a bad way."

If James had made those manikins, he was far more powerful than she was. The thought nagged at her. At first, she thought it was simple jealousy. Power was power, and she wasn't immune to the green-eyed monster. More power meant more interesting spells, and Carrie lived for an interesting spell. But that wasn't the source of her unease. James had seemed greedy, but also impetuous and irresponsible. Not the kind of person who could spend years in a difficult apprenticeship. Carrie suspected he had mesmerized Maggie because he needed a comfortable place to stay, and ready access to a credit card. Even evil had to sleep somewhere. But Maggie had a ferocious spirit, almost immovable when it came to protecting Reggie. Her insistence that James leave had infuriated him, enough that he retaliated with dark magic. Now that he was exposed and on the lam, there was no telling what he might do. But could that kind of flighty person work complex black magic? They had to find him.

"James is the only one who has the information we need. He must know how to destroy the dolls." The second the words came out of her mouth, a clear-eyed confidence suffused her body. James was the key to everything.

Her first investigatory step was uncomfortable, but necessary. She needed to know if Reggie had heard or seen anything related to the manikins. She made two cheese sandwiches and took them down by the river, where Reggie was trying to skip stones across the swollen brown water. The water was running too fast for stone skipping, but he didn't seem to mind. Grateful for the food, he endured Carrie's gentle questioning with tween stoicism. She was relieved to discover that James had kept him far away from any magical schemes. He had either ignored Reggie or bribed him into staying out of the way with gifts and screen time.

"He didn't mention anything about friends in Frognot? Other people? Anything?"

Reggie shook his head and whacked another chunk of stone into the river.

As she wandered back through her rows of acanthus, her dowsing pendulum weighed heavily in her pocket. It hadn't moved since aggressively directing her attention to the third manikin. She fiddled with it for a few minutes, keeping an image of James in her mind and waiting for guidance from the amethyst. The only time it moved was when a big gust of wind blew in over the hills. Carrie sighed. You couldn't expect magic to function like a GPS tracker. Maybe it was time to stop relying on magical solutions.

Carrie maintained a bare-bones social media presence on Facebook and Instagram. She despaired of the internet's many fake witches, mostly attractive goths who made harmless content about crystals and astrology. She knew of exactly two real witches with large social media followings. One made urban foraging TikToks, and one was a genius tarot reader. Neither revealed their real magical powers to their followers. They were still very popular, however, and they had both landed celebrity clients. The forager was now making enough money from sponsorships that she no longer needed to do magic for money. Carrie was jealous.

It had been several weeks since Carrie had logged onto Facebook. The blue-framed timeline popped up, and a pinging notification announced that she had a friend request from Luke Menkin. She hit 'accept,' and hoped he would appreciate it when he got out of jail. Fortunately, Luke's profile also gave her access to his friends list, and she quickly located the profile of Marcus Alvers that he had shown her in the car.

Carrie typed out a quick message telling Marcus she was looking for his brother. A few minutes later, she got back a terse response:

If he owes u money I can't help u

Carrie started to respond that she didn't need money, when all of a sudden the thread disappeared. Surprised, she tried to find the profile again, but it was gone. Marcus must have blocked her. Clearly, this wasn't the first time someone had come looking for his brother. If he knew where James was, he wasn't likely to tell some random woman on Facebook about it.

If she was James, where would she go? That kind of guy rarely left an unscorched bridge behind him. She doubted he had many friends.

Carrie rapped her nails on the table for a moment, then went to grab her keys. Desperate times might have sent him spiraling back to his exes. She had to warn Emily he might ooze out of the woodwork.

The parking lot of Dani and Emily's apartment was quiet, and Carrie donned her cloak against the evening chill as she got out of her truck. Almost immediately, something felt wrong. The hair on her neck rose to attention, and she scanned the area for threats. The sparse woods on the hillside stared back at her, revealing nothing. On high alert, she headed towards the stairs. As the gravel crunched under her feet, she thought she heard a rustle of branches. But when she stopped, the noise disappeared. When her feet hit the steps, however, a voice echoed behind her.

"You bitch," James said.

Carrie spun. The porch light shining in her eyes made it difficult to pick out the details. But James's silhouette was unmistakable. His hand went to his pocket. Carrie, who wasn't going to be taken down by a shiny purple gemstone a second time in a row, charged towards him at a run. As she did, she pushed her sleeve over her elbow to reveal a dark tattoo of an arrow. This time, he wouldn't catch her off guard.

Carrie traced the outline of the arrow with one finger, muttering an incantation softly as she ran. The arrow glowed purple under the moonlight, filling Carrie's arm with energy as she brought her fist down on James's skull.

The magic didn't turn her into a superhero. Rhonda Rousey in good form could hit harder. But still, it helped. And half of the attack's advantage was surprise. Very few men expected a woman to hit hard. James looked surprised as he hit the sidewalk with a solid thud. Carrie's energy reserves were dangerously low, but she traced the arrow again. As she did, a cloud fell across the moon. Carrie swore. She needed that lunar boost to make up for her flagging strength.

"Look down," James said, honey in his voice. He really

expected that mesmerizing trick to work a second time? Carrie slapped him without looking. He shouted, more in rage than pain, and twisted his body to reach for his boot. Carrie grabbed his wrist with her right hand, but the arrow tattoo was dull in the temporarily clouded night. James was stronger than her and squirmed out of her grip. A dangerous *schwing!* of metal on leather echoed in Carrie's ears, and in the next instant a blade was coming towards her face, a silver slice against the clouds. Carrie caught his hand, barely, and watery light haloed James's face as the moon glided back into the sky. Just in time.

Carrie dug her fingers hard into James's sinewy tendons, gripping his arm with her full strength. Moonlight rapidly charged her arrow tattoo again. The second the purple light glowed against her skin, she released James's hand and threw a punch into his head. Her fist exploded with pain and there was a faint cracking sound—the answering rush of adrenaline was so fierce she couldn't tell if the sound had come from her knuckles or James's skull. He fell limp against the ground.

Carrie caught her breath and rolled her weight off James's body. She reached two fingers towards his neck to check his pulse. A car was pulling into the parking lot, and soon whoever was inside would see her looming over the crumpled body. His heartbeat pulsed strongly below her fingers. Before her relieved sigh was out of her body, James's eyes shot open. With a scream, he sat upright, raising the knife over his head.

He was going to stab her. She had fallen for a stupid ruse, *again*, and now her body was a nice soft bullseye for that plummeting blade. Carrie dodged the flashing metal, but she could tell that she wasn't moving fast enough.

An aluminum baseball bat flew out of the sky and met James's knife arm in mid-air. He screamed, and the blade dropped out of his hand.

"I told you not to come here!" Dani said. Carrie thought she was talking to James, but she wasn't entirely sure.

Dani had left her car idling in the parking lot and jumped out to help. It said a lot about the kind of trouble James had caused that she was still traveling with a weapon.

Carrie snatched the knife from a half-dead patch of grass and scrambled breathlessly to her feet. James attempted to sit up, but Dani kicked him back to the ground with one foot.

"Tell me what you did to Maggie!" Carrie demanded, pushing her sleeve dramatically back over her elbow. She made sure James could see her trace the arrow with her finger. Under the moonlight, it glowed brighter and brighter. And now she had a knife.

"You have five seconds to tell me, or I kick you in the dick so hard your grandkids will have genetic trauma." She meant it, too. "I kind of hope you keep your mouth shut, because I would really enjoy that. Five, four, three, two, one."

"Stop," James screamed. His voice went into a higher register, and he pulled his knees to his chest. Dani, less of a fool than Carrie, choked up on her bat without relaxing an inch. "I can't tell you," he said.

"Good luck to your family tree," Carrie growled, and raised her boot.

"Stop! Stop! Okay. I used a basic mesmer on Maggie."

"That was way more than a basic mesmer. She was nearly catatonic."

James sneered. "Maggie was desperate to believe in love. The mesmer just pushed her over the cliff."

"And the manikin made it worse," Carrie added.

Dani looked confused "Manikins? Like, the ones in stores?"

"No. These are more like, like little magical dolls. Only evil."

"Like voodoo dolls?"

"Not exactly. The manikins make things go wrong. Their effects get worse over time."

"Like Emily's illness," Dani murmured.

Carrie hadn't thought about that. But it made perfect sense. She poked James with her toe. "Is there a manikin in Dani and Emily's apartment?" she demanded.

James flipped her the finger. Carrie, who wasn't in the mood, kicked him sharply in the side. He grunted in pain.

"Tell me!" Carrie demanded.

"Do you want the bat next?" Dani took a threatening step forward, knuckles choking up on the aluminum.

"It's in the stupid panda bear," James blurted before she got in range.

Dani looked incredulous. "What?"

"I sewed it in there one day while she was at work. It's her fault for still sleeping with a stuffed animal like a toddler. She could have been a grown-up and thrown it away any time."

Carrie and Dani exchanged a look.

Fuck. Quadruplets.

"I need to destroy the manikins," Carrie said.

"And I need a million bucks and a redhead with double Ds," James said. Carrie kicked him again. This time out of principle.

A dog barked in a nearby apartment, and after a moment, a light turned on inside.

"Get up," Carrie said. "Slowly. If you try to use a mesmer on me again, we're both going to find out how sharp you keep this knife."

When he was on his feet, albeit shakily, Carrie demanded that James raise his hands. Together, she and Dani marched him up the stairs and into the apartment. Emily met them at the door with a squeak of fear. If she had questions, she kept them to herself.

Carrie pushed James onto the sofa and withdrew a pale blue ribbon from her pocket.

"Hold out your hands," she said.

James's expression was pure contempt. "Are you gonna French braid my hair?" he asked. But with Dani at bat behind her, he obeyed. His contempt turned to alarm as the ribbon wrapped around his wrists. There was a light weakening spell woven into the silk. Not enough to paralyze him, but enough to put him at a serious disadvantage in a fight. He would certainly be weaker than Dani or Carrie. And he might be weaker than Emily. When he was secure, Carrie barked at Dani to guard him and charged into Emily's room.

"What is he doing here?" Emily asked, skittering behind Carrie.

"He was looking for a place to lay low. He was probably

going to see if he could weasel his way back into your good graces."

Emily protested as Carrie flung open the door into her room, but Carrie ignored her. Emily's tidiness had deteriorated alongside her health. Her bedding was piled in a mass against her wall.

"Where is the panda?" Carrie demanded.

Emily was so taken off guard that she snorted in shock. Carrie's face cut her laughter short. "What? What do you mean?"

"James put something in it," she said. "It's been making you sick."

Emily rifled through her blankets until a black and white head popped up.

"Don't touch it!" Carrie said. That explained why the curse she had felt had been localized in Emily's chest. If Emily had spent eight hours a night with her arms wrapped around the bear, the manikin could have caused all kinds of problems.

Carrie raised the knife. "Stop!" Emily said.

"I'm going to cut open a little piece of the seam," Carrie reassured her. "We can do reconstructive surgery later."

Emily's cheeks turned pink with embarrassment, but she nodded. Carrie carefully reverse-build-a-beared the stuffed animal, poking stuffing away until twisted black hair peeked out from the white fluff. Carrie dragged Emily into the apartment's tiny kitchen and demanded a pair of tongs, then carefully removed the manikin from the bear. She lay the bear carefully on the table and, an idea forming in her mind, took the manikin into the living room.

When James saw it, he squirmed, hands twisting

beneath the blue ribbon. Carrie set the manikin carefully next to him. James recoiled from the profane doll, torso flopping in the opposite direction. Once he was down, he was too weak to sit up.

Carrie pulled out a yellow vinyl chair from the dining table and sat across from James, turning her face so she could look him directly in the eye. "The spell on that ribbon is a minor curse, you know. The kind of curse that the manikin is *really* good at amplifying. Ordinarily, the ribbon would keep you compliant. With the manikin amplifying the ribbon's power, you'll get weak. It's going to suck the energy out of your muscles. It's going to turn your bones into jelly." Okay, she was taking some creative license there.

"No," James said, lip wobbling.

Carrie glared. "Oh, yes. You're the only one who can stop it, James. Tell me what I need to know, and I won't let it kill you." He groaned weakly, which Carrie took as a good sign. "First of all, how do I destroy the mesmer on Maggie? It's still affecting her."

James's mouth stretched weakly around his words, slurring as his lips moved out of sync.

"Can't. Not unless you destroy the manikin that was in her house. It's like a battery source. The connection between the manikin and the doll exists outside of normal physical space. Once the curse gets rolling, the only way to stop it is to destroy the manikin."

"You were going to let Emily get sick? And erase Maggie's mind? You were going to let the Menkin herd go crazy and die?"

"Why? Why would you do all this." Carrie was startled

to find Emily next to her. "Why, James?" Emily asked. Although the illness had taken its toll, her eyes were bright with forceful rage. Stuffing streamed out of the panda dangling from her hand.

James looked away. "I loved you, and you ruined my life. I wanted you to feel a fraction of what I felt."

"You made me get sick. And you cursed Menkin's cattle, so that I'd have trouble at work."

Emily's eyes were wide and glossy. "You started the Beckermeier fire, didn't you?"

Another twisted smile spread across James's face.

"What could you possibly gain from a forest fire?" Carrie asked.

"I went on a long run there every weekend. Before I got sick, anyways. I loved that trail," Emily said. "He destroyed it because I cared about it, just like the cattle."

"Now you know," he whispered. "Now you know how I feel."

"You've done terrible things, James. But there's still time to change," Carrie said. "If I destroy the manikins, I can turn back the clock on all the bad things you've done. But I need to know how."

James's face went blank and cold. He breathed hard, gathering his strength, then said, "I don't know how to destroy them. I didn't make them."

Shit. Of course, he might be lying. But Carrie thought back to her gut feeling about him. How he didn't have the patience for powerful, complex magic. She could easily believe he'd gotten the evil dolls from someone else. But who? And at what cost?

"Where did you get the manikins?" Carrie demanded.

He pressed his lips together, chin wobbling against the sofa cushion.

"He's been working with another witch?" Emily asked.

Carrie nodded. "Yeah. I knew he didn't have the gray matter to go solo."

James didn't look defiant, but he still wasn't speaking. Was the weakening ribbon messing with his mind? Carrie felt a spark of bloodthirsty triumph that he might be experiencing a fraction of what he'd done to Maggie. But her priority was destroying the manikins, and he couldn't help her if his brain was instant oatmeal. Carrie pushed the manikin away from him with the tongs. He sighed in relief.

"Give me a *name*, James," she said.

"I can't."

Carrie spun to the sisters. "Did he have any friends? Any people in his life who seemed, I don't know, witchy? Ex-girlfriends? Coworkers?"

"He wasn't very open about his life," Emily said.

Carrie almost snorted. No wonder, not with all the scheming he'd been up to. She turned back to the sofa, brandishing the tongs. "Give me a *name*, James," Carrie repeated.

"Paper and pen. I'll write it," he whispered.

Carrie frowned at this request. It seemed weird, but he was too weak to try another mesmer, and she was too exhausted to argue.

Dani fished a pen from a shelf and retrieved a piece of white printer paper from a desk in the corner. Carrie shoved James roughly upright. The friction in the room was getting worse by the minute. Presumably thanks to the now-free manikin. They all deserved to be free of these soul-sucking dolls. Maybe even James. Carrie gave him one of Dani's books to write on, a ridiculous bubblegum pink tome called *Girlboss Tarot*. She stayed on high alert as she handed him a pen, in case he tried to stab her.

The second James touched pen to paper, however, the energy in the room changed. James made a gurgling noise, and the pen fell from his fingers. Another ruse? When she shoved the pen back onto the paper, she saw that the edges of James's nails were blue. He brought his hands towards his throat, but he was too weak, and they fell back onto his lap.

The gurgling sound repeated itself, and James's lips opened and closed in a fish-like purse. His lips were blue, too.

"He's choking," Emily said, and rushed forward. As a former veterinary tech, she had more medical training than the rest of them. James's eyes were desperate, but he reached for the paper and pen. He barely got the nib halfway down the page before his hand went limp and he fell back against the sofa.

"It might be a trick," Carrie pulled Emily away, silently hoping that he was about to spring forward.

"Loosen his collar," Dani said, reaching for his highest button. As she undid it, she yelped and yanked her hand away.

"What's wrong?" Carrie asked.

A red welt rose on her finger. "I don't know but be careful. There's something on his throat. It's like touching a hot iron."

Careless of James's buttons, Carrie yanked open his high stiff collar. Heat radiated from the hollow of his throat, where the edges of his shirt exposed a tattoo-like marking. It was the ancient magical symbol for death. Heat and light radiated from the blazing mark.

Shit.

"What the hell is that?" Emily asked.

"It's a *geas,*" Carrie said grimly. The mark was fading before their eyes, until it looked like little more than a red tattoo. Carrie cursed, knowing what it meant. James was dead.

"I'm calling an ambulance," Emily said.

"No!" Carrie yanked the young woman's phone out of her hand. "It's too late. That's a powerful death mark. The second he tried to write down a name, he was gone."

"I don't understand. You mean that tattoo killed him?" Emily's voice was very small, but it was shot through with long-awaited relief.

"Sort of. A *geas* is a magical prohibition on a specific word or action. Like a magical deadman's switch," Carrie said. "I'm guessing it was set up to kill him if he tried to tell me the name of the witch who made those manikins."

Whoever it was, they didn't have a conscience.

"That's why he asked for the paper," Dani said.

Carrie shook her head, cursing her own stupidity. She should have predicted this. "Yeah. He must have thought that he could get around the prohibition with a pen and paper. Or he hoped he could. Stupid. He could have broken out a telegraph and tried morse code, and it still wouldn't have mattered. A *geas* is about the message, not medium."

"There's nothing we can do?" Dani asked. A glance at the frozen lump of James's face answered her question.

Carrie retrieved the printer paper from James's hand, hoping he might have managed a first letter. But all he had left was an incoherent scribble.

"We have to call the cops, right?" Emily asked.

"No!" Dani and Carrie said at the same time.

"They'll think we killed him," Carrie said.

"We did kill him," Emily cried.

Carrie spun on Emily, grabbing the young woman's frail shoulders. Emily winced as Carrie said, "No. We absolutely did not. He got mixed up in dark magic. You can't cast a *geas* on an unwilling person. He must have agreed to it in exchange for the manikins. Which are nasty pieces of work, by the way."

"He thought we were going to kill him," Emily said softly.

"He's dead. You can stop defending him," Dani said, clearly disgusted with her sister.

"I'm not defending him!"

"Oh, please. There's a reason he thought he could lay low here. You're a pushover."

"That's better than being a murderer!" Emily said.

Carrie began looking around the house. "We can clutch our pearls later. After we figure out how to get rid of his body."

"We don't have to chop him up into little pieces, do we?" Emily asked desperately. Carrie's stomach churned at the thought.

"What? No! Why would we do that?"

"To get him out of the house. Like, in our purses. I saw it in a movie."

Dani had turned the same shade of green as her sister.

"No one's chopping anyone up into little pieces, okay?" Carrie said. "We need to *think*."

"We could say he broke in," Dani said. "That he was threatening us? And then he collapsed? Like, a seizure?"

"That's barely a lie," Emily agreed.

"It won't be good enough. The sheriff's already suspicious of me."

"Interesting," Dani said coldly.

A chill ran up Carrie's spine as she endured a calculating appraisal. Dani was trying to decide if she could pin this crime on Carrie and keep herself and her sister clear of the aftermath.

"If I go down, you go down with me," Carrie said, cutting Dani off at the pass. "Thorne already thinks your sister poisoned the Menkin cattle. It's not a big leap to poisoning a person."

"She didn't poison anyone!" Dani said.

Deep underneath the anger and recrimination, Carrie knew the truth. Emily had been taken in by a bad man. Dani had tried to protect her. Carrie had tried to help both of them. But every time she reached for that shred of reason, rage hit her like a wave, sending her back into a dismal undertow. Dani's hands balled into fists as Emily ran to the kitchen and disgorged her stomach contents into the sink.

It's the manikin. It's interfering with your rationality. And it's getting worse.

A fresh wave of anger knocked the thought down, twisting her anger towards Emily. If Emily hadn't driven James away, he never would have wound up with Maggie.

And Carrie wouldn't be involved at all. The thought clawed at her, filling her with adrenaline.

This wasn't Emily's fault. But only a tiny clear voice, buried deep, seemed to recognize this. Everything else was a mangrove swamp of pessimism. If they didn't get some distance from the manikin, James wouldn't be the only dead body in the apartment at the end of the night.

Carrie, buffeted by fear, raced to the door.

"Oh no you don't!" Two of Dani's acrylics broke off as she swiped at Carrie, and she yelped in surprise. Carrie ignored the gouges in her arm and grabbed Dani in her right hand, her grip strengthened by the spell she'd cast earlier.

"Come on, Emily!" she yelled. Emily had the weakest will of the three, more inclined to terror and self-doubt than anger, and she padded obediently behind them. The manikin's dark energy dissipated as they gained distance from the apartment.

"What the fuck was that?" Emily asked.

"Whatever is going wrong in your life, the manikins make it worse. They don't just amplify curses. They amplify diseases, and negative emotions, and arguments. Something like a death," she lowered her voice, half-mouthing the word, "is going to create an emotional bomb."

"What do we do?" Emily asked.

The apartment complex was dark. Only Emily's window was a bright rectangle, looking out over a patch of dirt, where a newly planted sapling struggled up from the soil. There was a healthy patch of dirt on either side of it.

"Does that window open?" Carrie asked.

Emily, who was still holding her unstuffed panda by one paw, nodded.

"Wide enough to get a body out?" Carrie asked.

"Are you crazy? We'd never get it to the parking lot without someone seeing."

"We won't have to. We just need to get it outside."

"To do what? We're going to bury it in the yard? That's crazy. Half the people who live here have dogs, and all of them have windows." Dani, who had put a protective arm around her sister, was frantic.

Carrie, remembering lessons learned from her previous brushes with the law, checked the building's eaves and hallways. "Are there security cameras here?" she asked.

Dani shook her head. "I asked the super to put them in when James was harassing Emily. He said he'd look into it. Hah. The only thing that man ever looks into is the bottom of a Doritos bag."

"That's good. For once an asshole's incompetence is going to benefit us," Carrie said. "I need to make a call."

CHAPTER TWENTY-EIGHT

"Finn. I need you," Carrie said.

"More than you need me to stop evil magic from burning down your house?" Finn asked.

"Unfortunately, yes."

"What about the kid?" Finn asked.

The options weren't great. Leave Reggie in a house threatened by several mutually amplifying evil dolls or involve him in a plot to hide a dead body. Both were bad. Twelve-year-olds weren't known for their ability to keep secrets under pressure. But at the end of the day, Carrie would rather be arrested than see Reggie harmed.

"Bring him with you."

"It's late," Finn said gruffly.

"It's an emergency," Carrie said. "I'm sending someone to get you."

She handed the keys to the truck to Emily. "I need you to pick up my butler."

Twenty minutes later, Finn hopped out of Carrie's work truck. For a moment, she thought he'd left Reggie at home. As it turned out, the kid's seat was leaned all the way back, and he was curled up on top with a pillow and blanket. Finn held his fingers to his lips as he eased the car door shut. Carrie examined Finn's outfit. He was wearing shiny pink athletic shorts and a pearl-snap shirt covered in flamingos. His long white beard was French braided into pigtails. Emily clearly didn't know what to make of him.

"Who the hell are you?" Dani demanded, poking Finn in the middle of a flamingo.

"He works with me," Carrie said. "He's going to solve our...organic waste problem," Carrie said.

Finn's eyebrows went up in an explosion of wiry white hair. "You know Frognot has perfectly good garbagemen," he said.

"This service is...particularly hazardous."

"Did you dig up a big glowing nugget of plutonium?" Finn asked, his face increasingly grim.

There had, in fact, been a lot of uranium mining in the area in the past. Some of the bigger rapids in the Santa Sangre had arisen from mine tailings and would make a Geiger counter chirp like a cricket.

"Unfortunately, no. Plutonium would be easier to handle," Carrie admitted.

They left Emily outside to keep an eye on Reggie in the truck. As Carrie pointed Finn toward the apartment, Dani pulled her back.

"Can we trust him?"

"He's saved my life before," Carrie said.

"If we screw this up, this murder's going to have more accessories than a model at New York fashion week."

"It's not a murder," Carrie said. If she kept repeating it, it might become true.

The dead body did not elicit much surprise from Finn. He checked for a pulse but stopped when he saw the *geas* mark.

"We didn't see it. He tried to write a prohibited name down. With a *pen*," Carrie said, shaking her head.

Finn growled. "Stupid," he said. They were in perfect agreement about that. Finn also took note of the manikin. "Give you anything useful before he croaked?"

"He was working with another witch. But I don't know who."

"That's not good," Finn said.

"I know. But we can only solve one problem at a time."

Finn paced around the sofa, stomping occasionally on the floor. It made a hollow noise.

"I can't take him through the floor. Not unless you've got a power saw and are willing to share the TV room with a sinkhole."

"Definitely not," Dani said, looking confused. "And what do you mean *take him through the floor?*"

"Don't worry about it," Carrie said.

A faint pink wash rose on Dani's face, from her neck to the roots of her hair.

"Don't *worry* about it? Of course I'm *worried* about it. You're going to get us put in prison for life! Oh, god, does Colorado have the death penalty?" Dani spat.

Carrie's own anger roiled in response. How dare Dani question her competence?

Shit. The manikin's back up to its tricks.

Carrie reached for the tongs on the sofa table, planning to move the manikin into the bedroom at least. Finn pulled her back and removed a silver canister from his shoulder bag. He unscrewed it and held it open while Carrie deposited the doll inside, fighting through a tense atmosphere of worry and anger.

"I suspected we hadn't seen the last of these things. And I thought we might need to transport them if we couldn't destroy them."

"You don't think we can destroy them?" The thought sent her head spinning and she leaned against the sofa. When she opened her eyes, she was staring straight at James's rigid face and nearly fell over. But the dizzy spell passed, and the thick press of tension eased. Finn had screwed the lid of the protective canister on. A little of the tension eased off her shoulders.

"That'll buy us some time from this hostile soup," he said, gesturing between Carrie and Dani.

"We can relax now," she said.

Dani raised an eyebrow. "Sure. Let's chill. Who needs a massage when you can bask in the aura of a corpse?"

The whole thing was a macabre farce. Carrie let out a dark laugh, and Dani shot her a genuine if exhausted smile. "The apartment feels different. Better," Dani admitted.

Finn grunted in agreement and pulled them back to the task at hand. "Okay. The floor is a no go," he said, kicking it with the toe of one sneaker.

"Yes. But I have a plan," Carrie said. She pulled Finn into Emily's room, and threw open the window, pointing at the patch of dirt one story below.

"You want to drop a body out a window? Out in the open? Risky. This isn't an abandoned quarry," Finn muttered. He wasn't wrong. The window was definitely exposed. To underscore Finn's point, a car pulled into the parking lot, illuminating the wall. Finn backed away instinctively until the headlights went back off.

"We'll set a lookout. We're talking about a few seconds. Will you do it?" Carrie asked.

"I don't like it," he said.

"Neither do I. But this is our best option. I'm sure of it."

She would have to search the body. There was no way around it. She had coerced James into breaking his *geas* and couldn't ask Dani or Finn to do it. If there were any clues about how to destroy the manikins, she needed them.

Fishing through the greasy pockets made her sick, and Carrie did it as quickly as she possibly could. Her face was slick with nervous sweat by the time she was finished tossing his worldly belongings into a pillowcase. He had a few hundred bucks in cash. Keeping it seemed wrong, but when she reached to put it back in his jacket, Dani stopped her.

"There's no way in hell he earned that money," she said, counting off the bills and stuffing them in her pocket. "He owed Emily three hundred bucks. He never once took the high road. We don't owe him shit."

"Fine. But wave some sage over that stack before you go on a shopping spree," Carrie said. "It's the definition of ill-gotten gains."

Dani nodded. "I still don't understand what we're doing."

"That's fine. I do," Carrie said. "All you have to do is keep an eye out for anyone coming out of their apartment. If they do, do whatever you can to distract them."

The only thing left to do was the deed. Finn carried James's body to the bedroom and left it below the window before taking his place outside. Carrie posted herself at the entrance to the parking lot, overlooking the road leading up to the apartments. The approach was quiet and dark, so she raised her phone to give the others the signal. Three flashes of the light. The light in Emily's room went off, and a moment later, a dark shape dropped out of the window. Carrie heard the faintest grunt from Finn.

And then, Finn and the body began to sink into the soil. Finn held James in a bear hug, and the sound of packed soil being overturned reached Carrie's ears as the patch of ground below the window swallowed Finn's feet, and then his knees. Finn could burrow rapidly when he wanted to, and tonight he was trying to break his own speed record. The soil reached his chest, and then his chin, and then he took a single, deep breath as it swallowed his head. Finn's descent left a divot in the ground, like someone had dug a big hole and then filled it back in. Grains of soil were still dropping into the hole when Carrie went past to smooth it over. She breathed a sigh of relief. The cops could send all the forensics teams they wanted now, if worse came to worst. Finn had taken James deep underground, down into the bedrock, where only a gnome could go.

Gnome magic was enigmatic, the stuff of rocks and metal and dark spaces in the earth. She had asked Finn once how he was able to travel through solid ground. "It's not solid when I go through it," he'd said. She couldn't explain witchcraft either, so she'd let it go. Was this the first time he'd disposed of a body? He'd moved trash underground for her before. When they were building the greenhouse, they'd generated a debris pile so high that it brushed the porch roof. The only waste disposal service in her area had quoted a full few limbs over an arm and a leg to rent her a dumpster. When Finn found her crying over her checkbook, he'd told her to cancel the service. He spent the next four days tunneling in and out of the ground, disposing of the construction debris a few pieces at a time, pausing only for the occasional tuna fish sandwich. The slow diffusion of trash into the soil was amazing. That unflagging labor was the most generous thing a man had ever done for her. Up until today, that is.

Would Caleb Thorne help me hide a body? Probably not. He was a straight shooter, and he took his job as a peace officer seriously. A total boy scout, although she suspected that he was serious about justice as well as the letter of the law.

Carrie tamped down the last of the churned-up soil, sighing in relief. Was this justice? Carrie wasn't sure. Thorne could arrest all of them, and no one would be better off. Not Carrie. Not Emily and her sister. Certainly not Maggie. Guilt nagged at her when she remembered Marcus's voice on the phone. He'd never get closure for his brother's death, now. That was a fact. The pillowcase of James's earthly belongings was heavy in her hand. She could send a few things in an anonymous package, she supposed. But that would be risky. And the bond between the brothers had snapped a long time ago.

Dani jumped on Carrie the second she was back inside the sisters' apartment. "What the fuck was that?" she demanded.

"That was Finn," Carrie said evenly. This only made Dani angrier.

"You know what I mean. Is he a witch, too? Can witches turn dirt into, I don't know, quicksand?"

"I know what you mean. Of course I do. But that's all I can tell you. The rest of it isn't up to me. If you want to know more, you'll have to ask Finn." And Dani would never find Finn if he didn't want to be found. If he wanted to, he could go to ground for weeks. Literally.

Getting rid of the body might keep them out of jail, but they weren't out of the woods. Maggie was still brainwashed. Emily was still sick. The Beckermeir fire was still burning. The Menkins' cattle were still dying.

Emily, Carrie, and Dani sat in the living room. Emily lay on the sofa, and Dani sprawled across the floor. Reggie, ushered inside, was sleeping soundly in Emily's bed. Carrie expected the door to burst open at any moment, for Caleb Thorne to rush in and arrest them all. That seemed less and less likely as the hours ticked down.

"There's something I don't understand," Emily said.

"What's that?" Carrie asked.

"Why did I get sicker after you took my bracelet?"

"You said you felt better."

Dani and Emily looked at one another. "I wanted to feel better. I really did. I thought I did," Emily insisted, face flushing a little with embarrassment. "I knew you were trying to help me."

Ah, the placebo effect. Plus, Emily hadn't wanted to

offend her. Carrie understood, although she wished the young woman had told her the truth. She considered the situation. The bracelet was an energy drain. It should have weakened Emily. But somehow, it had been protecting her. Or reducing the manikin's negative effects, at least.

"Did you wear it all the time?" Carrie asked.

There was a sudden thaw in the room.

"I left it on Pandy," Emily whispered.

"Who?"

She grimaced in embarrassment. "The stuffed bear."

"The bracelet was always so cold. Emily wanted me to wear it, but I couldn't sleep at night with the freezing metal on my skin. I'd put it around Pandy's neck."

The last piece of the puzzle clicked into place. Carrie's mouth dropped in awe as she saw the whole picture.

There was still hope.

"The bracelet isn't really cursed. Not exactly. It's an energy drain. Instead of draining energy from you, it was draining energy from the manikin. When I took it from you, the curse got stronger, not weaker."

Carrie leapt to her feet.

"Don't look so excited," Emily said glumly, rubbing the swollen purple bags under her eyes.

"Don't you see? That's the solution. I figured it out." Insight blazed through her. "We can weaken the manikins with energy siphons."

The twisted little dolls would still be powerful. But maybe it would be enough.

"Come on," Carrie said.

Dani was exhausted, and Emily looked like she needed a coma's worth of sleep. But Carrie couldn't execute her new plan without them, and so she hauled Emily to her feet. "The spell we need to do takes four people."

"Who's the fourth?" Dani asked.

"Finn," Carrie said, praying he'd be back at the house by the time they got home.

CHAPTER TWENTY-NINE

The atmosphere at the oxbow was sharp and threatening. Under a sickly wash of moonlight, the house's Victorian embellishments were unforgiving black edges against the sky. The moon was only half-full tonight. By tomorrow, its power would be seriously diminished.

They had to destroy the manikins now. There was no more time to waste, not with Emily sick and Maggie hospitalized and the Beckermeir fire smoldering across the landscape. Carrie left Reggie sleeping in the car just inside the gate as she sprinted into the house. "Finn! Finn!" she screamed.

The door to the basement opened, and Finn emerged. Dirt darkened the creases of his face, and his beard was more muddy than snowy now. Carrie wrapped her arms around him. "We're not going for pie, are we?" he asked grimly.

"Not just yet," Carrie admitted. "We have to destroy the manikins, and then I will buy you all the pie in the world. I will commandeer a bakery for a week if I have to." When she shared her revelation about the energy drain, his eyes sparkled.

"Could work," he said. Coming from Finn, that was high praise. "It'll be a tight fit, all of us in the tower," he said.

The tower wasn't the right place. Carrie could feel it in her bones. Shaking her head, she reached down and began to unlace her shoes. "No. Not indoors. We'll do the spell out in the garden. Under the moon."

"Could be risky for your garden," Finn said.

"That's a risk I'll have to take." She hoped they would have enough time.

Dani and Emily were clearly terrified, but they trusted Carrie enough to take orders from her without arguing. She tasked them with clearing a circular plot in the middle of the garden as she and Finn readied the spell. They made three trips each to the tower, bringing down armfuls of ingredients and dumping them in piles along the edges of the newly cleared plot.

"Did your girlboss witch books teach you how to make a basic protective circle?" Carrie asked Dani, grabbing the younger woman by the shoulders.

"I think so," Dani said. Carrie nodded. "Okay. Get started. Use as much sage as you can, and chamomile, mugwort, and yarrow—in that order—for the rest. Do you know what those look like?"

"No, but I have an app," Dani said. Of course she did. Dani and Emily put their heads together over her phone, diving into plant identification.

She wished she had more time to fabricate the energy siphons. Silver medallions would have been best. But complicated metallurgy took time they didn't have. Instead, Carrie collected a canister of soft, moldable clay from her kitchen. The clay was mixed with colloidal silver —Carrie normally used it for minor spells and protective runes, but it would have to do heavier lifting today. It was cool under her hands as she rolled out a cylinder and sliced it into medallions with a kitchen knife.

Carrie retrieved Emily's silver bracelet from where it was still stored in a coffee mug on her kitchen counter. Using the siphoning charm as a guide, she carefully traced a matching sigil into the clay, then handed it to Finn to copy. Silvery muck soon covered the old grime on Finn's hands. When they were done, they had four coaster-sized medallions.

"You've been a lifesaver, Finn," Carrie said, suddenly emotional. A well of sad gratitude bubbled up from beneath her exhaustion.

"You've had my back before and you'll have it again," he said. "We'll toss that favor back and forth until one of us misses."

Like a game of hot potato with a reaper's scythe. The image was so bizarre that Carrie laughed. She tried to explain it to Finn, but she was too exhausted, and all she could do was laugh and wipe tears out of her eyes.

"Don't fall apart on me now, Moonshadow," Finn said. She stuck the makeshift medallions on a cookie tray to keep them from sticking together and carried them out into the garden. The ground underfoot was moist, its solidity a centering comfort.

Carrie set the cookie tray next to the cleared patch of ground. Dani had laid out a basic protective circle, creating the lines using sage and other plants. The greenery was attractive against the dark soil. It made Carrie regret not doing anything for Beltane this year.

"Take off your shoes," she said. Emily kicked off her flip-flops, already sockless. Dani sank to the ground and unlaced her sneakers, then stuffed in the socks and set them carefully aside.

"Why?" Emily asked, wiggling her toes in the dirt.

Dani looked like she was about to answer, but deferred to Carrie, who said, "The soil will ground you. Any physical sensation will. When you open a door to the spirit world, the opening goes both ways. You can pull magic out, but if you're not careful, that magic can pull back."

"What happens if you get pulled in?" Emily asked.

"It depends on the size of the door." What she didn't say was that tonight, they were opening a very big door.

Carrie divided the protective circle into quadrants and placed a clay medallion in each. "These are going to draw down the power of the manikins."

"Are we going to do them one at a time?" Dani asked.

"No. That's part of the plan. The manikins amplify curses, so we're going to stick a big fat curse in each of them. The siphons will draw down the magic that protects them, and they'll amplify the destructive curses until they amplify themselves to death."

"Mutually assured destruction," Emily said.

"Exactly," Carrie agreed.

With the siphoning medallions done, she set out to create a destructive curse strong enough to destroy the weakened manikins. Tucking a mortar and pestle under her arm, she headed to the greenhouse. Her finger flashed over the ward on the silver padlock that held the greenhouse door shut. Inside, Carrie pulled on elbow-length gloves and goggles, then stormed down the aisles of the greenhouse, pulling stems and leaves into a wicker basket. She harvested material from every corrosive, poisonous plant in the room. Black nightshade berries, shiny red rosary pea seeds, and scalloped jimsonweed leaves. Finally, she clipped a leafy stem from the Bitch Weed. "You owe me a favor," Carrie told the plant as she dropped it in her basket.

She took her harvest to a work table and, plant by plant, crushed the leaves and stems and berries into the mortar. Throwing her shoulder into it, she worked the plants with the pestle, crushing them together into an emerald paste. A surprising vegetal aroma wafted up from the mortar. The grassy scent contained no foul notes. No noxious odor to warn of the paste's toxicity. If it wasn't utterly life-threatening, she might have worn it as a perfume.

This part of the spell was not about sophistication. No complicated runes or careful measurements. This was about raw destruction. She was going to pound some Bitch Weed and belladonna into those freaky little dolls, and hope for the best.

Grabbing a gooseneck watering can, Carrie added several drops of water to the paste, loosening it. She scraped it carefully into a shallow bowl, careful to hold it with a rag so that none of the corrosive sap got onto the outside of the glass.

Back outside, Carrie issued a loud warning as she placed the shallow bowl next to the protective circle, piling dirt against it to steady it. She hoped they were ready.

Once they brought the manikins down from the tower, things would move very quickly.

Carrie reinforced the herbal stems with a layer of salt. They would need a lot of power, and fast. The whole thing was going to create a massive debt-stone, which meant they needed a sizable chunk of rock.

Carrie raced upstairs, thighs burning as she reached the tower. The atmosphere inside was intolerable. In addition to the oppressive dark aura, the manikins reeked. Would the acrid rot ever come out of the floors and walls? Could you paint over demon stink? A problem for tomorrow. If she even got to tomorrow.

Carrie pulled her black t-shirt over her nose as she retrieved the basketball-sized jade orb from her bookshelf. She had to trace the triangle tattoo on her arm to move it downstairs, and it made a deep dent in the soil when she dumped it into the protective circle.

"Are you sure you want to use that? I know how much you love that stupid jade bowling ball," Finn said.

"It's big enough, and it's here," Carrie said. "That's all we have time to worry about."

"That thing's gonna be pretty damn explosive," Finn said, poking the pale green stone with the toe of his fuzzy slipper.

"We'll get rid of it right away. And I mean immediately. The second those fucked up little hairballs dissolve in our magical Drano, we'll sprint it out to the forest."

"Are we ready for the manikins now?" Finn asked.

"Is anyone? But we have to move. We're running out of moonlight."

Finn nodded grimly and disappeared back across the

garden. It was time to pull the trigger on this ritual. Carrie guided Emily and Dani to their places at the points of the circle. "You don't move or speak unless I tell you. Understand?"

They nodded fearfully.

The windows of the tower were darkly shadowed, the grim aura of the manikins creating a fog that condensed against the glass. There was a flash of movement behind the panes, and several minutes later, Finn returned. He moved from the back door across the garden without stopping, carrying the plastic water bucket they'd been keeping in the tower out in front of him, stretched all the way away from his body.

Finn used kitchen tongs to distribute the manikins into the circle, spacing them like hot dogs on a grill. Carrie pulled four thick upholstery needles from her pockets, connecting them through the eyes with a waxed blue thread. She tied the ends together with an elaborate knot. "Tie the thread, tie the fate," she said softly. She repeated this as she secured the knot, leaving the looped needles on her knee. This would strengthen the connection between the dolls, which hopefully would magnify their mutual destruction.

Taking a deep breath, Carrie placed a polished black mirror beside the jade ball. She checked the protective circle one final time, and then drew a sigil on the surface of the mirror to open the circle to the magical realm. Energy bubbled up from the shining surface, and the herbs that formed the border changed, the greens and browns deepening in the moonlight. Carrie smiled at the sight, relishing the power flooding the circle. Her heart raced pleasurably at the commencement of the ritual. Illuminated by the magic, the manikins changed, surrounded by clinging black auras, evil, dense energy. It was dangerous, but Carrie's excitement surged at the complex interplay of spells.

She retrieved a ceramic bowl containing an herbal paste. A conventional paste, not the one she'd ground in the greenhouse. This was an old batch; one she'd made when she repaired the second-story joist. That seemed like a million years ago. She retrieved a sticky fingerful and passed the bowl to Finn. "Now everyone activate your energy drains. The clay is wet, so use a light touch." Working quickly, she re-traced the symbol on the clay medallion with the herbal paste. As she finished, the rush of energy in the immediate area diminished. A moment later, the stench of the manikins began to fade. The others followed her instructions, and soon the lively magic flowing out of the mirror drained into the individual medallions, splitting the surging current into four streams. Carrie grabbed the tongs and pushed the nearest manikin into the center of her current. The clinging black aura around the doll washed away in the flow, like ink from an inkpot diffusing in water. The aura regenerated continuously, but its power was diminished.

"It's working," Carrie said. She grabbed the needles and yarn from her knee. "Everyone take their needle, and dip it in this paste. Be very, very careful. It'll burn like hell if you get it on your skin, and it might do worse."

Somberly, her three companions dipped their needles in the toxic paste. Carrie sent a silent prayer of thanks to her poisoned garden, then turned her attention back to the circle.

"When I say go, plunge the needles into the middle of the manikins. Into their hearts. Which unfortunately I mean literally. Once the destructive curses start to resonate with each other, the manikins should be destroyed."

They gripped their needles. The air over the manikins was icy, the smell worse as she leaned forward. Carrie waited for the streams of magic to equalize, then nodded. "Now," she said, and drove her needle down. When the point penetrated the surging black aura, the metal turned so cold that it became painful to hold. "Fight through it," she said through gritted teeth, wishing she'd left her gardening gloves on. The manikin resisted the plunging metal, and the end of the needle bit into the meat of her thumb as she pressed. She had a brief horrible fear of the needle's eye piercing through her thumbnail, but the initial resistance dissolved and she found her target in the manikins' hearts. There was an audible squeal, like a kettle boiling.

Finn's needle went through his doll like butter, and Dani managed the procedure with gritted teeth. Emily cried out in pain, and by the time she was done, her finger was bloody.

"You'll be okay," Carrie said authoritatively. She took a glass phial and poured the dust inside into a quarter-sized pile on her palm. Then, she blew it over the dolls, swiveling her head so that the dust touched all four. The powder activated the curse, and Carrie had a sudden sensation of falling out of the light, away from the overhead stars. Emily squeaked, like a small mammal caught by a predator.

Weakened by the curse that had been cast on her, she was particularly susceptible to the dread permeating the atmosphere, dampened but not deadened by the protective circle.

The cursed black tendrils surrounding the dolls crept out of the needle holes up the threads, blackening the yarn.

Black hair twisted in her peripheral vision. When Carrie's head spun towards the doll, it was still. After a moment, however, a gap opened in the twisted black hairs at the center of its 'face.' A whistling wail escaped this horrible new mouth, and acrid black smoke like boiling tar escaped. The second doll screamed, and then the third, and finally a fourth demonic wail joined the chorus, the voices twisting together in an earsplitting cacophony.

"I'm going to open the circle, now," Carrie said. "Whatever happens. Whatever you see. Don't leave your station."

Finn settled into his spot and held out his hands. Dani glanced at the congealed dirt underneath his ratty fingernails, then grasped the offered hand. Carrie linked palms with Finn and Emily.

She took a deep breath. For a moment, the small noises of the others distracted her. Dani's flannel shirt rustling in the night breeze. The soil crunching beneath Finn's feet. Emily's labored breathing. Carrie dug her heels into the rich garden earth, the soil encroaching into the spaces between her toes. The dampness of the soil seeped into her jeans, the water cool against her skin. She stretched her awareness from the small circle to the greater reach of the garden, and finally to the whole valley. She was in an interconnected system of living organisms, connected by damp earth and chilling sky. She had been exhausted and struggling for weeks, and now she allowed the magic to rush over her, recharging her reserves. Every tattoo on her body was shining a subdued lavender. Emily gaped, awed by the sight. Jealousy pricked Dani's eyes.

If she knew the true cost of magic, she'd never be jealous. She would pay for this top-up later.

Carrie held hands with Emily and Finn, tightening her grip as Emily screamed in terror and tried to yank her hand away.

"Don't let go!" Carrie screamed.

"But the rot. The rotting bones," Emily said, staring straight through Carrie's hand. She was hallucinating, her eyes racing across the soil after some unseen nightmare. Carrie dug her nails into Emily's skin, and the sudden pain yanked the younger woman out of her delusions. She whimpered but tightened her grip on Carrie's hand. Carrie squeezed back.

She was grateful for Emily's renewed grip a moment later, when a burbling noise rose up from the earth.

"Do you hear that?" Carrie asked.

Finn gripped her hand. "Hear what?"

Another gurgle. It was the sound of sucking mud. Water began seeping out of the soil, turning the garden into a muddy morass.

The soil between her toes turned to mud, the ground below her liquefied by the upwelling water. Carrie told herself it wasn't real, but mud was so wet and cold on her body. If she could just let go of Finn and Emily's hands, she might be able to swim free. Carrie struggled, but they wouldn't let her go.

"It's not real," Finn shouted.

He didn't understand. Real mud rose up around her, its weight crushing her lungs as it pushed up over her shoulder. It was a landslide. They had to leave before they were buried. But as much as she struggled, she couldn't get her hands free. When she made one final effort to scream, black muck poured into her mouth and up her nose, cutting off her airways. She closed her eyes, and the liquefied soil pressed against her eyelids. She would be dead soon, her lungs crushed under the weight of the earth.

"Carrie! Don't you leave us," a voice, garbled by the mud, reached her ears. It was Finn, his rich baritone an immediate comfort. Hearing it made Carrie realize something important, which was that she wasn't dead. Her eyes flicked open. The other three were covered in mud, like golems, their eyes and mouths sodden pits. The clay figure on her right turned towards her.

"Come back to us," it shouted, the muddy hole of its mouth moving around the words. She focused on the voice, which had joined her own in so many spells and incantations. *It was Finn.*

It's not real. You have to push through.

Carrie screamed and imagined a warm wind. She pictured it flowing off the mountains, drying out the liquefied earth, caking the mud into a desiccated, cracked plateau. Emily and Finn's real faces flashed in her vision between blinks, and she kept the image of the warm wind going until the hallucination was gone.

"You okay?" Finn asked.

She gasped, "Yeah. The mannikins are making a final push to free themselves. Stay strong. We can do it."

The garden was dark now, the remaining plants sharp

and silent twists of leaf and stem. The Santa Sangre was loud, the rush of the water an oppressive blanket over all other noises.

Over the garden, the tower of the oxbow house loomed, its window a blind eye.

On a small hill on the other side of the river from the oxbow, a figure stood among the trees, watching a column of acrid smoke rise from the garden. The whistling wail of the manikins was just audible over the rushing Santa Sangre waters. A sneer rose on a shadowed face as the circle surrounding the manikins held fast. A single hiss escaped chapped lips. They were actually going to do it. They were actually going to destroy the supposedly inde-structible manikins. With a curse, the figure disappeared into the forest.

"What is it?" Dani asked, following Carrie's gaze.

"I thought, I mean, I feel like someone's watching us," she said. A breeze ruffled the hairs on the back of her neck, and she shivered.

Neither Carrie nor the others saw the figure move back into the forest, because the manikins quickly recaptured their attention. The doll directly in front of her Carrie had started moving. Not corner-of-the-eye hallucinations, this time, but proper movement. The twisted hair twitched and flailed. Carrie leaned in, amazed, wondering if she'd made a terrible mistake and brought the thing to life.

An earthworm wriggled through the doll, its wet flesh straining in the air. Carrie sighed in relief at the sight of the segmented pink body. Her garden was coming through for her in a time of need. The manikin's black hair turned gray and then white, the strands thinning and drying, and when the earthworm squirmed again, the doll split in two, like a clump of dry grass pulled apart by strong hands.

Earthworms could destroy anything, given enough time and the right conditions. Carrie sent a silent prayer of thanks into the earth, pressing the soles of her feet into the soil and wriggling her toes. The earthworm's appearance heralded the manikins' destruction. Within minutes, the other dolls had disintegrated. Finn's crumbled, the body splitting into chunks. The manikin in front of Emily was swallowed by black mold, the normal infinitesimal creep of the fungus accelerated by the cursed needles and string. Dani's manikin untwisted itself, the strands of hair writhing like snakes until the whole thing broke apart. The magic flowing out of the earth and into the clay medallions washed away the last black tendrils of the manikins' cursed aura. The wailing chorus faded as the dolls disintegrated, and a blanket of silence fell across the landscape.

"Did we do it?" Emily asked, still not letting go of Carrie's hands.

The purple gleam of Carrie's tattoos dulled under the shadows of the garden. Carrie nodded.

"We did it. You can let go now." They released hands. Carefully, Carrie traced the sigil on the black mirror in reverse, cutting off the flow of magical energy into the garden. She collected the clay medallions, smushing them into a big ball to destroy the siphoning spells. The clay was wet enough that she might be able to reuse it. Not that that was her biggest concern.

With mounting dread, Carrie stretched her hand towards the jade orb. They had used a tremendous amount of magic tonight. The stone would want to be repaid.

Reluctantly, Carrie placed her palm on the smooth green stone.

It was as bad as she had feared. Maybe worse. The orb was freezing to the touch, a gaping void hungry to be refilled. In a few hours, it would be as dangerous as nitroglycerin, capable of sucking the life out of everyone in a quarter-mile radius. She would treat it like a ticking time bomb, because it was.

Carrie planned to get the orb deep into the forest before that happened. Fighting exhaustion, she unfurled a bolt of red velvet embroidered with protective symbols and moved the jade ball on top. She rolled the velvet like a burrito, then wrapped the whole package in sage-imbued twine, chanting as she secured the knots. Carefully, she reached out and touched the remnants of the nearest manikin. Skin contact confirmed that the curse had faded. Still, she wouldn't take any chances. Carrie gathered the last fragments of the manikins into a small copper brazier. She added sage and dry kindling, plus a dollop of her poisoned poultice for good measure and lit the whole thing on fire. "Don't breathe this smoke," she cautioned the others, stepping away from the brazier. Still, the smoke made pretty blue tendrils as it rose into the sky.

When she finally checked her phone, a message from Caleb Thorne was waiting. What did he want now? Carrie reluctantly put the receiver to her ear.

"Carrie, this is Thorne. I'm calling because, ah, we still haven't found Reggie. We've got an alert out, but he hasn't turned up. Thing is, Maggie took a turn for the worse tonight. The doctors aren't sure what's wrong. But if you have *any* idea where Reggie is, he should really get to the hospital. Before it's too late. I thought you'd want to know."

Panic rising, Carrie repeated the message to Finn. If Maggie was permanently injured, Carrie was going to dig into the earth until she'd found James's body and kill him again. And she wasn't thrilled about the prospect of more encounters with law enforcement. Hopefully, with the manikins destroyed, Maggie would turn the corner. But Carrie couldn't keep Reggie away from his mom any longer.

"I'm taking the debt-stone out to the big stretch of BLM land past the south end of town. There's an old game trail there. The hospital's on the way. I'll drop Reggie off before I dispose of the debt stone."

"I'll come with you," Finn said.

"No," Carrie said. "The stone is dangerous. I don't want anybody at the drop site but me. We have a little time. It'll be okay. Take care of Emily and Dani. This is something I have to do on my own." She stuffed the jade orb in her antique backpack and hauled it to the truck.

Destroying a bunch of manikins hadn't been easy, but it was much easier than telling a twelve-year-old that his mom might be dying.

CHAPTER THIRTY

The debt-stone was heavy on Carrie's back. She had considered leaving it in the truck, but it was simply too dangerous. Even wrapped in the red velvet, it was cold, and Carrie shivered as she and Reggie walked through the bright sliding doors of the Frognot hospital. Carrie's arm was on his shoulder. When she'd told him his mom was very sick, his face had gone completely expressionless. He was a statue, feet shuffling across the smooth tile. When they'd arrived at the roundabout, any thought of sending him inside alone disappeared. She couldn't do that to Reggie. And so, struggling beneath the debt stone, they went in together.

Thorne's enthusiastic young deputy stood up from a chair beside the entrance to the waiting room. "Reggie!" she said. Her bright smile was nervous and insincere.

Reggie nodded.

"Your mom's doing a lot better," Mac said. "Why don't I take you to see her?"

The good news was a relief, and Carrie surged forwards with Reggie, squeezing his shoulder.

"Miss Moonshadow?" a voice said behind her. Thorne was behind her. *Even under these fucking fluorescents, he looks handsome.* She quickly dismissed the thought as she realized his hand was on his gun. "Can I speak to you for a moment?"

"I don't want to leave Reggie," Carrie said. Thorne's hand twitched, and she dropped her arm from Reggie's shoulder. The second she did, Mac yanked Reggie backwards. He let out a small yelp, and before Carrie could comfort him, Thorne raced down the hallway, tackling Carrie to the ground. She fell face-forward with an exhausted grunt, pressed into the antiseptic tile by the debt-stone on her back.

"Carrie?" Reggie said softly, but Mac was already hustling him away.

CHAPTER THIRTY-ONE

The hospital was quieter than usual that night, which was lucky for Thorne. The duty nurse had found him a private room to run his investigation out of. He was grateful, because it meant that Reggie could stay near his mom.

Maggie Lane was doing fine. He was guilty about the ruse, mostly because he had worried the kid. Twenty minutes or so before Reggie and Carrie had arrived, Maggie had regained consciousness. She understood where she was, although she was terrified about Reggie's being missing. Now that he was here, Thorne expected that she would quickly become her old librarian self. The doctors still didn't know what had happened to her. Some kind of rare seizure?

Carrie had been relieved by the news that her friend was okay but had erupted with rage when she had realized he had lied. Now, she was handcuffed to a chair in the private room he'd commandeered. He'd been shocked when he'd felt how heavy her backpack was. In fact, he'd barely been able to pull it off her.

Carrie had wrapped the object in her backpack so weirdly and tightly that he expected it to be some kind of drug. But it was only a large jade ball. He'd had one of the x-ray techs take a few slides to make sure it wasn't some kind of Trojan horse with a solid core. But no, it was just a chunk of rock.

He couldn't understand her panic. She'd begged him to let her go, and when begging hadn't worked, she'd screamed. When her voice had gone hoarse, she'd gone nearly catatonic, staring at the sphere with glazed-over eyes.

He sat down across from her, blocking her view of the sphere. She blinked.

"Will you tell me what's really going on?" he asked. "I am well aware that you're only here because of how much you care about Maggie and her son. If you tell me what the hell is happening, I might be able to get you out of this mess without kidnapping charges."

Carrie looked at him blankly. Her ordinarily lustrous dark hair was plastered against her skull with sweat, and her green eyes were foggy and faded. "You can charge me with anything you want, and I'll confess. But first you have to let me take that stone into the forest." Her tone made him shiver, and she immediately went back to staring at the clock.

"We only have an hour. Maybe less now that you've unwrapped it. Please," she croaked.

"It's just a rock, Carrie," Thorne said.

She shook her head violently. "It's not. Please. Help me

get it out of here. You have to take it to the forest. Or everyone's going to die."

Thorne's heart dipped. Carrie was clearly unwell. She was exhausted, and not making any sense. He should find a nurse and ask her to get a psych consult in here. But he wasn't willing to leave Carrie alone, not looking so disconsolate.

"People are going to die," she repeated. "How many people are in this hospital?"

"Carrie, you have to calm down. No one is going to die. Maggie's doing okay. Reggie's with her now."

"If you won't let me leave, please get them out of here. At least get Maggie and Reggie out. You should go, too."

"What are you afraid of?" Thorne asked. "Is there someone after you? Are you afraid someone's coming to this hospital to hurt you?"

"Not someone. *Something.*"

Carrie, exasperated, pressed her lips together. She looked terrified. He wanted to comfort her, but there were limits to what he could do. After a moment, she closed her eyes and began taking deep breaths. That was better than screaming about some kind of impending apocalypse, he supposed. For a moment, he thought he saw a flash of purple on her wrist, like a momentary violet sparkler.

"What was that?" he asked.

Her eyes flashed open. "What was what?" Her tone was light, but she knew what he meant.

"I saw a light," he said.

She raised an eyebrow. "And you think I'm crazy?"

He didn't respond. After a moment, she shut her eyes again. He leaned back into his uncomfortable hospital chair, trying to find a position where the hard plastic didn't dig into his tailbone. Squeaky wheels ran down the hallway, and there was quiet conversation outside the room. Thorne jumped as a metallic clang echoed out. At first, he thought it had come from outside. When Carrie rose from her chair, a shattered silver cuff dropping from her wrist, he realized what he'd heard.

"What the hell?"

She dove for the rock on the bed, scooping it under her arm. Thorne blocked the door, and she charged at him. She was so much smaller than him that he hardly braced for the hit, shocked when she knocked him down with far more force than her frame should have generated. As he tumbled, he thought he saw a glowing purple triangle. *So weird.*

The bleach-scented tile knocked the wind out of Thorne, and he gasped on his hands and knees before struggling to his feet to run after Carrie. She was already in the stairwell, and he hobbled through the door, feet thudding heavily onto every step.

"Carrie! Stop!" he gasped. His head swam, and he gripped the banister to pull himself upright.

Carrie paused at the doorway into the lobby. "I promise you. I'm doing this for everyone." And then she slipped out the door.

The lobby was chaos by the time he made it down. "Where did she go?" he demanded, grabbing a passing nurse's shoulder. She flinched away from him, clearly fearful, and he let go. "Dark hair, carrying a large rock?"

The nurse pointed out the main doors, and Thorne took off.

Outside, a disgruntled twentysomething man grabbed Thorne's arm.

"Sheriff! Sheriff! Someone stole my car!" he shouted.

Thorne paused. "What?"

"My wife just went into labor. I put the car in neutral while I helped her inside, and this crazy chick jumped into the front seat and drove away. I think she had a bowling ball under her arm?"

"What kind of car? What's the license plate?" Thone demanded. He memorized the first three letters and sprinted towards his Tahoe, shouting an APB into his radio as he went.

With his sirens and lights on, he raced up the road back to the main highway. Horns sounded in the distance to the south. He took a leap of faith and headed in that direction, pushing down on the accelerator as he shot through multiple red lights. One narrow miss sent an oncoming red sedan onto the curb, but he managed to avoid a collision.

The stolen Taurus appeared in the distance a few minutes later. He put on his lights, and the car sped away, veering with a rain of gravel onto a county road that led out to BLM land. The Tahoe was better equipped for a dirt road, and he quickly gained ground. Just as his headlights hit the Taurus's license plate, Carrie stopped. For a moment, she was in his high beams, a waning figure with stringy hair clutching a green ball like a baby. Then she was gone, stumbling into the forest.

Thorne cursed. He parked behind the Taurus and retrieved a high-power flashlight from the ceiling of his Tahoe, leaping onto the shoulder. Would he ever find her out there? The trees had swallowed her completely.

Thorne forced himself to breathe quietly and listened for something out of the ordinary amid the chirping insects and small rustling mammals. A branch cracked loudly in the distance, and an owl hooted in alarm.

Bingo. Thorne pointed himself at the noise and ran into the trees. The forest was a dark web of branches. Thorne's flashlight illuminated patches of the tangle as he stumbled towards the distant cracking of underbrush. Every few minutes, he had to pause to reorient himself. He was pretty sure he was losing ground until a branch snapped nearby. Maybe ten feet ahead of him.

"Carrie!"

The forest went silent.

Thorne shouted again, sweeping his flashlight over the trees. A flash of movement drew his gaze, but it was only a tree branch swaying in the wind. Were there bears out here? Thorne felt stupid. Of course they were. It was early autumn, too, right when they were fattening themselves for winter. Still, the expression on Carrie's face back at the hospital had been more frightening than any bear.

The ground sloped gently down into a ravine. As Thorne picked his way carefully down the side, there was a pained cry and crash of underbrush ahead of him. Thorne stumbled toward it. He tripped once, his ankle sending him sideways into a smooth aspen trunk. The leaves shook like coins as he righted himself and pursued a cry of pain on the hillside ahead.

"Carrie?"

A low moan answered him, and after a minute of frantic strobing, his flashlight beam found her. Carrie had collapsed at the bottom of the ravine. A branch had torn through her right arm, and her skin was clammy and cold. She was in shock.

A faint game trail dropped over the lip of the ravine, plummeting down hardpacked dirt overlain with fine gravel. About as stable as ball-bearings on tile. Carrie must have fallen down it.

"I have to go a little farther," Carrie whispered. She tried to push herself up on her injured arm but cried out in pain and collapsed back onto the dirt.

"We have to go back to the hospital," Thorne said. Her physical wounds were one thing, but Carrie was clearly unwell. She was resisting him even now.

"I twisted an ankle," she said stubbornly.

There was a sudden green glow as Carrie's phone lit up. "We don't have much time," she said. It was four in the morning.

"What are you talking about? Time for what?"

"The reckoning." Her voice was a wet rasp. She pushed off the ground again, and this time she made it to her feet. She jerked on the jade sphere, but it remained stubbornly on the ground. "Help me," she ordered, and Thorne found himself bending over to help pick up the sphere. When it was back in her arms, Carrie turned and marched towards where the game trail continued up the ravine.

"Little farther," she said.

"Carrie, stop!" Thorne touched her good left shoulder, but she shrugged him off.

"You're limping." Every other step, her gait hitched, and a strangled whimper escaped her throat.

"'S'just sprained," she said. "No time to fix it."

What the hell was Carrie Moonshadow doing? Not

escaping from him. It was too late for that by far. She was trying to do something with the jade sphere. And she was very, very serious about it.

"Just tell me what you're doing," he said.

There was a long, rasping pause, and then she said, "I'm taking this debt-stone at least a mile into the forest."

Thorne looked behind him. He guessed they had only gone half a mile, if that. He didn't know what the hell a debt-stone was, but it was clearly important to Carrie. And he remembered his own words to Alethea Murrow. *If she really is a witch, don't piss her off.* The whole thing made him deeply uneasy. They should be leaving the forest, not going deeper into it. He took the opportunity to dump out his left loafer, where a chunk of gravel the size of his little toenail had lodged in the arch of his foot. Would he even be able to stop her, if he wanted to? A memory of a golden frog popped up in his mind, seemingly out of nowhere. *What would make him think of that?*

She had destroyed a pair of police-issue steel handcuffs. That was a fact. He could tell himself that she'd picked the locks, or that the metal had rusted, but that would be a lie. It was time to start facing reality. If he managed to stop Carrie, he'd still be in the middle of nowhere with an unco-operative suspect. He was in good shape, but not good enough to carry a tall woman out of the forest along a hazardous game trail.

He was going to have to get Carrie Moonshadow's buy-in. Which meant he was going to have to play along.

"If I help you…finish whatever this is. But will you come with me, afterwards?" he asked.

"Yes," she said immediately. "Yes, of course."

"We're staying on this trail?" he asked.

When Carrie nodded curtly, he took the lead, lighting their way. A few times, the path grew so faint they had to bushwhack while they searched for it. But now that they were working together, more or less, they made much better time.

"Why did you take Reggie?" he finally asked.

"I wanted him to be somewhere safe," Carrie muttered. "Maggie's house wasn't safe."

"Whatever you're up to doesn't seem safe, either."

"No," Carrie agreed grimly. That was the last thing she said for a long time.

When a low hum reached Thorne's ears a few minutes later, he paid no attention to it. The deep rumble sounded like the spinning blades of a helicopter, and there had been a lot of helicopter activity in the county lately because of the forest fires. When the hum rose into a sucking whine, he finally took note. Carrie's footsteps went quiet behind him.

"Oh no," she said.

Thorne turned to her, and nearly jumped out of his skin as he realized that the evil vacuum noise was coming from the jade sphere.

"What the hell? How is it making that noise? I had it x-rayed!"

Carrie's face went white, and she dropped the sphere into the nearest scrub oak like it was made from hot iron. "It's starting. We have to go." She flinched as Thorne shone the light on her face. Her pupils were wide pits of fear.

"What's wrong? *What's* starting?" Thorne asked.

The bush where Carrie had thrown the jade crackled.

At first Caleb thought it was the sound of the rock settling into the branches. But no, the noise was coming from inside the rock, a rushing sound like a river. Thorne turned the flashlight beam towards the noise, trying to identify the source of the noise.

The scrub oak looked wrong. It slumped inwards, as if it was being crushed into mulch under its own weight. The twigs at the center of the bush had lost their color, turning from a silvery brown to a dead white. Thorne gasped in alarm as the whole oak changed color. The scalloped edges of the glossy scrub oak leaves paled, turning from green to a brownish gray, then crumbled at the edges. The jade sphere was sucking the life out of this oak, like some kind of tree vampire.

Carrie's hand was on his arm. Her nails dug into him, and the half-moon crescents of pain jolted him out of his amazed stupor.

"It's happening too soon," she said, pulling him back along the trail. She yanked his arm so hard that Thorne stumbled and fell, landing on his hip. The patch of grass illuminated by his dropped flashlight went white under the beam, the leading edge of the sucking desiccation marching out and away from the scrub oak where Carrie had dropped the jade ball. Everything around the green sphere was dying, and fast.

Thorne scrambled for his flashlight. By the time he grabbed it, the grass near his toes was white. For a terrifying second, his loafer-clad toes brushed against an icy force field. Thorne had never experienced anything like it. It was like plunging his toes into liquid nitrogen, an unfeeling cold so comprehensive that his teeth chattered. It was pure, needy nothingness, and it was going to swallow him alive.

Thorne was jolted from his fear by the sound of screaming. As he realized that he was the one doing the screaming, Carrie hauled him to his feet and pushed him down the trail. He looked back over his shoulder briefly, and gasped.

Carrie was glowing. Her tattoos shone with indigo light, bright enough to illuminate the trail at her feet. Beyond that, her whole skin sparkled purple, underlain with shifting currents of swirling woad and crackling violet. When had she found time to apply luminescent body paint?

"Run!" she shouted as they locked eyes. Her eyes, too, glowed with icy light, amethyst chips glinting amid the green. The whole effect was so formidable that he obeyed instantly. He jogged back along the trail, hopping over rocks and leaping branches, wishing he'd worn tennis shoes instead of his loafers.

To his left and right, the forest was changing. Branches blackened and snapped under their own weight, falling like an apocalyptic rain. Frantic, terrified shrieking rose from the forest in front of them, as animals and insects sensed the impending danger and fled. Birds fluttered and fled the death front.

Thorne was grateful for the pain in his feet and legs. It distracted him from the sheer terror that had gripped his spine like a clenched fist. He pumped his arms harder, heart slamming into his rib cage.

They were fast, but the apocalyptic front was faster. It advanced on either side of the trail, until it was a good fifteen feet in front of them on both sides. Thorne didn't understand what Carrie was doing, but it was clearly keeping them safe. The ground at his feet sparkled purple where his feet touched. She was keeping the life-sucking force away. When his pace flagged, her screams spurred him forwards.

Their flight felt interminable, although it couldn't have been more than ten minutes. Finally, the destruction along the sides of the trail began to slow. Thorne's heart pounded and acid rose in his mouth, but he maintained his pace.

And then he fell. A root the color of dirt caught his foot, and he flew forward, bare forearms scraping against the ground as he skidded to a stop. Carrie fell against him, tumbling onto the forest floor. Once again, the yawning void licked at his feet, an icy void lapping up his life force. He tried to crawl forward but banged his knee against a rock. Blinding pain blossomed in his leg as the tips of his toes froze. So, so cold.

Thorne screamed. Something horrible was happening inside his shoes. Needles of hot fire pricked his skin, threatening to surge up his legs. What kind of damage was being done? And then the pain dulled, the purple glow at his fingertips brightened.

CHAPTER THIRTY-TWO

When Thorne fell, Carrie's heart nearly stopped. She could hold off the debt-stone's advance, but not indefinitely, and only at a great cost.

She could have left him there. Part of her had wanted to leave him. If the jade sucked him dry, her debt would be repaid in full, and the risk to herself would be over. She could go back to the oxbow unencumbered, grab her go-bag, and hitchhike her way out of town. Finn would get evicted, eventually, but he'd be okay without her.

But then Thorne's sparkling eyes would be gone forever. And whoever replaced him as sheriff might not be as upstanding. Certainly, Frognot would feel the loss. That was why she had to save him, she decided, throwing herself over him and flooding the ground around them with protective magic. Frognot couldn't afford to lose him.

Thorne tried to scramble onto his knees, but Carrie pushed him down.

"Stay still," she instructed. He froze beneath her. The magic had overtaken them completely now. The few weeds sticking out of the game trail were wasted dust now, the rocks around them crumbling and unstable. They were on a small, glowing purple island, surrounded by death.

Black shadows appeared at the corners of Carrie's eyes as she poured her own life force into the protective magic surrounding them. She had thought she had nothing more to give, but impending death was a hell of an upper. But even a witch's body had hard limits.

The black marched inwards at the edges of her vision, until she was seeing the patch of purple dirt in front of her as if through poorly focused binoculars. The agitated noises at the leading edge of the destruction had gone much quieter. She just had to hold out a little bit longer.

Carrie plunged her hands into the soil at either side of Thorne's body, anchoring herself to the sensation of earth. Small pieces of gravel dug painfully into her palms. Far more grounding was the warm mass of Thorne's body beneath her. She concentrated on that sensation instead, of his practical musculature, the sound of his ragged breathing near her ear. The encroaching blackness blinded her, but she fought to stay conscious a few moments longer, pouring herself into the protective circle. Energy poured out of her skin, washing over Thorne and into the surrounding soil.

Just...a few...more...seconds.

Her fingers froze and went numb, and then the sensation of warmth beneath her faded away entirely. As Carrie lost consciousness, she prayed to the forest around her that she had done enough.

CHAPTER THIRTY-THREE

Thorne's face hovered above Carrie. If she was dead, he was too. She was appalled at the idea of an afterlife where she would feel this much pain but it was a possibility. At the very least, the soft surface beneath her suggested she was no longer in the forest.

Maybe she was in jail. It would have been rude of Thorne to arrest her right after she'd saved his life. But maybe he would consider that bribery and take her in anyways. And how much did he understand about what had happened? Did he realize how much of her own energy she'd spent to protect him from the imploding debt-stone?

Carrie raised her right hand in front of her face. The movement twisted a cut in her arm, sending a burning line of pain down from her shoulder. Carrie gasped and dropped her hand onto her stomach. It was enough time, however, to see that the tattoo on her hand and wrist had faded, the dark ink lines graying and blurring. *Damn.* Would she be able to get them re-inked? Certain types of magical power functioned like human organs. Once you destroyed them, they were gone for good. And she had really gone through it last night.

"Move," Carrie told Thorne. His expression settled halfway between surprised and relieved. He took a step back, and her dark blue ceiling, painted with golden constellations, came into focus above her. She was at home, in her own bedroom.

"I'm not in jail," Carrie said.

"Saves me the trouble of paying your bail with gold." Finn leaned against the doorframe, keeping a watchful eye on the sheriff.

Thorne raised an eyebrow. "Gold?"

"Don't worry. He means *solid* gold," Carrie said. To her delight, this only confused Thorne further.

"Would you give us a minute?" Thorne said to Finn.

"You gonna arrest her?" Finn asked.

"It's okay," Carrie said. "He can arrest me if he wants. I told him he could. If he helped me with the stone."

"I guess I'll go assemble my solid gold stores, then," Finn said. His footsteps faded down the hallway.

"I don't understand your inside jokes," Thorne said, eyes narrowed at the doorway. She let the comment slide, wondering if she could avoid this conversation by going back to sleep. She tried closing her eyes but remained stubbornly conscious.

"So," Carrie said.

"So," Thorne repeated. He crossed his arms over his chest. "I have questions."

"Then you should see if *Jeopardy!* is looking for contestants."

"You know, I could still arrest you," Thorne said.

Carrie felt like she'd been steamrolled and limply reinflated. She didn't have the energy to have the "magic is real" talk with Thorne. At the same time, he wasn't blind, or stupid.

"I thought I might have been hallucinating last night," Thorne said. "I thought maybe you drugged me."

"Okay," Carrie said.

"But I sent a buddy of mine at BLM out to take a look at that trail. He said a good half mile stretch of forest is just dead."

"You saw it yourself?"

"I–yeah. I guess I did."

"What happened after I passed out?" Carrie asked.

"I carried you back to my Tahoe."

Her eyebrows shot up. "Really?"

He nodded, embarrassed. "I was going to take you to the hospital, but–I thought–if there was something wrong with you, it would be something like that freaky green bomb stone. Something that a normal doctor couldn't help with. I brought you back to your–butler."

"That was smart. And I appreciate not waking up in jail. Are you going to arrest me now?"

He had clearly asked himself the same question. "You stole a car. One with a brand-new car seat in the back," he finally said.

"Shit."

"Yeah."

She was right. She had done it out of dire necessity, to save a town full of people from being sucked dry by a debt-stone meltdown. But that probably didn't help when you were trying to get a baby home from the hospital.

"Mac came out and drove the car back to the hospital before baby Kyrie was born. Six pounds, five ounces."

Carrie sighed in relief. Unfortunately, Thorne wasn't done.

"The thing is, security footage of the car theft already hit social media. And one of the local news stations picked it up, too."

"Ah."

"I've got to charge you with motor vehicle theft in the third degree. Your record's clean, so you should get off with community service."

"You don't know that. I could be a repeat offender."

Thorne rubbed his temples. "Actually, I *do* know. I am a real sheriff, Carrie. I ran you through our system."

"Oh."

It wasn't great, but it wasn't kidnapping. And it was a small price to pay to save a hospital full of people.

"Do we have to go now?" she asked.

Thorne was grim. "Pretty much. I'm not much happier about this than you, you know. I–I don't understand what happened out in the forest. But I know you saved my life. Thank you. I'll put in a good word for you with the prosecutor."

She assessed her own condition. Her ankle was wrapped, and there was a bandage on her arm. When Carrie lifted it, she found neat stitches underneath. Finn had taken good care of her.

"Well, I guess we'd better get this over with," Carrie said, climbing to her feet.

"How's your ankle?" Thorne asked.

"Just sprained, I think." She limped down the stairs.

Down in the kitchen, Emily jumped to her feet from Carrie's sofa. Carrie was taken aback when the young woman enfolded her in a bear hug.

Color had returned to Emily's face, and the circles under her eyes were gone. She looked so different, so much healthier, that Carrie almost didn't recognize her.

"I slept for nine hours," she announced enthusiastically. "I forgot what it felt like to wake up refreshed."

"I'm glad," Carrie said honestly. Emily gave Thorne the side-eye, then leaned in. "Dani says we're in your coven now. Is that true?"

Carrie snorted. The closest thing she'd ever had to a coven was her family, and that had been a disaster. Sure, she and Faye had worked a few spells together. But they'd hardly shared an abiding bond. "Very funny," she said. When Emily's face fell, Carrie realized that the younger woman hadn't been joking. "Oh. Um. I don't know. Let's talk about it later." Carrie would find time later to let Emily down easy. "I have to go to jail now," she added beatifically.

"You can't," Emily shouted at Thorne. "You have no idea what she's sacrificed. She saved my life."

Thorne cleared his throat. "That's a running theme."

"You're not going to let him do this," Emily told Carrie. Thorne made an offended noise.

"I am," Carrie said.

Finn's head popped out of the basement door. He had a small leather pouch in his hand. "Bail time?"

"Bail time," Carrie sighed.

Finn shoved the pouch into his pocket. "I'll be along shortly."

"He wasn't serious about the gold, was he?" Thorne asked as he led Carrie out to his car.

"I guess you'll find out."

Thorne sighed again. "I guess I'll read you your rights now."

CHAPTER THIRTY-FOUR

Carrie got booked, but she didn't have to spend any time in jail. As it turned out, she was released on her own recognizance just as Luke got released. This irritated Thorne immensely, which Carrie considered a huge bonus.

"Sweetheart!" Luke shouted, waving from across the room. He had a plastic bag with his belongings in it under his arm. The bag crinkled as he pulled her in for a kiss. She might have pushed Luke away, but Thorne was watching, and Carrie wanted to see his face turn bright red. "You didn't have to come by just for me," Luke said.

Thorne coughed. "She didn't," he said. "She stole a car."

To her consternation, Luke grinned. "Shoot. We're a regular Bonnie and Clyde. I guess that means you can't give me a ride home. If something happened to your car and you had to steal one."

"I don't mind," Finn said. Carrie kicked him in the foot, and he smiled blithely.

"I'll get you back," she whispered as the gnome trotted back out to the car. She was going to buy a really, really decadent garden gnome. Maybe she'd even commission one that looked just like Finn. With his stupid ugly hat and everything.

"How was jail?" Carrie asked. "Or I guess that's a stupid question."

"It was okay," Luke said. She noticed, now, that his hands were shaking. She guessed he didn't spend many nights outside of jail sober. Luke saw her looking.

"Don't you worry about that, now. I got my newcomer chip at the jailhouse AA meeting this morning, and I'm going to make it stick this time."

He didn't look or sound very sure of himself, but Carrie hoped he was right. He'd come through for her in a time of need. And he was the source of her favorite pitchfork.

"That's great, Luke," she said.

"I, uh, might need a few days before I can take you out on a proper date," Luke said. "I'm not feeling so hot, right now."

"Of course," Carrie said. She made a mental note to check her grimoires for anything that could help with the DTs. And she didn't have the heart to break things off with him. Not until he was feeling better. Plus, that would give her the opportunity to see how Menkin's cattle were doing. Still, guilt nagged at her when Luke kissed her on the cheek at the gate to the Menkin ranch.

"You're really an item?" Finn pulled a rough U-turn on the gravel road, sending Carrie flying into her seatbelt.

"No. I mean, sort of. I don't know," Carrie said. "He's kind of sweet. And it's not like I have anything else going."

Finn snorted so loudly that Carrie thought he was

having a stroke. "If you believe that, I'll sell you flood insurance for the oxbow."

"What?"

"Sheriff Caleb Thorne?" The lilt in his voice rankled her.

"What does my arresting officer have to do with this?"

"Oh, you think he's arresting, all right."

"Do not!"

Before they could launch into a mature adult conversation about who was rubber and who was glue, Finn turned on the radio. SUNN 98.9 was playing a twangy guitar song about love. Carrie endured Finn's amusement in silence.

"You owe me a slice of pie," Finn said as they neared the turnoff to the oxbow. "Care to settle all your debts?"

"I would, but I need to do some cooking."

Finn was incredulous. "Did the manikins give you brain damage? You don't cook."

"I'm turning over a new leaf," Carrie said. "And I need to do some experimentation."

She had decided to develop a new healing spell. She roped Finn into a quick grocery store trip and returned to the oxbow laden with a bounty of produce, ice cream, and cheese. Lots and lots of cheese. Sure, grinding poisonous plants into a deadly paste was fun, but Carrie wanted to try something different.

Three days later, she was standing on Maggie's steps with a Tupperware container. When the door opened, Carrie was relieved to see her old friend comfortably dressed in a vintage velour tracksuit and gleaming white sneakers. Carrie threw her arms around her friend, and Maggie went stiff.

"Is everything okay?" Carrie asked. She prayed that the mesmer wasn't still affecting Maggie.

"Yeah, it's fine," Maggie said. But she sounded strained.

Of course she did. A spell that destroyed your will would affect you for a long time. Mentally and emotionally, if not physically. Of course Maggie was still struggling. After all, that's why Carrie had come.

"I tried something new," she said, pulling the Tupperware lid dramatically off. A dozen round pimento cheese sandwiches were nestled inside. Carrie had garnished the tops with protective sigils constructed from green onions and red peppers.

"Behold, the healing power of cheese," Carrie held the plate out.

"More magic?" Maggie asked, her face drawn.

Carrie had expected more excitement about this innovation in healing magic. "I was inspired by your fondue party."

"I, um, I don't really remember that. Not very well, anyway. There are a lot of blank spaces in the last few weeks."

Maggie rubbed the empty space on her finger where the glittery purple ring had been.

"Oh. I'm so sorry," Carrie said. "I didn't mean to remind you of that time. I'm sorry I didn't see what was going on sooner."

Maggie shrugged. "It's not your fault. That asshole took me in."

"It's not your fault, either," Carrie said.

Maggie clearly didn't agree, but Carrie hoped she would come to the same conclusion in time.

Maggie wasn't inviting her in. Worried, Carrie took a step towards the door. "Where's Reggie? I cut the crusts off especially for him. I know he loves a good cheese sandwich."

"His dad flew out. They're staying at a cabin while I recover."

"Can I come in?" Carrie blurted. She'd been looking forward to having her friend back, but something was wrong.

"I'm pretty tired right now," Maggie said. "I'm sorry you went to the trouble, but I'm tired of magic. I just want to finish a depressing gothic novel and go to sleep. Get some rest before I go back to work tomorrow."

Carrie had wanted to ease into her planned conversation, but Maggie needed to know. "I don't know what the police have told you about James. But I need you to know that you don't have to worry about him. Ever."

"I thought so. I had a strong feeling. Plus, Reggie told me a crazy story. About a body disappearing into a parking lot."

They exchanged a long look. Carrie cursed. Reggie had been in the truck while they disposed of James's body. She thought he had been asleep. Had he seen something? "He had a nightmare about being buried alive."

"I'm so sorry, Maggie," Carrie said. For once, she meant it.

"How dare you get him involved in all this!" Maggie shouted.

"I couldn't leave him with you and Marcus. Not when you were out of it. And everything happened so quickly. I wish I could go back and change it, I really do. I was trying to save you. I was trying to save everyone."

Maggie's expression softened. "I know you were, Carrie. And you didn't just try. You did it. I'm going to be okay. Reggie and I are going to be okay. You were willing to go full Liam Neeson when you thought he had been kidnapped. I owe you so much. But I can't just think of myself. That's what got me into trouble with Marcus. Or James, I mean. I have to put Reggie first."

"Maggie–"

"You shouldn't come around here anymore. I can't put Reg in any more danger than I already have."

Carrie felt suddenly unsteady. A wave of dark emotion welled up inside her, so swiftly that she wondered if there could be another manikin under the porch. But no, this was good old-fashioned sorrow. She had had one friend in Frognot, but that was over now. Carrie tried not to cry as she secured the Tupperware lid onto the sandwiches. "I understand," she said. "Tell Reggie, I don't know. Whatever you think is right. You know I care about him."

"I know. Goodbye, Carrie."

Carrie's ears buzzed over her own goodbye, and she walked numbly back to her car. She made it one block before tears blocked her vision of the road and she had to pull over. Yanking the Tupperware lid off the container on the passenger seat, she stuffed a pimento cheese sandwich into her mouth. She had bought the good cheddar, from Ireland, and let it charge for a full night under a crescent moon. Warmth and replenishing energy flooded through her, but she was so sad it seemed like a sick joke.

She understood Maggie's perspective, she really did.

She had taken Reggie to her house, with a bunch of cursed manikins. He had maybe seen her dispose of a dead body. From personal experience, Carrie knew that kind of thing was no good for a twelve-year-old. Spending your childhood dodging curses would mess you up. Maggie was making the right choice.

Carrie let herself cry, anyways. Tears could be a potent magical ingredient. Maybe not as potent as Irish cheddar. But a witch had to take what she could get. After finishing a second sandwich, she was able to pull herself together enough to drive home.

The sun was low in the sky when she reached the turnoff to the oxbow. She admired a stand of yellow aspens, so engrossed in the fluttering yellow leaves that she almost did not see the figure standing in front of the fence at the end of the road.

Carrie thought it was Finn, at first, out for an afternoon walk. But no, the figure was tall. And wearing black, which Finn only did during burglaries. When Carrie's truck rumbled onto the road, the figure fled into the trees.

What the hell?

Carrie parked to open the gate and looked out into the woods.

"Hello?" she cried.

Aspens rustled in the breeze, and songbirds chirped.

"Hello!" Carrie said again. She listened for the sound of branches cracking or footsteps moving through the undergrowth.

Nothing, just more wind and birds. Feeling uneasy, she opened the gate.

When she told Finn what she had seen, he didn't seem surprised.

"Destroying those manikins took powerful magic. That kind of spell attracts attention. People are bound to come sniffing around, sizing you up. People, and *things.*"

Carrie liked the sound of that even less. "We'd better refresh the wards on the house. And maybe put some on the fence, too."

Finn nodded. "Sure," he said. "But not right now. Right now, I'm hungry for pie. I believe you promised to buy me a bakery?"

"I never said that. Did I? How about a slice at the Wildcat Diner?"

"I see your slice, and I raise you a whole pie."

Carrie sighed. "Fine. I'll buy you a whole pie. But only if you're willing to share."

She looked into the forest as they drove away from the house. All she saw was branches and trees. But deep inside her, she knew the truth.

Something was watching her.

THE STORY CONTINUES

The story continues in book two, *A Gnome's Wisdom,* coming soon on Amazon

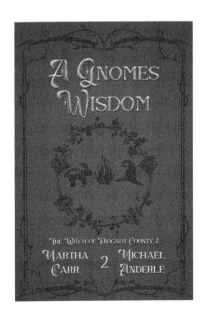

Carrie Moonshadow is a witch with a problem. Well, a few of them.

The local go-to for what ails anyone, especially the heart, is staring down a series of escalating pranks that are turning dangerous. Who knew a rubber duckie could turn on you?

Not what Carrie needed. It's only stirring up even more suspicion about her in the town.

Finn, her old friend and gnome assistant, has got some secrets from his past that could be tied to the chaos. Will he speak up in time?

As Carrie races to clear her name, she and Sheriff Thorne share a growing attraction.

Can Carrie uncover the true culprit behind the pranks before things spiral out of control?

Is the budding romance in trouble? Sheriff Thorne is drawn deeper into Carrie's world, but will his feelings cloud his judgment?

AUTHOR NOTES: MARTHA CARR

OCTOBER 17, 2024

I've always believed that the best life lessons come from unexpected places—like the grocery store checkout line or, in my case, my backyard garden that stretches across the entire yard and down the sides. The only large patch of grass is out front and HOA required.

My goal with the backyard garden was to provide a place for living things of all kinds to rest, drink, eat and thrive, and after three years it's really paying off. There are worms in the dirt, lizards darting everywhere, the occasional snake and grasshoppers and helpful spiders, along with dormice and birds and the occasional raccoon. Not to mention my good dog, Lois Lane.

My backyard garden is beautiful, organized chaos, where even the birds and the squirrels get in on the planting, taking seeds from the wildflower bed out front, or sunflower seeds they got from a feeder and planting them in back for me. I kind of never know exactly how the garden is going to completely look from one year to the next.

Here's another thing I love about being out there. Gardening is a constant reminder that control is an illusion, and things go more smoothly when I can go along with what the dirt wants, (it's often the dirt), or what the temperatures or rainfall are going to be. I can have the perfect plan for how your garden is going to look—like a mental Pinterest board of blooms and bounty—but my backyard oasis has other ideas. It's kind of like life in that way. You plant your seeds, water them, fertilize them and wait, but not everything will turn out the way you expect. Sometimes, a heatwave hits, and your lettuce wilts faster than a middle-aged woman in a sauna. Other times, a late frost sneaks in, and all your hard work turns into mush overnight. Or like last year, a baby boar finds his way into the garden and helps turn the soil in some large areas and I get to start with a blank slate again. It's just the way it is.

When I see a plant isn't doing well, I do my best to assist and ask questions over at the Natural Gardener. They actually have a designated person who will answer endless questions. I've tested it. And there's nothing toxic that will poison wildlife or the soil.

But sometimes, nothing works and a plant withers and dies. It happens. I learn the different areas of the garden. That spot doesn't keep the moisture as well, or that spot has a lot of sunlight that never ends. Or everything grows super well right there under the tree. It's a daily reminder to roll with what is because it will all be easier and work out beautifully. Plus, I keep reading those reports about how putting my hands in dirt will improve my own biome. Bring it on.

Speaking of rolling with it, let's talk about weeds. Oh,

weeds—they can be the bane of every gardener's existence. They return with the first good rain. Weeds are the gift that keeps on giving, popping up when you least expect them, often in the most inconvenient spots, like right next to your prized roses or smack dab in the middle of your lettuce patch. I spend a few minutes every morning as the sun rises pulling them up. It's like meditation and a good way to start the day.

Here's another way of looking at them. Weeds can be a lot like the little annoyances in life. You can spend all your time and energy trying to get rid of them, but more will pop up tomorrow. Instead of trying to eliminate every last one, I've learned to pick my battles. Some of the larger ones I let stick around during the hottest Texas days because they're shading plants underneath and keeping them alive. Everything can have a purpose. I've also made peace with the fact that my garden will never be completely weed-free—and that's okay. It's still beautiful in its own imperfect way.

Gardening has also taught me the fine art of patience. You can't rush a garden, no matter how much you want those tomatoes to ripen faster or those flowers to bloom on your schedule. Nature has its own timeline that's in perfect order. There's something strangely peaceful about it. In a world where everything is instant—fast food, fast Wi-Fi, fast everything—gardening reminds you that some things take time. It's a good reminder that not everything in life is meant to happen right away, and sometimes, the best things come to those who wait (and water diligently).

Finally, perhaps the most important lesson I've learned from my garden is the value of tending to something.

There's something incredibly grounding about caring for living things, watching them grow from tiny seeds into full-blown plants. You don't realize it while you're doing it, but there's a sense of accomplishment that comes from nurturing something and watching it flourish, even if it's not always perfect.

And isn't that the point of life, too? We may not always have control, weeds and pests will show up, and sometimes things don't grow as fast as we'd like. But with a little patience, care, and a sense of humor about the whole process, we can still create something beautiful—even if it's a little messy.

the next time you're feeling overwhelmed by life's chaos, consider taking a page from the garden playbook. Get your hands dirty, tend to what's in front of you, and remember: perfection isn't the goal, just being present is. And if all else fails, there's always another season. More adventures to follow

AUTHOR NOTES: MICHAEL ANDERLE

NOVEMBER 20, 2024

First, thank you for not only reading this story but for taking the time to dive into these author notes! You rock.

Dusty Books and Digital Dreams

So picture this: a few years ago, amidst juggling story ideas and sipping way too much Coke (the drink, not the white stuff), I decided to pick up Leonard Shatzkin's *In Cold Type*. Yep, I took a deep dive into the world of traditional publishing as it existed over 40 years ago.

Why, you ask? Well, *sometimes to understand where we are, we've got to look at where we've been.*

Now, I'll admit, like many indie authors, I've had my fair share of gripes with traditional publishing. It's easy to sit on this side of the fence and point fingers, thinking we've got it all figured out. But honestly, you shouldn't point a finger if you don't know WHY they did something in the first place.

From our vantage point here in the third decade of the 2000s (seriously, where did the time go?), it's tempting to think traditional publishers were stuck in the Stone Age. But back then, they had reasons—good ones, even—for doing things the way they did. Crazy, right?

If you're a bit of a history buff or just curious about the behind-the-scenes of the book world, I highly recommend giving *In Cold Type* a read. It's like cracking open a time capsule from 1982, just before everything started to change.

Now, if you've been following the epic battles in the publishing world a few years ago (decades even)—first between Borders and Barnes & Noble, and now the juggernaut that is Amazon—you'll know there's been a fundamental shift going on. Each side claims the moral high ground in the endless quest for profits, and it's a real PITA.

Dig a little deeper, and the name Shatzkin pops up again. Mike Shatzkin, Leonard's son, has been a prominent voice in the industry. I've read his blog. Now, Mike sees the world through the eyes of traditional publishing (he retired mostly a few years ago). I'm not a fan of some of the comments he made as (even in 2016 and 2017 when I was reviewing some of this) he made assertions that didn't connect with my reality.

However, back to history. Well, farther history.

In Cold Type is a gold mine of insights. Written for folks like us, it's packed with contrarian views about the industry as it stood on the brink of upheaval.

He talks about the inefficiencies—the dreaded remainder system, for one. Imagine printing thousands of books only to have a huge chunk of them returned unsold, then sold off at a loss. Insanity! Even Leonard thought so back in '82. It's like baking a hundred cupcakes and tossing fifty because they didn't sell fast enough.

Come to think about it, this does happen in some bakeries.

Then there's the warehousing woes—thanks to the infamous Thor decision (no, not the hammer-wielding god, unfortunately). It was the IRS decision about taxing products sitting in a warehouse made storing books expensive and added another layer of complication.

But here's the kicker: so many of these problems are solved by the eBook revolution that I am a part of.

No more returns, no warehousing, instant global distribution, and the ability to keep books available forever. Prices come down, and authors have more control. It's a win-win, right?

Unless you think that you must keep the eBook price high to keep getting the high prices for paper books.

So, what's the point of all my rambling? Maybe it's to remind ourselves not to be too quick to judge. Understanding the past helps us appreciate how far we've come—and maybe, just maybe, gives us insight into where we're headed.

I hope you enjoyed this little detour into the quirks of publishing history. Sometimes, looking back can be just as enlightening as looking ahead.

Here's to learning from the past and embracing the future.

Until next time,

Ad Aeternitatem,

Michael Anderle

P.S. If you've got thoughts on this—or just want to share your own ironic typos—drop me a line or leave a review. I love hearing from you.

P.P.S. For more musings, sneak peeks, and general shenanigans, don't forget to subscribe to the MORE STORIES with Michael newsletter: https://michael.beehi iv.com/

OTHER SERIES IN THE ORICERAN UNIVERSE:

THE LEIRA CHRONICLES
CASE FILES OF AN URBAN WITCH
THE EVERMORES CHRONICLES
SOUL STONE MAGE
THE KACY CHRONICLES
MIDWEST MAGIC CHRONICLES
THE FAIRHAVEN CHRONICLES
I FEAR NO EVIL
THE DANIEL CODEX SERIES
SCHOOL OF NECESSARY MAGIC
SCHOOL OF NECESSARY MAGIC: RAINE CAMPBELL
ALISON BROWNSTONE
FEDERAL AGENTS OF MAGIC
SCIONS OF MAGIC
THE UNBELIEVABLE MR. BROWNSTONE
DWARF BOUNTY HUNTER
ACADEMY OF NECESSARY MAGIC
MAGIC CITY CHRONICLES
ROGUE AGENTS OF MAGIC

OTHER BOOKS BY JUDITH BERENS

OTHER BOOKS BY MARTHA CARR

JOIN THE ORICERAN UNIVERSE FAN GROUP ON FACEBOOK!

CONNECT WITH THE AUTHORS

Martha Carr Social

Website: http://www.marthacarr.com

Facebook: https://www.facebook.com/groups/
MarthaCarrFans/

Michael Anderle Social

Website: http://lmbpn.com

Email List: https://michael.beehiiv.com/

https://www.facebook.com/LMBPNPublishing

https://twitter.com/MichaelAnderle

https://www.instagram.com/lmbpn_publishing/

https://www.bookbub.com/authors/michael-anderle

BOOKS BY MICHAEL ANDERLE

Sign up for the LMBPN email list to be notified of new releases
and special deals!

https://lmbpn.com/email/

For a complete list of books by Michael Anderle, please visit:

www.lmbpn.com/ma-books/

Made in the USA
Columbia, SC
23 March 2025

55556881R00190